ROAR OF TOMORROW . . .

"He's down! We've lost the echo!"

Mac and Howard were already outside the truck, racing toward the runway through the thick fog.

What was upon them within seconds could never have been expected. It broke through the veil of rain that concealed the runway like a curtain. Ahead of it, battering their deafened and incredulous ears, was a sound such as they had never heard before in all their lives. Instead of the familiar deep-throated roar of piston engines, there came a screaming banshee wail, like the voice of a million demons escaping from hell. It tore at their eardrums and set their teeth on edge, leaving them stunned yet at the same moment exhilarated by the sheer impact of overwhelming power. As the low, squat aircraft, half shrouded in flying spray, hurtled down the runway and disappeared once more into the mist, they felt the fiery breath of its passage lick across their faces.

Oblivious to the pouring rain, even forgetful of what they had just achieved, Alan and his companions remained staring along the empty runway. In that moment they knew that the age of the propeller was coming to its end. The sound still echoing in their memories was the voice of the future.

Books by Arthur C. Clarke

NONFICTION
Ascent to Orbit: A Scientific
    Autobiography
Astounding Days
Boy Beneath the Sea
The Challenge of the Sea
The Challenge of the Spaceship
The Coast of Coral
The Exploration of the Moon
The Exploration of Space
The First Five Fathoms
Going into Space
Indian Ocean Adventure
Indian Ocean Treasure
Interplanetary Flight
The Making of a Moon
Profiles of the Future
The Promise of Space
The Reefs of Taprobane
Report on Planet Three
The Treasure of the Great Reef
The View from Serendip
Voice across the Sea
Voices from the Sky
1984: Spring

WITH THE EDITORS OF *LIFE*
Man and Space

WITH THE ASTRONAUTS
First on the Moon

WITH ROBERT SILVERBERG
Into Space

WITH CHESLEY BONESTELL
Beyond Jupiter

**WITH SIMON WELFARE AND JOHN
    FAIRLEY**
Arthur C. Clarke's Mysterious
    World

Arthur C. Clarke's World of
    Strange Powers

FICTION
Across the Sea of Stars
Against the Fall of Night
Childhood's End
The City and the Stars
The Deep Range
Dolphin Island
Earthlight
Expedition to Earth
A Fall of Moondust
The Fountains of Paradise
From the Oceans, from the Stars
Glide Path
Imperial Earth
Islands in the Sky
The Lion of Comarre
The Lost Worlds of 2001
The Nine Billion Names of God
The Other Side of the Sky
Prelude to Mars
Prelude to Space
Reach for Tomorrow
Rendezvous with Rama
The Sands of Mars
The Sentinel
Tales from Planet Earth
Tales from the "White Hart"
Tales of Ten Worlds
The Wind from the Sun
2001: A Space Odyssey
2010: Odyssey Two
2061: Odyssey Three

WITH GENTRY LEE
Cradle
Rama II

ARTHUR C. CLARKE

GLIDE PATH

BANTAM BOOKS
SPECTRA ™ NEW YORK·TORONTO·LONDON·SYDNEY·AUCKLAND

GLIDE PATH

A Bantam Spectra Book / published by arrangement with
Harcourt Brace Jovanovich, Inc.

PRINTING HISTORY

Harcourt Brace Jovanovich edition published 1963

Bantam edition / June 1991

SPECTRA and the portrayal of a boxed "s"
are trademarks of Bantam Books, a division of
Bantam Doubleday Dell Publishing Group, Inc.

ISBN 0-553-29052-5

PUBLISHED SIMULTANEOUSLY IN THE UNITED STATES AND CANADA

Bantam Books are published by Bantam Books, a division of Bantam Doubleday Dell
Publishing Group, Inc. Its trademark, consisting of the words "Bantam Books" and
the portrayal of a rooster, is Registered in U.S. Patent and Trademark Office and in
other countries. Marca Registrada. Bantam Books, 666 Fifth Avenue, New York, New
York 10103.

PRINTED IN THE UNITED STATES OF AMERICA

OPM   0 9 8 7 6 5 4 3 2 1

PREFACE TO THE 1963 EDITION

AS MANY OF the incidents in this book are based upon real events, and a few are, indeed, unadorned reminiscence, some readers may be tempted to identify the leading characters with actual people. I would therefore like to stress, with even more than the usual emphasis, that *all* the characters in the following pages (except the Mark I) are entirely imaginary. They are not in any way based upon, or intended to depict, the men who developed and perfected the radar talk-down system, known in real life as GCA (Ground Controlled Approach).

The sequence of events also departs completely from historical facts, which seldom arrange themselves for the convenience of storytellers. Nevertheless, I hope that this novel does justice to the skill, enthusiasm, and devotion of those to whom it is dedicated.

INTRODUCTION TO THE 1987 EDITION

AS THE PRECEDING note indicates, *Glide Path* is my only work of *non*-science fiction. Yet if, by some miracle, it could have been published thirty years earlier, it would have been a perfect example of hard-core s.f. So the literary frontier moves, and classifications change.

Perhaps because of its close links with what is laughingly called reality, *Glide Path* gave me more trouble than any of my other novels. After writing *The Deep Range* in 1956, I produced a whole series of short stories, but found it impossible to get involved with any full-length work. Though it was the closest I've ever come to the dreaded "writer's block",* there were no subconscious factors involved, because I knew exactly why I hesitated to attempt another s.f. novel. Before my memories were eroded by time, I felt it was my duty to pay a tribute to my wartime colleagues and to record a piece of important technological history. Not

---

* My experience here, I am happy to say, is similar to Robert Silverberg's. Quoting from memory: "Writer's block? Yes, I once had one—for thirty minutes on a Saturday morning in 1953."

until I had done that could I let my imagination run wild again.

The first draft of *Glide Path* was begun in 1958, restarted in 1959, revised in 1960—and promptly rejected by my publishers. I put it aside until 1963, but the fourth version still wasn't right. At this point Julian Muller, my editor at Harcourt, Brace, took it in hand, and I shall always be grateful to Julian for whipping it into shape. It was a great relief to know that my conscience was clear and that I could now get back to my proper business of writing pure science fiction. Just as well: Stanley Kubrick had recently finished *Dr. Strangelove* and was thinking about *his* next project . . .

But back to 1945 and real history. Although GCA saved many Bomber Command aircraft returning from missions, it came too late to have much impact on the European war. It received its baptism of fire in the Pacific, sometimes on islands that it shared with very uncooperative Japanese troops. I am indebted to Lieutenant Neal Jolley—one of our original team—for sending me his lively account of these events.

GCA's greatest hour, however, came after the war was over. Stalin's 1948–49 Berlin blockade is now an almost forgotten piece of history, but for eleven months a fleet of Allied aircraft kept the city supplied with essential food, fuel, and other supplies—more than two million tons in all. This would have been impossible without the round-the-clock use of GCA; so if it did not change the course of the war, it may have helped decide the peace.

Soon afterwards I published an account of GCA's pioneering days in the British journal *The Aeroplane* (September 23, 1949) under the not altogether tongue-in-cheek title, "You're on the Glide Path—I think." It has recently been reprinted in my collection of technical essays, *Ascent to Orbit* (John Wiley, 1984). In this volume I give credit to GCA for introducing me to the narrow microwave beams that are essential for communications satellites; in fact, today's "K"-band is the old GCA "X"-band.

Not until October 1971 did I catch up again with most of

the real-life characters in this story, when the GCA team—scientists and service personnel alike—had a thirtieth anniversary reunion near Cambridge, Mass. It was strange to search for the young GIs I vaguely remembered in the prosperous middle-aged businessmen in the Marriott Motor Hotel, singing indelicate songs I'd last heard a quarter of a century ago at RAF bases.

Sadly, Dr. George Comstock—who provided *some* of the elements in "Dr. Wendt"—died only a month after the reunion. And although I did meet Neal Jolley briefly in the hectic chaos of the *2010* premiere, the only members of the old gang I am still in touch with are Bert (Charles) Fowler and Luis Alvarez. After retiring as vice-president of the MITRE Corporation, Bert is now busier than ever as chairman of the prestigious Defense Science Board. He has several times tried to lure me into the Pentagon to advise his colleagues: luckily for the safety of the free world, we have so far been unable to arrange a date.

As for Luie—well, it's been very hard to keep up with him. He had already left the GCA team when I arrived on the scene, and was busy inventing the implosion mechanism for the A-bomb. (He was an airborne observer above Trinity—and Hiroshima.) I did not catch up with him until 1952, when he took me for a walk through the huge Berkeley "Bevatron."

Although I must again stress that—apart from unavoidable historical parallels—there's nothing of Luie in my fictional inventory of "GCD," I am modestly pleased with the prediction in the last paragraph of Chapter 13: "Professor Schuster would be a Nobel prize-winner in the 1950's." Luie almost let me down: he didn't get invited to Stockholm until 1968.*

His other activities during the last three decades have included a hunt for hidden chambers in the Great Pyramid by examining the intensity of the cosmic radiation passing

---

* The Bob Hope incident a few paragraphs earlier in the novel occurred exactly as described. Little did Bob know that Luie was on his way to end the war.

through it, and an expedition to the South Pole in search of magnetic monopoles—both quests, alas, unsuccessful. More recently Luie and his geologist son Walter have hit the headlines with their discovery—he claims it's no longer a theory —that the dinosaurs were wiped out by global ecological changes triggered by the impact of a gigantic meteor some seventy-five million years ago. This event—the Cretaceous–Tertiary extinction—has underscored the ability of Earth's currently dominant species to arrange an encore, without any external help.

Yet perhaps Luie's most important achievement—and here I'm wearing my science-fiction hat again—was the discovery of *cold* (room temperature!) nuclear fusion. ("The catalysis of nuclear reactions by mu mesons," University of California Radiation Laboratory Report 3620, 10.12.56.) As he once patiently explained to me, it is very unlikely that this will lead to results of practical value. Well, the great Lord Rutherford said exactly the same thing about atomic energy back in the 1930s. . . .

Nuclear-powered scooters, anyone?

—ARTHUR C. CLARKE
Colombo, Sri Lanka
September 25, 1986

GLIDE PATH

✳ CHAPTER 1

FLYING OFFICER ALAN BISHOP found it singularly peaceful on this tiny metal platform a hundred feet above the North Sea. The fact that Adolf Hitler was undoubtedly preparing some sort of mischief over there on the Continent, and that it was his duty to watch out for it, seemed quite irrelevant on such a warm autumn afternoon. Nothing moved in the whole expanse of sea and sky; even the big concave dish of the radar scanner had ceased its restless searching and was staring straight toward Holland. If it did start to spin, Alan would have to move smartly; it was not very practical to share the platform with a whirling ten-foot saucer standing on its rim.

Below him, the rest of the station appeared equally relaxed. But this, Alan knew, was an illusion. In the wooden hut at the base of the tower, Sergeant Campbell was attacking a defective wave monitor with liberal doses of solder and profanity. Over there inside that mysterious barbed-wire enclosure, Flight Lieutenant Hicks, Royal New Zealand Air Force, was assembling his Gee installation—whatever *that* might be. F/O Bishop resented the existence of any radar device that was secret to him, but all his attempts to winkle information out of Hicks had been wholly unsuccessful. At least, he consoled himself, by the look of the antenna arrays it was only old-fashioned meter-wave-length stuff, so it couldn't be very interesting.

There were probably fifty people hard at work within a hundred yards of him, but the only signs of life were the bored Service Policeman on duty at the main gate and a Woman's Auxiliary Air Force operator doing some voluntary gardening on the skimpy flower bed around the Orderly Room. At least, Alan assumed it was voluntary; the WAAF Commanding Officer had not, as far as he knew, started doling out horticultural exercises to criminous airwomen.

The parabolic bowl looming above him gave a premonitory creak and twisted toward the south, as if tired of staring for so long in one direction. There was no danger that it would start spinning at full speed—Sergeant Campbell knew that he was up here—but Alan thought he had better move.

The big dish was aimed straight at him, and he was sitting in a radio beam of a frequency and strength no one would have dreamed possible only a few years ago. It might be imagination, but he felt that he was already starting to cook.

Half a million watts were squirting silently, invisibly toward Holland, focused into a narrow beam by the big radio searchlight. Not a billionth of that energy was coming back, reflected from whatever obstacles it had encountered before it skimmed clear of the horizon and headed out into space. Yet that feeble echo was enough to betray the presence of any ships or low-flying aircraft within a hundred miles of the coast, and to pinpoint them accurately on the cathode-ray screen in the receiver hut.

There were times, however, when old-fashioned vision was better than radar, and this was such a moment. A mere half mile away was an approaching target of much more interest than Nazi torpedo boats or low-level bombers. As soon as Alan spotted the brown van weaving along the narrow lane, he started to descend the tower with reckless speed.

Despite his early warning, the news was all over the station before he reached ground level. By the time he sauntered through the main gate (it was, of course, undignified for officers to run) the queue for the NAAFI van was so long that it seemed incredible that the station could still be fully operational. If Hitler only knew, thought Alan, he could sabotage the entire radar chain by organizing a simultaneous onslaught of NAAFI vans loaded with off-ration chocolates and cigarettes.

The two charming but slightly distraught elderly ladies were doing their best to cope with the ravening horde that had boiled out of Orderly Room and Operations Blocks. Whenever he saw them, Alan was irresistibly reminded of a phrase he had once come across in some tattered Victorian romance—"distressed gentlewomen." There was no doubt that they were gentlewomen, and their distress was equally obvious as they tried to portion out their limited supply of Players, Mars Bars, and Cadbury's chocolate without favoritism. In the background, brisk bargaining was already in progress between smokers and nonsmokers as chocolates and cigarettes changed hands. It was hard to believe, Alan told himself, that once upon a time you could walk into a shop and buy as many sweets or fags as you could carry. . . .

He was retreating with his spoils when he saw the Commanding Officer heading purposefully toward him. He liked Flight Lieutenant Williams, but at the same time felt rather sorry for him; these Admin types must have such drab and tedious lives, dealing with their endless paperwork and quite unable to understand the electronic marvels all around them. But someone had to read and sign the bumph that emerged from Group Headquarters in a ceaseless stream; not everybody had enough brains to be a technical officer.

"I've news for you, Bish." Williams grinned amiably. "You've been posted."

Alan stared at him, disbelief and indignation striving for

mastery. "But that's ridiculous!" he finally blurted out. "I've only been here a fortnight. That's not even time to learn how the gear works!"

"Are you presuming," purred Williams, "to doubt the inscrutable wisdom of Group HQ?"

"Yes," retorted Alan, without hesitation. "What's it all about? Where are they sending me?"

"I haven't a clue—the signal didn't say. But they want you in a hurry; you've got to report to a Wing Commander Stevens tomorrow afternoon. So you'll have to pack your things right away—you won't have much time if you're going to catch the 6:30."

"What about my inventory? It'll take hours to check."

"You're not short of anything, are you?"

"I hope not."

"Well, Hicks will sign for it, unless you both want to stay up all night counting bits and pieces."

Alan was shocked at this casual attitude, but if his successor was willing to accept responsibility, sight unseen, for a hundred thousand pounds' worth of radar equipment, that was his business. There was certainly no chance of catching that morning train if every spare part and every secret document had to be accounted for before he left the station.

F/O Bishop was a chronic worrier, and halfway back to the radar hut he suddenly recalled an item well worth worrying about. A few weeks ago, some mysterious interference had blotted out the radar signals on several of the local sets and had, naturally, been blamed on enemy jamming. It occurred at the same time every morning and for a few minutes only; after several days of intensive research, the antijamming expert from Group Headquarters had proved that the interference came, not from the other side of the North Sea, but from Alan's electric shaver. By great good fortune, the electronic sleuth was an old classmater from Alan's radar course, and between them they had managed to contrive an innocuous report. But suppose the truth had leaked out, and he was now being called back to Group to be told that his old rank of acting corporal was yearning for him? He remembered a film about Dreyfus he had seen, years ago; he could still recall, with the utmost vividness, the scene in which the unfortunate Captain was stripped of rank and honors. He doubted if Group would arrange anything quite so spectacular (after all, no one could match the French at this kind of thing), but he found himself possessively clutching the thin blue band stitched to his sleeve.

These pessimistic reveries never lasted very long; by the time he was back inside the receiver hut he had already reconciled himself to whatever adventures the morrow might bring. Everyone had already heard of the posting, and Sergeant Campbell knew exactly what it implied.

"They're getting mobile units ready for the Invasion," he informed Alan with gloomy relish. "That's going to be a pretty tough job, sir. It's been nice knowing you."

Alan doubted the sincerity of the tribute; he had not been with the unit long enough to have been of much use, and all the work had fallen on the Sergeant. Yet he felt surprisingly sentimental as he walked over to take a last look at the picture on the tube. It was always a wrench when you left one station and prepared for the unknown hazards of another.

The echoes were abnormally strong today. Instead of slicing straight on out into space as the curve of the earth fell away beneath it, the radar beam was being bent downward by some peculiarity of the atmosphere. It was wave-hopping all the way across the North Sea, bouncing off the Dutch coast, and—little more than a thousandth of a second after it had started its journey—returning along the same curving path with the secrets it had gathered.

There they were, displayed at the extreme edge of the cathode-ray tube, beyond the hundred-mile-range mark. The delicately quivering line of green light reared upward to profile a jumble of peaks which the WAAF operators, through long practice, could read at a glance. Even Alan, whose job was to provide the signals, not to interpret them, could pick out the smaller spikes which were surface ships, and the more distant and solid ones which marked the coast of occupied Europe. The pattern shifted and changed as the beam swept back and forth, racing along that distant, unapproachable shore like an invisible searchlight. On the plotting board were the results of its probing, drawn in colored crayons—the tracks of convoys moving cautiously out from Rotterdam, the route of an Air-Sea Rescue boat patrolling on some special mission, the suspected signature of a periscope in a spot where the Admiralty felt no periscope had any right to be. . . .

Well, good-by to all this, Alan told himself; it was no longer his concern. He gathered up his papers, grandly bequeathed some unread paperback books to the operators, signed the log, and shook hands with Sergeant Campbell. Then he turned his back forever upon Coast Defence Radar, and the first half of his life.

✻ CHAPTER 2

AS HE CYCLED up the gravel drive of Elvesham Manor, whose reluctant hospitality he shared with the two other officers on the radar station, Alan wondered if his next billet would be quite so memorable. The big house, with its stables and aviaries, its private chapel and crypt, its bay windows and battlements, its acres of park and woodland, had been the residence of the Elvesham family for more than five hundred years.

But not, judging by the current residents, for much longer. Mrs. Elvesham was an octogenarian dragon who had taken a very dim view of RAF officers ever since her late dear husband had told her of a World War I Royal Flying Corps bounder who had actually boasted, in the Mess, of shooting a fox. Her daughter, Mrs. Esme Elvesham-Boyle, ran all the Women's Institutes for miles around with an iron hand, and terrorized the neighborhood with her good works. The third generation was represented by Miss Felicia Elvesham-Boyle, a sprightly, giggling maiden in her quite early forties, who had sometimes alarmed Alan with her not altogether mock flirtatiousness. It was a weird and pathetic household, decaying in the faded glory of the past, doomed soon to be dispossessed by the bureaucrats of the National Coal Board.

Alan had been treated very kindly, and had been splendidly fed on the products of the Elvesham farm. But he was never given a chance of forgetting the social gulf across which this hospitality—paid for in any event by the RAF—was tendered. F/Lt. Williams swore that when he had first presented himself at the Manor and asked the butler if one dressed for dinner, he had been told, "Don't worry, mate. You're eating with us."

Sometimes Alan wished it had been arranged that way; when he dined with the Elveshams, he always felt on the verge of some appalling social *gaffe*. And once, indeed, he had started on the soup with the dessert spoon. . . .

He reached his room on the second floor of the east wing without interception; the family was out for the day, and the servants were probably taking it easy in their own quarters. Alan's bedroom had an impressive approach, for the corridor leading to it was lined with huge glass cases, each holding half a dozen birds of Paradise. These stuffed mementos of Mrs. Elvesham's hobby were getting a little moth-eaten, but even after forty or fifty years their feathers still blazed with iridescent glory. It must have cost a fortune to bring them to England, and to provide the artificially heated jungles they needed in this cold and alien land. The last of them had died before Alan was born, but the old lady remembered all their names. To her, they were still alive; she had once found Alan examining them, and had taken him on a tour of inspection, introducing him to every one of the winged jewels her wealth had snatched across the world. For the rest of his life, when he recalled Elvesham Manor, Alan would always think of birds of Paradise.

He was halfway through his packing when he came across the last letter from home. It had arrived almost a week ago, and he had locked it in his suitcase away from prying eyes. At least, that was the reason he had given himself, and it was true as far as it went. But it would be just as true to say that he had hidden the letter from himself, until he could face the problem of answering it.

Well, he'd have to answer now; it couldn't be put off until the weekend, as he had intended. With a sigh, he settled down at the bureau and pulled a sheet of the Manor's embossed notepaper out of the drawer.

"Dear Father," he began. Then he nibbled his fountain pen morosely for five minutes, as he stared out across the park in search of inspiration. When it came, he put the words down in a breathless rush and scarcely lifted pen from paper until he had signed his name.

> *I'm very sorry to know that you have been poorly again and trust that you're much better now. I'd hoped to write a longer letter this time, but I have just been posted to a new station and have to pack in a great hurry. I don't know what the new job is but hope to find out tomorrow. As soon as I know where I'm going, I'll let you have my new address. Meanwhile, please don't send any more letters to the Manor.*
>
> *I'm sorry this is so short but I have only a few hours to wind everything up here. I'll have more news next week.*
>
> *Love to Miss Hadley and yourself,*
> *Your affectionate son,*
> *Alan*

It was hardly an inspired letter, but it was not quite finished yet. Alan glanced once again at his father's inevitable postscript, then prepared to add his own. First, however, he opened his wallet and carefully counted the thin wad of notes.

> *P.S.   I wish I could send you as much as you asked for, but I shall need all my spare cash for*

> *traveling expenses during the next few days. This is*
> *all I can manage now.*

He wrapped the solitary pound note in a separate sheet of paper so that its crinkling would not betray it. Miss Hadley would be annoyed if she caught him sending the Captain money—little though it was. Every penny, of course, would be spent in the dockside bars; but what else could he do? It was easy enough to say that one should be ruthless—that it was for the Captain's own good not to put temptation in his way. Unfortunately—or otherwise—Alan lacked that kind of ruthlessness.

One could, indeed, make out a fairly good case for considering him something of a moral coward. That thought crossed Alan's mind (not for the first time) as the ivy-covered battlements of the Manor faded behind him in the dismal, predawn light. Yet it was not his fault that he had to catch the milk train, and so was unable to say good-by to the ladies of the house. If that Whist Drive in aid of the church roof had ended at a reasonable hour, he would have stayed up to make his farewells, but now he was sneaking off like a hotel guest who hadn't paid his bills.

He had left a note to the old lady, thanking her for her hospitality and conveying his best wishes to daughter and granddaughter. Perhaps he should, after all, have given something to the servants, but how was he to be sure that they wouldn't be insulted? The aged butler had given him a reproachful look, now that he came to think of it. . . .

Well, it was no use worrying about the past. Another episode of his life had closed, and it was of no concern to him if the Elveshams recalled him only as that uncouth young Flying Officer who left without saying good-by. He wondered if, when they woke up, they would start anxiously counting the silverware.

The train was already waiting when he paid off the antique taxi. There was no one else traveling first class, so he had the whole compartment to himself. That was fine; at this time in the morning he did not feel at all sociable, and with any luck he might be able to catch up on some lost sleep.

London was three hours away, assuming that he arrived on time. Even if he did not, it would scarcely matter; he had four hours to wait between trains, and the railroad would really have to exert itself to make him miss the connection. But four hours was an annoyingly useless sort of interval; when he'd switched from Liverpool Street to Paddington, and had a snack at some café, there'd be no time to go anywhere or do anything. "Gone With the Wind" was out of the question, and there was nothing else that he really wanted to see. He thought of revisiting "Fantasia," still running at Studio One, but he'd seen it for the second time only a few months ago, and those cherubs and centaurs were beginning to pall.

Alan was confronted with an old problem, and did not know London well enough to solve it. He had never visited the city until the war; for the first two decades of his life it had been remote, vast, and mysterious. It was no longer remote, but its vastness and mystery remained. Nor would they ever be dispelled, for as long as he lived he would remember that magic moment (could it have been only two years ago?) when he had crested the rise of the hills and been confronted by a London no man had ever seen before, or would ever see again.

With thirty boisterous companions he had been driven down from the training camp where they had been fitted out with their new uniforms, taught how to march, when to salute, and how to behave without disgracing the Royal Air Force. The weeding-out process had already taken place; now they were on their way to learn a trade—that of wireless mechanic. They were also on the way to London, and the fact that the *Luftwaffe* had an identical goal did not dampen their enthusiasm in the least. The RAF bus that was carrying them reverberated with the bawdy songs they had acquired with their basic training.

The songs and the laughter ebbed suddenly into silence. The bus was no longer climbing, but had topped the hills and was now coasting down the gentle slope that stretched for miles ahead of them, down into the valley of the Thames. Still far off, yet spanning half the horizon, London was catching the last light of the day.

But no one had eyes for the city. Floating a mile or more above it were scores—no, hundreds—of brilliant silver tear-drops, like a fleet of strange ships at anchor upon the surface of some invisible sea. Though Alan had seen barrage balloons often enough in the past, they had always been in small clusters around some isolated target; he had never imagined the armada that floated above London, and which now transformed the city into a scene from another world.

The sunlight glancing from the acres of aluminized fabric made the ungainly gas bags look like drops of mercury, almost blindingly brilliant against the darkening sky. It was an unforgettable sight, but even as he admired it, Alan wondered how much protection this airborne shield really provided. In several places, thin columns of smoke were still rising from fires left by the last raid; with a slight sinking feeling, Alan—who had never yet heard a bomb drop in anger—reminded himself that for the next ten weeks he would be living in the middle of the world's number-one target.

They were lucky; the Blitz was not yet over, but it had spent its force. Apart from the blackout and the restrictions that now seemed part of life, one could even forget that London was a city at war. The thirty Aircraftsmen Class II (Under Training) who made up Alan's course were billeted in an infant's school in the East End, whose pupils had long ago been evacuated into the unfamiliar countryside. Classrooms had been packed with beds and turned into dormitories; there was much ribald mirth about the tiny toilets, but they had to suffice. Discipline was minimal, being enforced by a plump and friendly Sergeant and a remote Pilot Officer who emerged once a day when all the Courses were on parade, and had never been known to reprimand anyone for anything.

On the whole, it had been a happy time; they had no responsibilities and no worries. At 8:00 A.M. the squads were lined up in the playground, briefly inspected, and marched along the Mile End Road—to the great inconvenience of traffic—until they reached the Thomas Coram Technical Institute, where for six hours a day they were introduced to the fundamentals of radio.

No—"introduced" was too mild and gentle a word. It had been a high-pressure course designed to pump brains of average intelligence full of electronics in the minimum period of time. Within a few weeks, boys who had previously been unable to change a burned-out fuse were building radios and using cathode-ray oscileographs.

Alan had expected to find the course easy; after all, had he not been repairing radio sets for a living ever since he left school? He had soon discovered his mistake.

The empirical trial-and-error skill he had acquired while working in Mr. Morris's shop (RADIO AND TELEVISION A SPECIALTY, the sign said, though no television set had ever been seen within a hundred miles) was valuable, but totally inadequate for this job. Alan quickly realized that though he could repair a radio, he had never really understood how it worked. His grammarschool physics had stopped short at alternating currents, and had barely hinted at the existence of the electron. As for his mathematics—the less said about that, the better. Alan could still remember the horrified amazement with which he had first encountered the square root of minus one.

Yet he had made the grade; and now, only two years later, he was an officer, while most of his classmates were corporals or sergeants. He was still not quite certain how it had happened; when he remembered the grim-faced inquisitors of the commissioning board that had interviewed him at Adastral House, it seemed something of a miracle.

But the ways of the Air Ministry were beyond mortal understanding; and so were those of Group Headquarters.

In a few hours he would know what they wanted of him, and meanwhile there was no point in worrying about matters outside his immediate control.

While the train made its leisurely journey to London, no duties or responsibilities could touch him, and there was nothing that he could do about them even if he wished. He was beyond the reach of the world.

✳ CHAPTER 3

ORIGINALLY, 61 GROUP HEADQUARTERS had been built as a country seat by some Victorian merchant prince; its size, impeccable bad taste and brilliantly contrived inconvenience had made it an irresistible target for the Royal Air Force, which had promptly requisitioned it on the outbreak of war. The current owners, it was rumored, now occupied one of the numerous lodges scattered around the estate—the smallest of which would have accommodated a normal-sized twentieth-century family.

Wing Commander Stevens's office, which had once been the third nursery, commanded a fine view of the gardens surrounding the house. To be brutally accurate, it provided an excellent view of where the gardens *had* been. At the moment it showed a series of prefabricated wooden huts accommodating stores and clerical staff, and an expanse of badly beat-up lawn that was used as a parking place in good weather. In winter it was known as the Slough of Despond and was impassable to all except amphibious vehicles.

Despite Alan's fears, the interview had been pleasant enough; indeed, the wingco seemed positively friendly.

"We need someone," he said, "for a rather unusual job—someone who picks up new ideas quickly and can put them across to others. Someone who has practical experience, yet can lecture in the classroom. Do you think you qualify?"

"I really don't know, sir," said Alan cautiously. He was still very much on guard, not wishing to show any enthusiasm until he knew what all this was about. One of the first rules he had learned in the Air Force was "Never volunteer for anything." Like most rules, it sometimes had to be broken, but it had served him well in the past.

"You spent eight months as a lecturer at No. 7 Radio School, and the Chief Instructor has given you a very high recommendation."

"He *has,* sir?" said Alan, genuinely surprised. It was true that he had enjoyed teaching, and getting down to the fundamentals of new equipment; but it had not really occurred to him that he was good at it. Anyway, he was by no means sure that he wanted to go back to school, with its parades and discipline, after the easygoing life of an operational radar station. By this time, he had practically forgotten how to give a word of command; when he addressed one of his men, he was much more likely to say "Pass the soldering iron, Joe" than "LAC Jones! On the double!"

The Wing Commander continued to leaf through the dossier on which Alan could see his name and number tantalizingly displayed. He would give a good deal to see what was inside that file, but of course he never would. At least he could now be fairly sure that the electric-shaver incident was not recorded there, and that was a considerable relief.

Abruptly, W/Cdr. Stevens started to fire a series of technical questions at him. They were all about ten-centimeter radar: how do you tune a klystron; what is the principle of the cavity magnetron; what advantage have wave guides got over transmission lines? It was elementary stuff, and he had no difficulty in dealing with it. At last the Wing Commander seemed satisfied; he closed Alan's personal file and dropped it decisively in his out-tray.

"I'm posting you," he said, "to a Coastal Command airfield in Cornwall, not far from Land's End. You'll be joining a very small but very important unit; at the moment it has just one officer, Flight Lieutenant Basil Deveraux, who is attached to a team of civilian scientists. You are to assist him, and if everything works as we hope, then RAF personnel will take over from the scientists and the unit will grow rapidly. That's all I can tell you; the whole thing is even more secret than ordinary radar, and I can promise that you'll find it interesting. Ops 4a—second door on the left—will have your travel documents. Good luck!"

And that was all he saw of 61 Signals Group HQ. Fifteen minutes later, a van picked him up at what had once been the tradesmen's entrance, and dumped him back at the railway station. Flying Officer Alan Bishop, after two and a half years in the RAF, was now actually on his way to an airfield.

He was used to these sudden changes of status, but this was the most unexpected yet. When he looked back upon his service life, it appeared to be divided into distinct and almost unconnected strata, like the rock layers pictured in geology books. When you were in one layer, you could not imagine any other existence. Then, suddenly, you were in another—and what lay behind you in time was already dead and fossilized.

The earliest, or Eocene, layer of this RAF career was already gone almost beyond recall: he even had to think hard to remember the name of the place where it had started. Southbridge—of course! That was where he had said good-by to his civilian clothes, and drawn his first uniform from Stores. (It had fitted very well, too, despite all the jokes, but it was several days before he could stop his cap from falling off every time he saluted.)

At Southbridge he had been given the number whose last three figures he would remember all his life, for it had been branded into his mind at scores of Pay Parades. When the money was counted out and his name was called, he would step forth from the ranks and reply smartly: "Sir! 727!" Then he would collect his pay, salute, and merge once more into the sea of blue. Being so near the beginning of the alphabet was a great advantage. You never had to wait long for anything, whether it was pay or punishment. The poor W's and Y's were sometimes kept in suspense for hours.

It was at Southbridge that he had learned to drill, and had discovered, to his great surprise, that he enjoyed it. He felt a sense both of solidarity and of achievement when he marched in formation with his fellow airmen, tracing precise geometrical patterns on the parade ground—though according to the Drill Sergeant a flotilla of drunken jellyfish would have done better. He had also discovered—and this was another surprise—that noncommissioned officers were quite human off duty, and not averse to borrowing money from innocent recruits.

Yes, he had learned a lot at Southbridge, though he had been stationed there for little more than two weeks. It had been the dividing line between two worlds, for once you had put on uniform you were never quite the same again. You had exchanged the freedom and indiscipline of Civvy Street for a planned and regulated existence, in which the very clothes you wore and the way you walked were subject to rules. Even your sex life, according to the widely believed rumor, was suppressed by the Medical Officer, via the medium of bromides in the tea. Not until Alan became an officer himself, and had to inspect the cookhouse as part of his duties, was this ghost laid to rest in his own mind.

The rabble that had entered Southbridge emerged as fledgling airmen, already steeped in service lore and, in most cases, feeling some pride in their uniform. But at this stage they were good for nothing but sweeping floors, cleaning latrines, and peeling potatoes; they had yet to master a trade, and must now learn the multitudinous skills that were required to fight an aerial war.

Hence the Thomas Coram Technical Institute, and a hundred similar establishments. Alan had been lucky to receive his basic wireless training in the heart of London, even though it was a London of sandbags and blackouts and air-raid sirens. He had not been quite so fortunate on the next stage of his electronic saga.

High, cold, and windy on the Wiltshire moors, No. 7 Radio School had been Alan's university and, later, his home. It was a dismal prospect of barrack huts, parade grounds, and wooden radio towers, yet he had grown to love it. For it was here that he had said good-by to the simple, old-fashioned world of "wireless" and had come for the first time face to face with the unsuspected marvels of radar. Here he had also been introduced to Security.

It was exciting to feel that every word and drawing in your notebooks was so secret that not a scrap of paper could be taken out of the classroom. The Radio School was a closely guarded enclave set in a remote corner of the camp, surrounded by barbed wire and service policemen. At the beginning of the day the trainees would assemble on the parade ground in the main camp, and would then march almost a mile to their classrooms. When they arrived, the safes would be unlocked and their individually numbered notebooks issued to them; at the end of the day, the books would be collected again. On the rare occasions when one was lost, the whole school was turned upside down until it was discovered.

Alan had vivid memories of his first radar instructor—a thin, soft-spoken Canadian with a fine gift for sarcasm. Sergeant Lebrun had been a schoolteacher in civilian life and never had any need to fall back upon his three stripes to enforce discipline. His tongue was quite sufficient, and like all good teachers he appeared to have eyes in the back of his head.

Sergeant Lebrun had smiled with obvious relish at the thirty expectant faces staring back at him, on that first morning in class. "I've a surprise for you," he said. "You think you've come here to learn about wireless; some of you may even imagine you know it already. Well, we don't teach wireless here. We teach RDF—Radio Direction Finding—and even that isn't what you might suppose.

"RDF is a means of locating aircraft by radio waves;

another name for it is Radiolocation. It's one of the best-kept secrets of the war, and it's got to stay that way. That's why you're not allowed to take your notebooks over to the main camp, and if you're ever heard talking about your work here, you'll be in real trouble. Understand?"

Course 47 understood.

"The principle's very simple. RDF works by sending out a short, sudden radio pulse, and then detecting the echo when it comes back. We have RDF sets here that can spot aircraft two hundred miles away, and can pinpoint them on a map to within a fraction of a mile. That's how the Battle of Britain was won . . . with a little help from Fighter Command, of course."

No one laughed. The Sergeant's face did not encourage it.

"And RDF can do better than that. It can count the number of aircraft in a formation, and tell how high they are flying. It works just as well by day or by night, in rain or in fog, so Jerry can no longer rely on the English weather for protection."

A nervous titter started from the back of the room and spread swiftly across the class. Sergeant Lebrun seemed neither pleased nor annoyed—merely a little surprised.

"If we want to measure distances by radio," he continued, "there's one slight problem. Radio waves travel at the speed of light, and that's the fastest thing in the universe." He turned to the blackboard and wrote on it, in large, clear figures:

$$186,240$$

"This is how many miles a radio wave travels *in a single second*—more than seven times around the world. So we've got to be pretty slick to catch an echo from an aircraft only a few miles away. This is how we do it. . . ."

He turned once more to the blackboard, and began to sketch, while behind him thirty Secret Notebooks lost their blank virginity.

An hour and several pages later, Alan laid down his pen with a sigh of relief. He was suffering not only from writer's cramp, but from mental indigestion. Sergeant Lebrun had not, however, quite finished with Course 47.

"Before you go to Practical class, I've an announcement that may interest some of you. There's a gramophone recital tonight at 1700 in Hut 10b. The program will consist of Beethoven's "Pastoral" Symphony and Sibelius' Symphony No. 2. Flight Lieutenant Horsley will give an analysis of the Beethoven. Class dismissed."

That was typical, Alan soon discovered, of Gatesbury. The place was an absolute hotbed of culture. Despite the pressure of work, staff and trainees found time to run camp newspapers, music-appreciation classes, debating societies, and even a small symphony orchestra. No airman who entered No. 7 Radio School had a chance of leaving it again if he was a good performer on a musical instrument. He might fail dismally as a radar mechanic; no matter, if he could play the violin.

Alan stayed at Gatesbury for a different reason. The school happened to be short of instructors when his course had finished its training, and he had been near the top of the class—through hard work, certainly not through brilliance. When the remainder of the class had been posted to radar stations all over the British Isles, he and a few others had remained. Whether he liked it or not, he was a teacher from now on, already destined for the dizzy rank of acting corporal.

"Congratulations, Bishop," Sergeant Lebrun had said when the news came through. "As Shaw puts it, 'He who can, does. He who cannot, teaches.' Welcome to the ranks of the teachers."

That was a remark to make one think, and Alan had never forgotten it, even when he had at last shaken the mud of Gatesbury from his feet and gone out to work on the radar chain. He wondered whether, in the months that lay ahead, he would Do as much as he would Teach.

But before he could attempt either, he had first to learn. And just *what* he was expected to learn on an airfield a few miles from Land's End, he had not the faintest idea.

CHAPTER 4

"HE'S AT THE Guardroom? Right—I'll come and fetch him," said Flight Lieutenant Deveraux. As he put the receiver down, he felt a pleased surprise that Group had acted so quickly. Of course, the fellow might be no damned use—though he thought this unlikely, since he had considerable faith in Steve's judgment. They were old friends; at the beginning of the war they had been flying officers together. Now Steve had jumped three steps to wingco—while he had gone up just one to flight looey.

The reason for this he knew perfectly well. If only he could keep his temper, and suffer fools gladly . . . especially when said fools were air commodores and upward. But he couldn't, and hadn't; so he was still *Flight Lieutenant* Deveraux.

His first sight of Alan was reassuring. The officer waiting for him at the Guardroom was a smart, not bad-looking youngster in his early twenties—rather thin, dark-haired, and obviously nervous. But that was understandable; everyone felt a little lost on a new posting.

In fact, Alan was not so much nervous as surprised; the

contrast between the label "Basil Deveraux" and the reality was somewhat unexpected. The Flight Lieutenant was a rugged and battered six-foot-two, and his broken nose gave him the appearance of a retired prize fighter. All in all, he looked as if he would have been more at home in a combat unit than in the most highly technical of all professions.

They exchanged polite formalities as Deveraux drove the jeep away from the main gate, past Admin Blocks Orderly Room, camp cinema, Officers' Mess, Technical Stores, and hangar after hangar. If the radar stations he had known were villages, Alan told himself, *this* was a city. It would take him weeks to find his way around, and his first job must be to requisition a bike. That was the only form of transport you could always count on when you needed it.

Now they were out on the perimeter track—the great ring-road that linked the ends of the airfield's three intersecting runways. They seemed to be heading away from the main camp and all its buildings; then, miles away on the horizon, Alan saw a group of low wooden huts.

" 'D' Flight," said Deveraux. "That's where we live. But first I want to show you something."

He cut off the track, drove for a few hundred yards across flat grass, and wound his way between massive embankments spattered with NO SMOKING and OUT OF BOUNDS TO ALL UNAUTHORIZED PERSONNEL signs. Alan guessed that these were bomb dumps; by the time they were in open territory again, he had quite lost his bearings. Before he could recover them, they were out in the middle of a sea of concrete that appeared to stretch indefinitely in all directions.

Deveraux glanced quickly around the sky, then brought the jeep to a halt.

"We shouldn't be here," he said, "but there's no one in the circuit and we won't stay for long. Do you know where we are?"

It was obviously one of the runways; but were they all *this* huge? Not wishing to show his ignorance, Alan shook his head.

"This is the biggest runway in the world," Deveraux answered rather proudly. He stood up in the jeep and spread his arms, making a figure like an Old Testament prophet. *"Four hundred and fifty feet wide*—three times the normal width. In fact, it's really three runways side by side. Damaged aircraft can come in on Number One strip—here on the left, and if they prang, the center strip goes into action until the bulldozers can clear away the mess. And if the *second* strip is blocked, then we move over to the third. Impressive, isn't it?"

"It certainly is," agreed Alan, wondering what this had to do with him.

Deveraux started up the jeep.

"Here endeth the First Lesson," he said. "Now for Number Two."

Lesson Number Two was a good deal smaller, but possibly even more expensive. It was a graveyard of smashed aircraft, just off the edge of the vast runway. Liberators and Wellingtons in the white livery of Coastal Command lay side by side with Blenheims, Ansons, Spitfires, and Hurricanes. Some seemed almost intact; others had wings and control surfaces pock-marked with the tiny gaping craters of machine-gun bullets.

"This is where they get pushed by the bulldozers, until they can be repaired or carted away for scrap. At a guess, there's a couple of million quid in this little lot, and perhaps a dozen lives. And the sad thing is that most of the damage isn't due to Jerry. Half of these are just crashes in bad weather or at night."

"But aren't there radio aids to prevent that?" asked Alan.

"Oh, there are. But they don't always work, and even at their best they're not much good close to the ground, or in zero visibility. Especially to an exhausted pilot in a shot-up bomber, watching fifty needles at once and trying to tell whether he's on the glide path by sorting out dots and dashes in his earphones."

"I see," said Alan, as a light began to dawn. "So you have something better."

"A *lot* better—so they tell me. Not that I've seen it working yet," Deveraux added gloomily.

As they continued their circuit of the airfield, he gave Alan a quick briefing.

"It's an American project, called GCD, and it's being run by the scientists who invented it. In fact, they *built* it. If it's successful, we'll take over from them and train RAF crews; that's why we wanted someone with a Radio School background. But the problem at the moment is maintenance; this is an experimental prototype, and it doesn't like the British climate. These damned Cornish mists have a wonderful time shorting out our twenty-thousand-volt power supply."

"What does GCD stand for?" asked Alan.

"Oh, sorry—should have said that at the beginning. It means Ground Controlled Descent. The idea's extremely simple, even if the equipment isn't. What we have is a very precise radar set, capable of tracking an aircraft to within a few feet. A controller on the ground has this information presented to him, and he talks to the pilot over the radio, telling him what course to fly in order to keep on the glide path. If the pilot obeys orders, and everything's working OK, he'll find himself over the end of the runway. The Americans call it a 'talk-down' system, which is a good way of describing it."

Alan was vaguely disappointed. This sounded clever, but not very interesting. Moreover, he knew even less about American radar than he did about Americans, and was not at all sure that he wanted to make the acquaintance of either.

"The beauty of the system," Deveraux continued, "is that it puts all the equipment on the ground, where it can be as complicated as you like. The aircraft doesn't need any special gear—only a radio, which it has already. *We* do all the work; the pilot simply has to obey orders. That's the theory, anyhow."

The jeep drew up at a typical wooden barracks hut; quite a comedown, thought Alan, after the country-house luxury of Elvesham Manor. The private barbed wire fence and the two RAF Regiment guards patrolling with rifles at the ready added to the homely atmosphere.

Deveraux saw Alan's expression, and grinned.

"Sorry about this," he said. "The Station Adj keeps promising us a better billet, but it's always 'Next week, old chap.' Besides, there's a security problem; the boffins are talking shop all the time, so it's best to keep them isolated."

Effortlessly, using only one hand, he swung Alan's luggage out of the vehicle.

"There are plenty of spare bunks—so make yourself at home. I'll get over to the unit to see what luck they've had. We'll be back here by lunchtime to drive you to the Mess."

As the jeep roared away, Alan walked thoughtfully into his new home. The long hut with its bare rafters and all-too-familiar iron stove (on how many winter nights had he struggled to keep one of those monstrosities alive!) held some twenty beds and was completely empty at the moment. However, it had a distinctly lived-in appearance; RAF and civilian clothing shared the coat hangers indiscriminately, and the bedside lockers were stuffed with books, toilet gear, discarded radio tubes, soldering irons, electrical components, meters. . . . This was no longer an anonymous hut, but a home for people who couldn't care less about service discipline. My old Flight Sergeant, thought Alan, would have heart failure if he could see this.

There were more books scattered over the tables, and once he had dumped his belongings on the most comfortable of the spare beds, Alan walked over to investigate the literary tastes of his new companions. He found two dog-eared copies of *Esquire,* Terman's *Radio Engineering,* Millman and Seely's *Electronics,* four copies of the *Proceedings of the Institute of Radio Engineers,* James Hadley Chase's *No Orchids for Miss Blandish,* Louis Untermeyer's *Albatross Book of Living Verse,* Janke and Emde's *Tables of Functions,* James Branch Cabell's *Jurgen,* a dozen copies of *Astounding Science Fiction* and *Wonder Stories,* and a pile of miscellaneous westerns and thrillers.

This was all reassuringly normal; he might have been

back at No. 7 Radio School. But he knew perfectly well that he was not, and he felt very lost and lonely. He returned to his bunk, kicked off his shoes, and lay on the coarse blankets, staring up at the ceiling.

For better or worse, he had come to a major turning point in his life—like that summer morning, long ago, when he had met Miss Hadley for the first time aboard the *Channel Queen*. His thoughts always went to her at crucial moments, when his destiny was being reshaped; for she had done so much to shape it in the past.

It was curious that so refined and aristocratic an elderly lady should be traveling on a pleasure steamer loaded with trippers. Alan was aware of the oddness now, but to a small boy of five the *Channel Queen* had all the glamour and romance of an Atlantic liner. Nor did it occur to him, in those innocent days, that a retired governess—even one who had taught princes—would not have enough money for more far-ranging cruises, and that this was the best substitute she could contrive for the adventures of her youth.

He had been leaning over the ship's side, watching the foam spread out from the slowly churning paddle wheels. To get a better view, he had balanced himself on the rail, and was seesawing happily back and forth when a firm hand grasped him by the shoulder.

"Young man," said a cultured voice (he could hear it still, every syllable precisely articulated), "if you fall in, we shall have to stop the ship to pick you up."

Alan dropped back on the deck and twisted free from the restraining grip. "That's all right," he replied haughtily. "I can swim, and my father owns the *Channel Queen*." It was the first and last time he had ever been impertinent to Miss Hadley; what he said was true enough, but the delivery lacked politeness.

He turned to face his would-be rescuer. She was very old, so it seemed to him—he realized now that she must have been in her late fifties—and leaned slightly on an intricately carved ebony stick. Even then, her silk dress appeared old-fashioned, her wide-brimmed hat with its ribbons and lace something that might have come from an Edwardian fashion plate. A huge cameo brooch was pinned to her breast, and below it dangled a pair of pince-nez on a black ribbon. They were the first that Alan had ever seen, and they fascinated him as they pendulumed to and fro with the roll of the ship. He wished that she would put them on, but it was a long time before that desire was granted, because she used them only to read the finest print. For all else, the vision of those keen, exceedingly blue eyes was as good as Alan's.

They were staring at him now, most disconcertingly, and it occurred to Alan that she doubted his claim to be the Captain's son.

"It's true," he said defensively. "Captain Bishop is my father."

"I believe you," she replied. There was a slight pause before she added, as neither a boast nor a threat, but merely as a statement of fact, "No one ever lies to me."

That was the beginning of the intense yet curiously unemotional friendship between the lonely spinster and the lonely boy. To Alan, Miss Hadley provided a partial substitute for the mother whose memory was already lost beyond tears in a nightmare world of whispered conferences with solemn doctors, of prim, starched nurses dehumanized by carbolic, of black-clad uncles and aunts patting him on the head with commiserating clucks. And to Miss Hadley, Alan was, if not the son she might have had, then at least a successor to the royal pupils she had taught during her days in the East.

Alan grew to know them across the years, from the dark, hawk-faced features that stared out of the faded photographs in Miss Hadley's scrapbooks. Most of them were dead now—not many through natural causes—but sometimes letters would come from strange places, bearing wonderful stamps; and then Miss Hadley would be very remote and abstracted for a few days, and Alan would know better than to bother her with questions.

For more than half his life she had been his window on the world, widening his horizons beyond the circle of ports around which the *Channel Queen* thumped her impecunious way, losing a little more money every season. Miss Hadley had given him a glimpse of art and culture, as well as of geography; she had tried, not with complete success, to make him speak and behave like a gentleman, even though this had led to endless fights with the fisher-boys, trades-men's sons, and farm lads who made up the majority of his schoolmates. She had, indeed, been a much greater influence than the Captain—who, though Alan did not know it then, was slowly going down before his ship.

It was a pity that there was no radar to guide one across the trackless seas of life. Every man had to find his own way, steered by some secret compass of the soul. And sometimes, late or early, the compass lost its power and spun aimlessly on its bearings.

So it had been with the Captain. He had begun to drink soon after his wife had died, and though Alan had never seen him intoxicated, he could remember him wholly sober only once in the last ten years.

That was when he had taken the *Channel Queen* to Dun-kirk, to meet their last shared hour of glory. The Captain alone had returned, untouched by bombs or bullets.

But all the love that had not followed his wife to the churchyard had gone with his lost ship. There was nothing left for his son.

❈ CHAPTER 5

THE ORIGIN OF the word "boffin" has never been satisfactorily explained. One farfetched theory connects it with a puffin—a marine bird whose ellipsoidal eggs, it is said, always roll back to the original spot when an attempt is made to push them away. As many disgruntled air marshals can testify, this is highly typical of ideas put forward by boffins.

Dr. Theodore Hatton was a King Boffin, in constant communion with such Olympian entities as Watson-Watt, Bernal, Blackett, and the other scientists who were rapidly changing the whole nature of warfare. But unlike most of them, he was not a physicist; he was a biologist with a flair for math. He could see the things that had to be done, and could evaluate their results; it was up to the engineers to produce the necessary hardware.

At the moment, he thought gloomily, the engineers were not doing too well. Perhaps it was all his fault; for once, he had been unscientific, and had let his emotions overrule his intellect. But when he had seen Professor Schuster and his team at work on that airfield outside Boston, calling down aircraft from the sky with uncanny accuracy, it had been like a religious revelation. He had known at once that this was the answer to the blind-landing problem; it could save countless lives and aircraft—perhaps even change the course of the war.

So he had bullied and pleaded, had made promises and told flat lies, had written MOST SECRET reports and lectured eloquently to generals and air marshals. At first no one had taken much notice; then things had started to happen with surprising speed. The still experimental and unproved GCD prototype, plus the scientists who had built it, had been loaded on an aircraft carrier and shipped across the Atlantic.

"What you want," Hutton had told the somewhat reluctant Schuster, "is an operational airfield where you can see exactly what we're up against. We know that the system *works;* now it has to be integrated into Flying Control and sold to the pilots. We've just the place for you."

Well, here they all were, while the rain poured down in buckets, and over in the hangar Deveraux and the Americans wrestled with the recalcitrant Mark I. (At this rate, there would never be a Mark II.) As he had no electronic training or skill, there was nothing that he could do to help them; he could only sit here in the hut, sending off a daily no-progress report to his anxious colleagues at the Air Ministry, and answering F/O Bishop's questions.

Alan was now sitting at the hut's solitary table, which was completely covered with large circuit diagrams, all labeled SECRET. He was carefully copying them into a foolscap-sized notebook, as he tried to reduce the Mark I's five hundred radio tubes to some sort of order; already he had learned to call them "tubes," not "valves."

He glanced up when he saw that Dr. Hatton's eye was on him. When he first arrived, he had been overawed by the massed talent surrounding him, but he had quickly discovered that scientists are indistinguishable from other human beings. Though he had not yet met Professor Schuster, he was already on first-name terms with his plump, bearded deputy, Dr. Wendt, and the three absurdly young graduate engineers who had helped to design and build the gear.

"It's a funny thing," he said to Hatton, "but the Americans just can't draw circuit diagrams. I've never seen such a mess as these."

The biologist, who could barely cope with a crystal set, had no strong views on the subject, but he suspected that Alan's condemnation was a little unfair.

"They were probably so busy *making* the gear that they had no time to draw pretty pictures. Anyway, why are you so keen on it? You've done nothing else for the last three days."

Alan carefully inked in another line before answering.

"It's the only way to learn how a new piece of equipment works," he answered. "Besides, if I've got to train RAF mechs to run it, I must make sure I'm one jump ahead of them."

That was not the only answer, though it was a good one. Alan's aesthetic sense was rudimentary, but he derived considerable artistic pleasure from a well-laid-out circuit diagram. The problem was that of arranging, on a single sheet of paper, the symbols for several hundred resistors, capacitors, and electron tubes—and then showing all the connecting wires in such a way that the functioning of the circuit was made perfectly clear. One of the rules of the game was that there should be the minimum number of points where wires crossed each other; another was that the wiring should be of the least possible length. The two goals were not always compatible.

Until Alan had completed his notes, he was having as little as possible to do with the Mark I; in any case, at this stage, he would only be in the way. He had paid a single visit to the guarded hangar housing the gear, and had departed both shaken and impressed.

As usual, it had been raining when Deveraux and Hatton had driven him out to the hangar in T6, the Ford truck that was the unit's chief means of transportation. The vehicle had arrived from the United States with the GCD team, but did not seem to have any legal owner. Probably it still belonged to the Massachusetts Institute of Technology, and probably MIT was still looking for it.

When they had presented their passes to the armed guard, they had been allowed into the great metal cavern, lit inadequately by a few naked light bulbs thirty feet above the ground, which threw isolated pools of radiance on the oil-stained concrete. In one of these pools were standing two large, black-painted vehicles.

The smaller truck was about the size and shape of a furniture removal van, and was in no way unusual apart from the stubby aircraft-type aerials jutting from its roof. Alan did not give it a second glance; he was too busy staring at the larger vehicle, which was quite the oddest thing he had ever seen on wheels.

From the forward end of the roof, just above the driver's cab, sprouted a large cylinder, proportioned like one of the stovepipe hats beloved by the Victorians. From the other end reared a rectangular structure—a long, thin box stretching all the way from the ground to a point at least fifteen feet in the air. In addition to this, one side of the truck bulged out into a plywood-covered bay window. Presumably all these excrescences concealed radar scanners, but from their shape they must be unlike any that Alan had ever encountered before.

"That's the transmitter truck," explained Hatton. "It holds our mobile power plant—a big diesel-electric set—and the antennas that produce our radar beams. It's nothing but a radar station on wheels, and there's no room inside it for any operators. They're here in the control van; this is where the actual talking down is done. *When* it's done," he added gloomily.

He pulled open the door, drew aside a heavily weighted blackout curtain, and waved Alan into the van. Almost the whole interior was occupied by a massive rack of electronic gear, stretching from floor to ceiling. There were no fewer than four radar screens, as well as a prominent vertical panel carrying three large meters. One was labeled ELEVA-

TION, another AZIMUTH, the third RANGE. It needed no great intelligence to deduce that this was where the controller sat, and that these meters told him what was happening to the aircraft he was talking down.

One of the display units lay on the controller's desk, its wiring scattered around it in a tangled maze as Dr. Wendt performed some surgical operation upon it. The prevailing smell, however, was not that of ether and antiseptics, but of soldering irons, burned insulation, and tobacco smoke. There was something peculiarly dead and depressing, Alan had always thought, about any large radar set when the power was switched off, and he had never received that impression as strongly as now. The needles of the meters all lay supine against their zero stops; no lights were gleaming, either in red warning or green reassurance, on the banked racks and panels. The display screens themselves were like blind windows, looking onto nothingness—until Dr. Wendt could give them vision again.

Alexander Wendt was the oldest member of the team; he had reached the ripe age of thirty-three, and his companions never let him forget it. He was a striking figure, thanks to his magnificent spade beard and the slender cigarette holder he usually carried clenched between his teeth. This, Alan soon discovered, served as a kind of emotional semaphore whose angle accurately signaled all its owner's moods, from despondency to elation.

Sprawling full-length under the controller's bench were Pat Connor and Howard Rawlings III. ("What does the III stand for?" Alan had asked. "It means that he was one of triplets, but they drowned the other two," was Pat's explanation.) Howard was prodding hopefully around with the probes of a test meter, calling out the readings while Pat checked them against figures in a notebook. They were too busy to look up when the visitors all but walked over their prostrate bodies.

"Where's Benny?" asked Hatton.

Wendt nodded vaguely toward the door.

"Over in the transmitter truck. He's trying to run the X-band maggie up to twenty-five Kv."

Hatton pressed a key on the controller's desk and spoke into a microphone.

"How's it going, Benny?" he asked.

There was a brief pause. Then a loud-speaker somewhere in the massed banks of electronic equipment made a short announcement. No knowledge of Yiddish whatsoever was necessary to deduce that the X-band maggie had *not* run up to twenty-five Kv.

"I'll go over and give him a hand," said Deveraux. "He sounds a bit browned off."

"Thanks, Dev," remarked Pat's voice from the floor. "I always wondered what a typically British understatement was like. That'll do very nicely until a better one comes along."

As they retreated from the battlefield—stepping carefully over the recumbent bodies—Hatton asked Alan, with a mixture of pride and exasperation, "Well, what do you think of it?"

"It looks an awful lot of equipment just to land an aircraft."

Hatton, who normally walked with a slight stoop, reared up in annoyance. Like Deveraux, with whom he had a great deal in common, he was impatient of silly remarks, and he had heard this one so many times that it was beginning to rankle.

"I know a case," he said, controlling himself with an obvious effort, "where a Bomber Command squadron lost three Lancs and four Stirlings on a single op, because fog closed in before they could get home. If they'd had GCD, it would have paid for itself in one night."

Suitably abashed, Alan quickly changed the subject.

"When are we going to see Professor Schuster?" he asked. "I'm anxious to meet him."

"He's still on a scrounging-*cum*-propaganda tour," answered Hatton. "No one knows when he'll be back—and at the moment no one is at *all* anxious to see him."

Alan was quite shocked by this.

"Why," he said, "I thought he was very popular."

Hatton cracked a rather glacial smile.

"We're all very fond of him," he answered. "But you don't know the Professor. As a theoretician he's superb; as a *practical* man . . ."

He gave an eloquent shrug of his shoulders and pointed back at the hangar.

"We can consider ourselves lucky that he's not in there helping the boys. If he was, they'd *never* get the Mark I working again."

Alan's naïve remarks had an unexpected sequel a few days later, when Hatton suddenly announced: "Better pack your toothbrush and spare socks; we're going away for a couple of days."

"Where?" asked Alan, reasonably enough. Hatton often made mysterious trips away from the station, as befitted a King Boffin, but this was the first time he had invited anyone to go with him.

"There's a spot of trouble at a Bomber Command station, and it's time you saw some Ops. Until you do, you won't understand what all this is about."

Alan never did discover exactly what the "spot of trouble" was, even after Hatton had whipped him right across England by train and special car; apparently it concerned some long-range navigational aid that was misbehaving. For as soon as they arrived at the airfield, the scientist handed him over to the Senior Flying Control Officer, who appeared to be an old friend.

"Here he is," he said ambiguously, leaving Alan wondering what build-up he had received. "Park him in a corner of the tower where he won't be in the way. I'll collect him when I'm through." Alan was given a chair, a small desk, a mug of tea, a generous supply of official documents—and left to his own devices.

Around him, as evening fell, the airfield came to life. Out of the darkness, from the dispersals where they had already been fueled and bombed-up, the Lancasters were revving their engines. Thousands of horsepower—perhaps more power than any army in history had ever mustered before this age—was concentrated within these few square miles, waiting to be unleashed. What the target was, only a few men knew; that was the secret upon which the lives of all these crews, and the success of their mission, depended. Security was so strict that, for hours before the operation, the station had been virtually sealed off from the outside world.

And now the control tower was crackling with messages and orders as the squadrons were set rolling along the perimeter track. An intricate machine—as intricate as any that man had ever built—was being set in motion. It comprised hundreds of aircraft, scattered over many bases; vast communications networks and radar chains; Air-Sea Rescue boats already setting out into the dark waters of the North Sea; agents far inside enemy territory; and, in the very center of it, the pilots and navigators, engineers and gunners, who flew mission after mission despite the odds mounting inexorably against them.

One by one A Able, B Baker, C Charlie, and their companions acknowledged the flashing Aldis light from the control tower and went roaring down the runway to face the known and unknown hazards that lay ahead. Only Y Yoke failed to join that eastward-flowing stream of destruction; some mechanical failure developed at the last moment, and it had to taxi off into a dispersal site. Alan felt very sorry for the crew; it must be a terrible anticlimax, after you had steeled yourself for a mission, for it to be aborted. It was true that the grounding might have saved your life, but you could never prove it, and would always feel that you had let the squadron down.

The sky ceased to reverberate; the last red glow from incandescent exhaust faded among the stars. The English countryside turned to sleep, but in a few hours some German town would wake to nightmare.

There would be no sleep, however, for anyone in the control tower. Now that the raid was under way, the waiting had begun. The tension seemed to focus on a single loudspeaker, high on the wall above the Senior Controller's desk. No sound came from it except a faint crackling, but, if all went well, at some undisclosed hour it would call a few words which would mean nothing except to a few men at the Air Ministry. It would tell them that the squadron was over the target; or that it was under heavy attack, or that it had turned back—or many other things.

Time passed. Cups of coffee circulated; so did little jokes and reminiscences, but no one seemed to be taking any notice of them. Alan had never intended to stay this long, and miss a night's sleep, but now he found it impossible to leave.

It was after 2:00 A.M. when the loudspeaker woke to life. "The hounds of spring," it announced, "are on winter's traces." That was all; the words were clear and unhurried, as if spoken into a telephone in some peaceful office. Even the background of engine noise was quite subdued: there was no trace of the concussions that Alan had half expected to hear.

Whether it was a message of triumph or disaster, there was no way of telling. It certainly sounded reassuring—but even that might be a blind.

Half an hour later, the speaker gave the unexpected news that the price of Spam had gone up by sixpence a pound. This did not sound quite so good, but there was little point in worrying about it. However, the messages did allow Alan to deduce one piece of information. Assuming that the return journey would be quicker than the outward one, the bombers should be back just before dawn.

Across one wall of the control tower was a large blackboard, divided into rows and columns. The columns read A Able, B Baker, C Charlie, D Dove, and most of the way through the alphabet, with the name of the pilot against each aircraft. There were also columns for call signs, frequencies, and other information, and a final column for notes blank except for the disgraced Y Yoke.

As the small hours became steadily larger, eyes could be seen straying more and more frequently toward this silent reminder. The tension, which had slackened off after those radio messages, began to grow again. Wireless operators sat hunched over their dials, making minute adjustments from time to time; the Flying Control Officer seemed on the brink of making phone calls, but kept changing his mind; the WAAF clerks had dropped their knitting and their magazines. Everyone was waiting.

At 6:30 A.M., a telephone rang. The FCO grabbed it, listened for a minute, then turned to his assistant.

"F Freddie—he's landed at Hornchurch. Starboard outer feathered, but otherwise OK."

The information was chalked up on the board, and thereafter things began to happen quickly. Over telephone and radio, news of the returning squadron flowed in. Twenty minutes later, the thunder of the first approaching engines disturbed the dawn.

S Sugar was first to touch down, and the blanks on the blackboard started to fill up. It was like watching a jigsaw puzzle being completed; by 7:15 most of the pieces had been fitted back into place: two like F Freddie were absent but accounted for, and three were missing.

This, thought Alan, as he watched the dawn of a lovely winter day, must be the worse part of the whole job. P Peter, T Tommy, and X X-Ray might still be on their way home, staggering along on two or three engines, and might need all the help they could get. On the other hand, their troubles might have ended hours ago.

By the time hunger and fatigue sent Alan to breakfast, T Tommy had been rubbed off the board. The returning aircrews had seen it spiral down over the target; some parachutes had emerged, they could not say how many. But of P Peter and X X-Ray, there was still no news when Alan and Hatton left the station. There never would be, now.

CHAPTER 6

"WE'RE GROWING," said Deveraux to Alan, as they left the Officers' Mess after breakfast. "The Adj tells me that three WAAF operators and one radar mech arrived last night. He's just discovered that they belong to us."

"I hope we've got some work for them," said Alan. "What rank is the mech?"

"Sergeant—R double-A F. Probably a bit Bolshie, like most Australians. I don't think I've ever seen one salute an officer."

He said this without any particular rancor; as long as an airman was efficient and kept out of trouble, that was all that mattered. Deveraux himself was efficient—highly so—but he had not always succeeded in keeping out of trouble. This time, though, Group could hardly turn down that overdue promotion—if GCD lived up to its claims and he could train the RAF to use it. . . .

When they arrived at "D" Flight, the newcomers were waiting for them in the cramped office that served as HQ. The WAAFs were capable-looking girls, ranging in appearance from homely to passable; the Sergeant was a tough little bantam of a man in the dark-blue uniform of the Royal Australian Air Force.

He saluted smartly, thus refuting Deveraux.

"Nice to see you again, sir," he said to Alan. "Remember me?" That "sir" was the first and very nearly the last that he ever received from Sgt. McGregor.

Alan did a swift double take. During his term as an instructor, several hundred airmen had passed through his classes. They had been from all parts of the world—Britain, Canada, South Africa, Australia, France, Poland—and though at one time he had known the names of every one of them, most of them had faded from memory after the farewell party that terminated each course.

But it did not take him long to place the Sergeant; even as a humble aircraftsman II, McGregor had not been a very forgettable person. Like Alan, he had been that rare phenomenon—a radar mech who actually knew something about radio when he entered the service. Indeed, he was an amateur with his own license, operating a shortwave station somewhere in the Australian outback.

Alan was genuinely pleased to meet one of his old pupils, and to find that he had gone up in the world despite his tuition.

"It seems a long time ago since we had that passing-out party in the NAAFI," he said. "I hope the sheep farm's still managing without you. And why haven't you got your commission yet? You were always talking about it."

"*Station,* not far," corrected McGregor with a grimace of disapproval. "And as for the commission, I've changed my mind. Above sergeant you have too many responsibilities; below it, not enough privilege. So I'll stick here, if that's all right with everyone."

Similar thoughts had often passed through Alan's mind, but he was intelligent enough to reject them—as, he was sure, did McGregor. The balance between responsibility and privilege could be struck at any level, if one had the ability to function at that level. Alan had met miserable Aircraftsmen II—and suspected that there might even be happy air chief marshals.

The arrival of Dr. Hatton in T6 cut short these musings. It was the first time that Alan had seen the scientist looking really cheerful, and he guessed the reason.

"They've fixed it?" he asked hopefully.

Hatton nodded.

"Looks like it, touch wood. They're just getting ready to roll out of the hangar, so I came to collect you."

He caught sight of the newcomers, then added: "They've timed their arrival nicely. Maybe our luck's changing."

"We still don't know," complained Sgt. McGregor, "what we're supposed to be doing here."

"Jump in the truck," said Alan. "This is the quickest way to find out. You, too, girls," he added courteously.

The WAAFs took one look into the gloomy interior, at the oil stained fuel drums that served as seats, and declined the invitation.

"No thank you, sir," they said with one voice. "If it's only round the airfield, we'll follow on our bikes."

Alan could hardly blame them; he was still trying to remove diesel oil from his own battle dress. But he wished he knew how they'd managed to get hold of bikes so quickly; *he'd* been trying ever since he arrived. . . .

T6 arrived at the hangar just as the monstrous metal doors creaked apart on their steel rollers. They moved with understandable reluctance, for it was a full week since they had last opened; then the transmitter truck, followed by the smaller control van, drove out into the pale sunlight of the winter morning.

Alan had never before seen them in the open; he had to admit that they did not form a very handsome couple. With its cylindrical pillbox perched on the roof, protruding bay window, and square chimney, the transmitter truck looked rather like some kind of siege engine, built to storm a medieval castle.

"By the way," Alan asked Deveraux, "why do the Yanks call that antenna housing a 'Chick Sale'?"

"I haven't a clue," answered Deveraux, whose reading had not extended to *The Specialist*. "It seems some kind of private joke; probably Chick Sale's one of their folklore heroes, like—er—Buffalo Bill or Rip van Winkle."

The control van rolled to a halt beside them, and Pat Connor leaned out of the cab. He was unshaven but cheerful.

"And so we say farewell," he intoned, "to glamorous Hangar F, scene of strange native orgies and primitive fertility rites, while the sun sinks slowly in the east—doing it the hard way."

"*We* shall sink slowly in the east," said Hatton, "unless you've got the bugs out of the system. I've checked with Flying Control; we can use Runway 270. As soon as we're ready, they'll send up an Anson to do approaches and overshoots. So let's go."

The RAF's way of labeling runways was one of the dozens of new concepts that Alan had had to absorb at St. Erryn. It was simple and obvious, once one got used to it. Every runway was known by its compass heading, and therefore had two numbers, according to the direction of approach. Runway 270 thus pointed due west—and 090 was the same runway, looking east.

When the convoy arrived at the site, after trundling around more than a mile of perimeter track, Howard Rawlings gave a neat display of precision driving. Leaning out of the cab, he inched the huge transmitter truck back and forth until it was exactly aligned with some yellow survey marks already painted on the concrete.

"I laid those out with a theodolite a couple of weeks ago," explained Hatton. "One thing about this job—you never know what you'll have to try your hand at next."

With a great wheezing and snorting of hydraulic jacks, the truck was then leveled. As it heaved this way and that, inching itself higher and higher off the ground, it looked rather like an elephant getting to its feet. But at last it was properly positioned, so that the radar antennas were aimed along the runway, pointing in the direction from which an aircraft would approach.

While all this was going on, Alan stood well back and observed the proceedings. Everyone knew exactly what to do; it was like watching an orchestra going full steam ahead without a conductor. Pat Connor was starting the big Caterpillar Diesel in the transmitter truck; it gave several annoyed coughs and then broke into a full-throated roar. Benny Schwartz and Dr. Hatton were unreeling the thick cables that linked the two trucks, and plugging them into their sockets; as they dragged them across the concrete, they looked like firemen wrestling with recalcitrant hoses.

When Alan followed Hatton and Deveraux into the control van, power was already on and green bars of light glowed across the faces of the radar screens. But the bars were stationary, not yet painting their pictures—for the antennas with which they were linked had not yet started to sweep the sky.

Dr. Wendt was sitting on one of the operators' stools, staring at the dozens of meters, lights, and oscilloscopes but taking no action about any of them. His eyes roamed from panel to panel, and his nose twitched occasionally as it strained for the acrid, telltale stink of burning insulation. The cigarette holder had risen to the horizontal, indicating cautious optimism.

Howard's voice, relayed from the transmitter truck, boomed over the intercom speaker.

"Everything fine here. I'm starting the scan."

"Go ahead," answered Wendt. "We're ready."

On the radar screens, the lines began to move. Each left behind it a ghostly afterimage that slowly faded—so slowly that it had not vanished completely before the electronic brush, sweeping back and forth, had returned to re-create it. The whole cycle lasted about two seconds; it was as if a television set had been slowed down a hundredfold, so that one could see each separate line of the image being formed. At the moment, the glowing rectangles were empty—frames awaiting their pictures.

Suddenly, flecks of brightness mottled the blank faces of the radar screen. Howard was tuning the receivers; the first signals were coming in, as the questing beams searched heaven and earth. Fuzzy, softly glowing pictures, meaningless except to those who knew how to read their messages of life and death, were appearing as if by magic. And it *was* magic; though he had watched countless radar displays, Alan had not yet lost his sense of wonder. He was seeing the world around him by waves a hundred thousand times longer than visible light. The images were blurred, and it would take him some time to interpret them, but that was to be expected. The patterns it perceives mean nothing to a baby when it first opens its eyes.

"We're getting some nice, juicy echoes," said Wendt with satisfaction. He pointed to a cluster of four closely spaced blobs forming a tiny square near the center of one screen.

"See that bunch? Those are the towers of Filey Radar Station, about six miles from here."

Old-fashioned stuff, thought Alan smugly; compared with *this* equipment, the great radar chain that guarded England against the *Luftwaffe* already seemed like one of Marconi's first experiments, and its three-hundred-foot masts as obsolete as dinosaurs.

"What about our aircraft?" asked Deveraux. "Shall I tell Flying Control to get it airborne?"

"Yes," answered Wendt. "Ask the pilot to make a visual approach from five miles, overshooting and going around again until we tell him to stop. We won't attempt to control him; I just want to see that everything's working OK."

Deveraux passed these instructions over the radio; a few minutes later Alan heard a faint roar of motors as the twin-engined trainer swept past them and climbed into the sky.

Dr. Hatton glanced at his wrist watch.

"We should see him in about four minutes," he said, "coming in from the left."

They waited in expectant silence; then, just as Hatton had predicted, a moving fleck of light appeared at the extreme left of the radar map. With each sweep of the scan it edged in toward the center of the screen, leaving a curving comet tail behind it.

Now the creeping glowworm had straightened out, and was moving on a course that led directly toward the airfield. It seemed to Alan, as he watched the fluorescent rectangle hanging there in the semidarkness, that he was really looking down upon the earth and the approaching aircraft from an enormous height. Every twist and turn was revealed in such detail that one could almost read the pilot's mind; now he had realized that he was too far to the right, and the crawling blip had begun to edge back toward the invisible line of the runway.

Alan had met this type of azimuth or plan display before, though never one with such a degree of precision. But the elevation display was something quite new to him, for it showed a *vertical* cross section of space, from ground level up to a height of five thousand feet. Along the bottom of the screen the ground was clearly defined by a line of bright echoes, strung one behind the other like beads on a necklace. Above that was nothing—except in one spot, where the isolated blip of the approaching aircraft hung in space. Alan could see from its slowly fading afterglow that it was flying at a constant altitude, for its comet tail was parallel to the ground far beneath.

But presently it began to descend, dropping down toward the line of ground echoes as the pilot started his approach; on the azimuth display, he was maintaining his steady course toward the runway, deviating neither to the right nor to the left. Then, about a mile from the edge of the airfield, he began to pull out; the descending curve flattened into a line parallel to the ground, and not many seconds later the truck shook slightly as the Anson roared past overhead. At almost the same moment, the echo disappeared from both of the display screens as the aircraft shot into the blind area behind the radar scanners.

"Next time round, we'll start tracking," said Deveraux. "Bishop—bring in the WAAFs—I want them to see this."

Alan collected the girls, who had now arrived on their

bikes and were sitting patiently in the driving cab of T6, exchanging gossip about the radar stations they'd known.

"Sorry we haven't had time to explain anything," he said, "but you'll soon get the hang of it." When he ushered them into the control van, he found that the others were already seated side by side in the operating positions, waiting for the echo to make its next appearance. Deveraux was on the left, in front of the elevation display; Hatton was on the right, watching the azimuth display. Between them sat Dr. Wendt, watching everything. Alan parked a WAAF behind each of the three swivel seats, the style and arrangement of which always reminded him of the line-up at a milk bar.

When the echo appeared, five miles away, Dr. Wendt threw a switch and a thin, bright line appeared on the azimuth screen. He spun a handwheel, and the line chased after the moving echo until it caught up with it.

"He's tracking the echo in range," Alan explained to the WAAFs. "That line has to be kept right on the blip. You can move it backward or forward by turning that small brass knob."

Deveraux and Hatton were also busily turning wheels, each controlling the position of a little needle of light with which he was trying to spear his echo. When all three operators were on target, then the echo was being properly tracked in range, elevation, and azimuth. Then, and only then, would the mechanical brain of the landing system "know" exactly where the aircraft was in space.

"This is where the answer comes out," said Alan, as he led the girls to the controller's panel at the other end of the truck. The three meters were no longer blank; they were now illuminated and their needles were moving across the scales. Range said three and a half miles; elevation said fifty feet above the glide path; azimuth said one hundred feet left. Even as they watched, both the azimuth and elevation needles crept slowly toward zero error, while range shortened to three miles.

The girls were obviously impressed, but they were no more impressed than Alan. He certainly had no intention of revealing that this was the very first time that he, too, had seen the equipment at work. It was one thing to study the circuits and to know, in theory, how all this mass of electronics functioned. Yet somehow no amount of study could match a few seconds of the real thing. It was uncanny to stand here and to see these pointers recording every movement of that distant aircraft—and to know that they could do so with equal ease by day or night, in clear weather or blinding fog.

One and a half miles, said the range meter; zero error, said the azimuth meter, confirming that the aircraft was right on the center line of the runway. But the elevation meter was rapidly climbing, as the pilot broke off his approach and started to overshoot. A few seconds later, there was that familiar roar from outside, and the lights on all the controller's meters went out as the trackers lost their echo.

So it went on, all through the morning. For the pilot of the Anson, it was probably monotonous; indeed, toward the end he was obviously getting careless, and lining up on the runway in a somewhat perfunctory manner. His azimuth error swung wildly from left to right; but nobody minded, for it was excellent practice for the trackers. By lunchtime, everyone had tried his hand at the game, and Alan had discovered that it was not so easy as it looked. That shining blip on the screen moved quickly, and unless you were alert, it would escape from your electronic needle. Once, when Alan let his thoughts wander for a few seconds, he found that he was several hundred feet off—and then compounded his error by turning the tracking handwheel in the wrong direction as he started to pursue the evasive blip.

"Remarkable aircraft you British make," said Pat Connor, who had been watching this performance. "That's the first time I knew an Anson could fly a thousand feet in three seconds—sideways."

"That's nothing," retorted Alan with spirit. "Just now it flew *backward*—when a certain American scientist was tracking."

"*Touché*," said Dr. Wendt. "Maybe we'd better leave it to

the girls. They've only done a couple of runs, and they're better than us already."

That was almost true, but it was not particularly surprising. These WAAFs were highly trained operators who had spent hundreds of hours tracking echoes on every type of ground radar in the RAF. They could take this job in their stride.

That evening, after the trucks had been driven back to the hangar, there was a small celebration in the Mess. Everyone knew that their main task was just beginning, but at least the equipment was now functioning well. *That* deserved a few drinks, and a greatly relieved Dr. Hatton was only too glad to buy the first round. He had already sent off a signal to Group HQ, asking for a couple of Flying Control officers who could be trained in the talk-down technique.

The Mess anteroom, where the party took place, had given Alan his first glimpse of the *real* RAF—the world of operational aircrews. Here, at any time of the day, flying types of all ranks from wing commander to humble pilot officer might be found sprawled in the overstuffed chairs, hidden behind *Punch* or the *Illustrated London News*—or, more likely, studying the current exposure of "Jane" in the *Daily Mirror*'s celebrated comic strip.

Most of these aircrewmen, even many of the senior officers, seemed little older than Alan, yet almost all had two or three ribbon bands on their tunics and jackets. What sights had they seen, what experiences had they passed through, that he could never share? Alan regarded them with a good deal of admiration and some awe, as well as a growing envy; for that night at Bomber Command had planted a seed in his mind.

In theory, none of the station personnel was supposed to know what GCD was all about. In practice, everyone did, and Alan had grown a little tired of flying types coming up to him and saying, "When are you going to get that gadget of yours working, old man?" Until now his reply had been: "Sorry—I'm not allowed to talk about it." That was still the only reply he was supposed to give; but tonight the general behavior of the GCD team spoke volumes.

The party was a well-behaved one; the time for a lavish celebration had not yet come. No one went around with scissors cutting off ties; no one poured beer into the grand piano or tried to leave footprints on the ceiling. Deveraux and Hatton astonished everybody by doing a sprightly Cossack dance; Pat (after checking that the Padre was out of earshot) recited the saga of the Good Ship *Venus,* and the exploits of its ingenious but single-minded crew. It was Benny Schwartz, however, who stole the show.

He had a splendid voice ("How can I help it? My grandfathers and uncles, as far as the eye can reach, have *all* been cantors"), and his rendering of "Summertime" was completely professional. On this cold, dreary winter night, with the rain and fog now rolling in from the Atlantic, it expressed all the yearning of the heart for sun and warmth—and peace. When Benny had finished, there was that silence that is a greater tribute than any applause.

It was broken at last by a sound from outside. The deep-throated roar of an ascending bomber set the room vibrating, starting the beer mugs dancing on the glass-topped tables. Louder and louder grew the thunder of the engines as the outward-bound Liberator climbed off the runway, heading for its long and lonely mission over the Atlantic.

All around him, Alan suddenly realized, the Mess had become tense and expectant. He was merely listening to an aircraft taking off—but these men were hearing the departure of friends they might not see again.

In that moment, something happened to Alan. Until now —despite the object lessons that Deveraux and Hatton had been careful to give him on his arrival—this project had not really involved his emotions. It was fascinating, he enjoyed the company, and he was prepared to work until he dropped; but it was just another of the jobs that had to be done to win the war.

Perhaps the trouble had been that the war was too big to grasp. But now he was engaged on something that he could see as a whole—something whose aims were direct and obvious. And, moreover, something in which he could play a share that was not altogether insignificant.

The voice of the Liberator died away over Land's End; it was a sound, Alan knew, that must hereafter haunt his nights and days. It symbolized his new life; in the years to come, whenever he recalled St. Erryn, he would remember with both brain and heart the reverberation of those steadfast engines making their way across the western seas.

CHAPTER 7

PROFESSOR SCHUSTER'S ARRIVAL could not possibly have been better timed. The GCD trucks had just positioned themselves by the side of the enormous main runway when Flying Control called.

"Longstop to Ranger. Your aircraft S Sugar will be landing in twenty minutes. Requests your assistance. Can you provide it? Over."

As it was a cold but brilliant morning with unlimited visibility, this appeal was hardly a serious one. However, it was received with great satisfaction by the entire team, and Deveraux answered at once:

"Ranger to Longstop. Wilco. Please inform S Sugar that we will be watching for him and listening on this frequency. Out."

In the trucks, there was a flurry of well-co-ordinated activity. While Sgt. McGregor and Benny Schwartz tuned the transmitters, Howard Rawlings and Pat Connor checked the radar line-up; it would never do to tell the Professor that he was bang on the center of the runway when he could look down and see that he was a hundred feet off. The three

WAAF operators were already in position, fingers resting lightly on their tracking wheels—though it would be at least fifteen minutes before they would have anything on their screens.

The first person to see S Sugar would be Dr. Hatton, who was crouching over the search display that showed everything within fifty miles of the airfield. The GCD trucks, Alan had been surprised and impressed to discover, contained two quite separate radars. The fantastically accurate landing system had only a short range and a very narrow field of view; it was blind around ninety-five per cent of the sky. It therefore had to be backed up by a search radar that could sweep right around the horizon, to locate and direct aircraft that might approach from any point of the compass.

This preliminary shepherding—known as traffic direction —was as important and as specialized as the talkdown itself; for unless the Traffic Director could steer the aircraft into the landing system's restricted field of view, there would be no talk-down. At the moment, Dr. Hatton was trying his hand at the game, while Alan stood and watched over his shoulder.

Hatton's display was the conventional circular map, painted by a line of light spinning around like the hand of a clock. Scattered here and there over the face of the disk were glowing patches of light—the reflection of hills, buildings, and other ground objects. Also superimposed upon it were concentric circles at ten-mile intervals, and an illuminated compass grid. The operator could thus not only read the range of an aircraft and observe the course on which it was flying, but could also see instantly how well it responded to his orders.

"I have him," said Hatton suddenly. "Bearing zero eight zero, range fifty miles."

Yes, there was S Sugar—a tiny blip at the very edge of the screen. The luminous brush of the scan repainted it every two seconds, as the big antenna on top of the transmitter truck swept around the sky. After three or four reappearances, one could see that it had moved, crawling slowly in toward the center of the picture. The pilot was, obviously, on a course that would bring him to St. Erryn without any assistance from GCD, and there was little for Hatton to do except make radio contact.

"Hello, S Sugar," said Hatton. "This is Ranger. I have you in contact. Are you receiving me? Over."

There was a brief pause; then a deep, slow American voice came from the speaker.

"Hello, Ted. This is S Sugar. Receiving you loud and clear. Awaiting your instructions. Over."

"Continue on present course, and remain listening on this channel."

"Wilco," acknowledged S Sugar, and for a moment there was silence on the air, save for the inevitable background of distant static.

Alan, peering into the search display, watched the little glowworm crawl in toward the forty-mile-range circle. It was not the only aircraft on the screen, for a much fatter one was heading straight out from the center. Somebody had just taken off; Alan had heard the roar of engines only a few seconds ago.

"Calling S Sugar," said Hatton again. "Change course to two fife zero and reduce height to fifteen hundred feet."

That "fife," thought Alan, sounded very affected; but it had a good survival value in a noisy background. He would soon grow so used to it that it would require a distinct effort of will to say "five" in normal conversation.

"This isn't as easy as it looks," Deveraux whispered in Alan's ear. "Although he's already almost lined up, Ted has to allow for wind—and that often changes at different altitudes."

Alan didn't think it looked at all easy, as he tried to visualize what was happening up there in the sky. Perhaps one day he would have a compass card in his mind, with 0 at north, 180 at south, and so on. Then all these figures and courses would be instantly transformed into actual movements through the heavens; but for the moment he had to stop and draw a little mental picture every time he heard Hatton call a new number.

Slowly the echo crawled in toward the center of the map, while from time to time Dr. Hatton gave it a slight course correction. At fifteen miles, as far as Alan could tell, S Sugar was exactly lined up with the runway; but he knew that the scale of this hundred-mile-wide picture was much too small to judge that accurately.

Suddenly, one of the WAAFs gave an excited squeak.

"I've got him on elevation!" Almost at once another said, "I have him on azimuth!"

Alan looked up from the search display, its work now done, and glanced at Dr. Wendt, who was preparing to do the talk-down. The scientist was studying the meters intently, as the trackers fed their information to him, mentally judging the position and behavior of the still far-off S Sugar. Then the cigarette holder lifted to a jaunty angle, and he said to Hatton: "Not bad, Ted. I'll take him."

Alan was looking forward eagerly to seeing a controller in action for the first time, but Deveraux had other ideas.

"I want to watch this from the runway," he said. "Come along, Bishop—will you bring the Hallicrafter?"

The portable short-wave radio was no light weight, but Alan was outranked. As he emerged from the gloom of the control van and stood blinking in the sunlight, he felt a momentary surprise that there was no sight or sound of S Sugar, but, of course, the aircraft was still many miles away.

It was fifty yards from the trucks to the edge of the runway—Alan sometimes wondered if this safety margin was sufficient—and when they had reached the edge of the great concrete strip, they paused to tune in the radio. Deveraux pulled out the whip aerial, fiddled with the controls, and at once the peaceful airfield was assaulted by an adenoidal humorist telling vapid jokes to an audience of what appeared to be fifty thousand hysterical factory girls.

" 'Worker's Playtime,' " Deveraux muttered in disgust. "Sometimes makes me wonder if we deserve to win. Still, I suppose it keeps them happy." Having expressed these democratic sentiments, he rejected the program with a scornful twist of the waveband switch, and tuned the receiver with great care to an ink mark on the ten-meter band. At once, faint but clear, came the voice of S Sugar acknowledging the controller's first instructions. They were just in time to hear, blastingly powerful at this short range, a sonorous American voice say: "Hello, S Sugar. I have you in contact, seven miles from the airfield. Maintain present altitude and change course to two seven zero. How are you reading me? Over."

It was the beginning of a litany that Alan was soon to know by heart, though on this first hearing he could grasp only a part of its meaning. He hardly recognized Dr. Wendt's voice; it seemed to have become an octave lower as he talked to the oncoming S Sugar in his best bedside manner.

"Receiving you loud and clear," replied S Sugar. "Changing course to two seven zero. Over."

"Remain on receive," ordered Wendt, who would have to talk almost continuously for the next few minutes and so did not want any back-chat from the pilot. "Now change course fife degrees right; I say again, fife degrees right."

("We repeat instructions," commented Deveraux, "to reduce the chance of errors. Dr. Wendt shouldn't have much difficulty bringing him in; there's practically no cross wind today.")

"I have you lined up, six miles from touchdown. Change course fife degrees right; I say again, fife degrees right."

("Hmm—that's ten degrees he's given altogether. There must be more wind up there than I thought.")

"You are now fife miles from touchdown," continued that omniscient voice. "Start descending at fife hundred feet a minute. Change course three degrees left; I say again, three degrees left. You are nicely on the glide path."

"There he is!" said Alan suddenly. For the last couple of minutes he had been searching the heavens with such lack of success that he had realized very vividly the advantages of radar over ordinary vision, even on a clear day like this. But now a tiny spot had appeared low in the eastern sky; it was still so far away that it was quite impossible to tell how accurately it was headed toward the runway. Yet Dr. Wendt, sitting in semidarkness in front of his three meters, knew exactly what that remote speck was doing. . . .

"Increase rate of descent slightly. You are a hundred feet above the glide path. Four miles to go. Now fly three degrees left; I say again, three degrees left. Three and a half miles to go. Resume normal rate of descent. You are now on the glide path. Check wheels down."

The descending plane was now near enough to be identified as an Anson, but it was still difficult for the eye to judge how accurately it was following the invisible line that led to the end of the runway. One had to take Wendt's word for it that it was coming along nicely.

"Two and a half miles to go. Reduce rate of descent slightly. You are a hundred and fifty feet low; a hundred feet low; fifty feet; on the glide path. Now back to normal rate of descent. Two miles to go. You are cleared to land on this approach. Fly three degrees right; I say again, three degrees right."

The plane was now dropping swiftly toward them, the roar of its twin engines beginning to fill the sky. Deveraux turned up the gain of the receiver.

"One and a half miles to go. Getting a little low again. Reduce rate of descent slightly. You're lined up with the runway. One mile to go. Hold present rate of descent. Three quarters of a mile; half a mile; one thousand feet—go ahead and land visually."

With a roar, the aircraft swept in over the far end of the runway, made a perfect touchdown, and came hurtling toward them with an intermittent squealing of brakes. Long before it had drawn level with the trucks, its tail had come down and it was taxiing with engines throttled back; Alan was not surprised when it came to a halt a few yards away and disgorged one of its passengers.

He was a shorter-than-average man, about thirty years old, wearing an unbuttoned raincoat and walking with the aid of a stick. Apart from his limp, which did not seem to slow him down greatly, and his unruly shock of hair, there was nothing that would make one look twice at Professor Schuster. He might have been a schoolmaster or a bank clerk, rather than one of the finest scientific brains of the Western world. Alan had not known what to expect, yet he was somehow disappointed.

"Nice to have you back, Prof," said Deveraux, with obvious warmth and sincerity. "This is Alan Bishop, who's just joined us." They shook hands, and Deveraux continued. "That was a good approach—Doc had you right on the center line."

"Well, let's say about twenty feet to the left, but because we're both out of practice, we can't grumble at *that*."

It was then that Alan realized, a little belatedly, that Schuster had been flying the aircraft himself. Alan had a great (though well-concealed) admiration for anyone who could fly, and he looked at the Professor with increased respect.

"Have you got all the spares we wanted?" asked Deveraux as S Sugar's copilot taxied the Anson away down the runway.

"Most of them," answered Schuster. "With luck, we'll keep the gear running now—well enough, at any rate, to prove our point. But it was a close thing; you got the equipment serviceable just in time."

Deveraux made a face.

"As bad as that, eh?"

"I'm afraid so. There's some tough opposition, especially among the pilots. You know the argument—'I'm damned if I'll let anyone on the ground tell *me* what to do!' Well, we have to convince them by good salesmanship and actual demonstration. So from now on we'll be having a continual string of VIPs descending on us. If we deliver the goods, the news will get around soon enough. But if we don't, then we might just as well pack up and go home."

"*We'll* deliver," said Deveraux confidently. "Won't we, Bishop?"

Both touched and surprised, for a moment Alan could only nod his head in agreement. Then he said, with all the determination he could muster: "We certainly will."

He was not much use yet, but he had been accepted as one of the team; and that was a fine, heart-warming experience.

CHAPTER 8

NOW THAT THE Mark I had recovered from its ocean voyage and its brush with the British climate, the unit began to grow rapidly. Sergeant McGregor and the three WAAF operators were only the beginning; soon they were joined by two Flying Control officers to be trained in the talk-down technique, four radar mechanics, three more operators, and a complete flying unit.

"D" Flight—GCD's private air force—would not have scared the *Luftwaffe,* but it was enough for the job in hand. It consisted of two yellow-painted trainers—an Oxford and an Anson—together with the necessary pilots, navigators, fitters, and mechanics. The flying personnel were all experienced with instrument-approach and blind-landing systems, and looked upon GCD with interested skepticism.

In an experimental unit operating with a single complex and temperamental piece of equipment, there was no such thing as a normal working day. There were uneventful days and there were catastrophic days, but no two were ever quite the same. It all depended on the gremlins.

Like Abominable Snowmen, gremlins have never actually

been seen; but nobody who has worked with electronic gear doubts the existence of these mischievous and elusive entities. There are too many malfunctions and failures that can have no other explanation.

On mornings when the gods smiled and the gremlins hibernated, the GCD trucks would drive out to the runway in use at 8:00 A.M. There Alan and his radar mechs would set up the equipment under the watchful (and often anxious) eyes of its American inventors, and report back when all was satisfactory. The WAAF operators would put away their knitting and climb on their bicycles—except when the weather was really bad; then a bus would be grudgingly provided by the station's hard-pressed Motor Transport Section. At the same time, "D" Flight would warm up its aircraft, check their radios, and send them off into the sky. By 9:00 A.M., if all went well, the operators would be tracking the radar echoes across their screens, and the controllers would be calling S Sugar and F Fox down from the clouds like homing pigeons.

On the whole, it was a happy family, despite the mingling of nationalities and occupations. Scientists, pilots, controllers, mechanics, operators—all were united by the importance of their work, and the privilege of being in at the beginning of a new and vital project. The pilots' initial skepticism had quickly vanished, and the fact that all the officers and civilians shared the same hut added to the family feeling. They could discuss their problems and difficulties, suggest new procedures, hold post-mortems on bad approaches —and, occasionally, blow off steam. The biggest blowup occurred one miserable afternoon when the aircraft had been grounded by bad weather and there was nothing to do but sit in the hut and talk.

Though there were some good talkers in the unit, the best was undoubtedly Pat Connor. Not only did he have a ready wit, but he was an excellent mimic. Like many Americans, he was fascinated by the English and could not altogether believe that they were true.

"Look at Dennis Collins," he would say. "Is he *real,* or am I imagining him?"

F/Lt. Collins, DFC, was the twenty-four-year-old commanding officer of "D" Flight. A veteran of the Battle of Britain, with an impressive row of medal ribbons, he was waiting with some impatience for his return to operational flying. Although enthusiastic about GCD, he was not too happy about his present status, maintaining that he was a fighter pilot, not a blasted bus driver.

With his handlebar mustache, carefully unbuttoned tunic, wilting cap, and knotted scarf, he was almost a caricature of his species. To make matters worse, he had a public-school drawl that sounded peculiar even to most of his compatriots, and often baffled the Americans. Even the gentle and good-natured Benny Schwartz, who normally spoke pure Bostonian, made a point of relapsing into deep Brooklynese when Dennis was around. This delighted Alan, for reasons that he would not admit even to himself. His own accent—especially under stress—was a long way from the playing fields of Eton; and he was secretly jealous of those ribbons and that Distinguished Flying Cross.

The cause of the trouble was Pat's latest limerick; on the average, he produced one a day. Though few could be repeated in polite society, this one, by a miracle, was both amusing *and* clean. Putting on an accent hardly distinguishable from Dennis Collins's, he declaimed:

> I sat next to the Duchess at tea;
> It was just as I feared it would be.
> Her rumblings abdominal
> Were simply phenomenal—
> And everyone thought it was me.

Even Dennis, who had little sense of humor, would have enjoyed this had it not been for two unfortunate coincidences. In the first place, it *was* teatime, and everyone was drinking from the usual battered RAF mugs. And secondly, he was sitting next to Pat.

"I don't think that's at all funny," said Dennis belligerently. This only focused attention on him and made everybody laugh harder.

"And indaid, 'tis sorry I am to hear it," replied Pat, switching accents quickly to the other side of the Irish Sea. "But my poor muither, just before they shot her in the Troubles, always said the English couldn't see a joke."

"*My* mother," said Dennis, with more wit than Alan would have given him credit for, "always said that the Yanks couldn't see a war, until it was nearly over and they knew which side would win."

"Perhaps you English wouldn't *have* so many wars," said Pat sweetly, "if you spent less time chasing foxes, and a little more keeping an eye on gangsters like Hitler."

That word "gangster," Alan realized, left Pat wide open; but Dennis had used up his single flash of brilliance and missed the opportunity. Instead, he lost his temper.

"We've done more to stop Hitler than anyone!" he retorted, truthfully enough. "As for keeping an eye on him, thank your lucky stars that we invented radar back in 1936. The only thing *you* contributed to it was the name."

This monumental injustice stung Pat to the quick.

"Why," he snorted, "we've got more physicists working at the Radiation Lab than you have in the whole of this lousy little island."

"Quite so," drawled Dennis in his most infuriating manner. "You always confuse quantity with quality. If it's big, or costs a lot, it must be good. That's the American Way of Life."

"The trouble with you Limeys," retorted Pat, "is that you're jealous of—"

How far this schoolboy quarrel would have gone, no one would ever know. For at that moment Professor Schuster, wearing his usual uniform of slacks, turtleneck sweater, and flying jacket, emerged from his little room at the end of the long hut.

It was the first time that Alan had seen him angry; indeed, it was the first time that anyone had seen him angry.

He had even left his stick behind, and was supporting himself against the door with his right hand.

At first he said nothing, but just looked, while silence fell abruptly upon the room. Then he said: "Come here, Pat," and Pat went like a lamb.

There was no one who outranked Dennis, so he was safe from reprimand, but he looked extremely uncomfortable, and for the next half hour was pointedly ignored by everybody.

While Pat was receiving his rocket from the Professor, and Dennis was being sent to Coventry, Alan tackled Benny Schwartz, who was a mine of obscure and erudite information.

"Benny," he said, "who *did* invent radar? I always thought it was Watson-Watt."

Benny looked at him like a wise young owl.

"It depends what you mean by *invent*," he said. "You can thank Watson-Watt for the fact that England had the world's most advanced radar at the beginning of the war. But a lot of people had *described* it long before then."

He thought for a moment, running through the card index in his well-ordered mind.

"As far as I know," he said, "the first accurate description of radar, complete with diagram, appeared in a dreadful but fascinating science-fiction novel called *Ralph 124 C 14+*; the pun in the title gives you a good idea of its literary quality. It was written by an American inventor named Hugo Gernsback, and you'll never guess when."

"Well, when?" said Alan, as intended.

"Nineteen-eleven, believe it or not," answered Benny smugly, as if it settled the matter; and Alan was in no position to argue with him.

Pat Connor was incarcerated with the Professor for no more than five minutes, but he emerged in a very subdued and thoughtful mood. It took him a full hour to return to his normal cheerful self, and the episode had taught everyone a lesson.

Compared with the vivacious Dr. Wendt, who sometimes

gave the impression of being everywhere at once, Schuster was so quiet and reserved that one could easily overlook him completely. He spent little time at the trucks; usually he was locked up, immersed in mysterious calculations, in the tiny cubicle at the end of the hut that served him both as bedroom and office.

He emerged only for meals and crises; but there was no doubt at all who really ran the show.

CHAPTER 9

ALAN HAD BEEN with the unit for almost a month before he had a chance of seeing the customer's point of view. So far, he had managed to keep secret the fact that he had never been in the air, even on a five-bob joy-ride. Until now, he had had neither occasion nor opportunity to do so; like most of the Air Force, he was one of the humble penguins who helped to keep the flyers aloft.

It was a good day for the test—a dull, drizzly afternoon with thick clouds forming a leaden roof only a thousand feet above the ground. The twin-engined, low-wing Anson was being fueled up at the dispersal point when Alan followed Flight Lieutenant Collins up the ladder and into the cramped fuselage. The interior smelled of oil, rubber, and a dozen other odors that Alan could not identify, yet were somehow businesslike and reassuring. But abruptly, as his nose unraveled the symphony of scents, he noticed a faint but unmistakable smell which no amount of scrubbing and disinfectant had been able to eliminate. It brought back, all too vividly, memories of stormy trips aboard the *Channel Queen*.

"What's the matter?" asked Dennis as he paused in the entrance.

"Nothing," lied Alan, "nothing at all." He reminded himself that he had never been seasick, even in the roughest weather. That should be a good indication that his stomach would behave in the air.

He listened and watched carefully as Dennis showed him how to attach and operate the parachute harness, then settled down in the seat immediately behind the Canadian Warrant Officer who was acting as copilot. There were no other passengers; though the ground crews and GCD operators often went up on joy rides when they were not wanted for other duties, this was hardly a day that promised pleasure, and Alan had the rear of the plane all to himself.

While the cockpit drill was in progress, he listened over the intercom and tried to interpret what was happening. He knew very little about the detailed mechanics of flight—it was not his business, and he had picked up no more about it than would be gathered by anyone who had a general interest in engineering and technology. As Dennis went through the preflight routine, talking of flaps and boosts and revs, like a magician intoning a spell, it made Alan realize how utterly incomprehensible his own technical jargon must be to an outsider. He reminded himself, with some satisfaction, that Dennis would be completely baffled to hear him talking glibly of sweeps, triggers, clamps, gates, pip generators, main bangs, and all the other picturesque terms in the lively language of radar.

Alan did not often stop to wonder why he disliked Dennis, but his antipathy had been steadily growing ever since the pilot had joined the unit. Resentment of someone from a better social background was only one of the elements involved. Another—perhaps slightly more excusable—was the jealousy of one male for a more successful rival.

The advent of the WAAFs had set all sorts of emotional cross currents swirling back and forth in the little world of GCD. There were now six operators with the unit, most of them girls in their teens, though one corporal was an old crone of twenty-three. With few exceptions, they were intelligent and attractive girls, and there were times when Alan found it a considerable strain being in close proximity to such large amounts of nubile womanhood, especially in these dimly lit surroundings.

He never got to know their full names; they were simply Anne or Daphne or Iris. Their well-being in the midst of all these brutal and licentious radar technicians was the concern of a diminutive but fierce little Flight Officer who visited them every day, listened to their tales of woe, and then raised several kinds of hell if she thought that her poor little girls were being ill-treated.

They very seldom were; on the contrary, in fact. Several romances, Platonic and otherwise, were already in full blast. Pat and Howard (Alan was not sure about Benny, who was a little too deep for him) both had their steady girl friends; and so, it seemed, did most of the airmen.

It was easy enough for the Americans, who did not have to bother with service regulations, but for officers to become too familiar with WAAF other ranks was "conduct prejudicial to good order and discipline." This did not appear to worry F/Lt. Collins; he seemed to regard himself as God's gift to the female sex, and flirted outrageously with all the operators. Alan suspected darkly that he did a good deal more than that, for he would frequently disappear from camp for the evening, and come back with a most annoyingly self-satisfied expression.

None of these things affected his efficiency, and Alan had no lack of confidence in his pilot, even when the long, broad strip of concrete stretched before him, its far end already lost in the haze. He felt himself pressed back into his seat as the straining, quivering aircraft built up speed, moving faster and faster in its attempt to reach its natural element. Before they had covered a thousand feet, Alan was already moving more swiftly than he had ever traveled in his life; how must it feel, he wondered, to take off in a *really* high-powered aircraft, and not a humble trainer like this?

He never noticed the exact moment they became air-

borne; they were already climbing as they swept past the
GCD trucks and the vehicles clustered around them, fifty
yards off to the left of the runway. There was someone waving down there—Mac, by the look of it—and he waved back
without really expecting that he would be seen.

Nobody, not even the architects who had designed it,
could have known the layout of the airfield better than Alan
did by this time; he had spent so many hours poring over
maps and plans when discussing siting problems with
Deveraux. It was somewhat absurd, therefore, to feel a mild
sense of surprise that everything was exactly where he expected it to be, and that he could identify almost at a glance
the hangars and workshops and living quarters, the bomb
dumps and dispersal sites, the camp cinema and Stores Section, the education officer's little classroom, the Sergeants'
Mess—even the "D" Flight hut. The only thing he couldn't
label to his own satisfaction was in the area to the right of
Runway 140, just beyond the perimeter track. There was a
lot of construction work going on there, and no one was
supposed to ask questions about it. The Air Ministry Works
Department was up to something mysterious, and seemed to
be getting more of a move on than usual. Large circular
structures that looked as if they were the foundations of
storage tanks had already been built. Well, an airfield had to
use a lot of gas; what was mysterious about that? Alan dismissed the problem, and a moment later St. Erryn was lost
from sight as they entered the first layer of cloud.

He could see no farther than the tips of the wings, and
streaks of rain began to materialize from nowhere on the
Perspex window beside him, moving straight backward owing to the speed of the aircraft. Clouds were more interesting
from below than from close quarters, Alan decided. He remembered that there were other aircraft besides S Sugar
stooging around inside this damp cotton wool; it was about
time to see what the GCD Traffic Director was doing.

The truck came in loud and clear on Channel B, and
Alan was just in time to hear his own aircraft vectored onto
the downwind leg. They were still climbing, though they

were already at three thousand feet and were not supposed
to go any higher. But presumably Dennis knew what he was
doing, and Alan made no comment. He let his eyes wander
over the instruments that crammed the cockpit, noting their
readings and interpreting them as far as possible. It all
looked very complicated at first sight, but he knew from his
own experience how swiftly one learned to understand—if
not to master—even the most elaborate pieces of technical
equipment.

The swift and total transformation took him completely
by surprise. One moment they were plowing through the
gloom and drizzle of a November fog; seconds later, with
the briefest of warnings, they had broken through into blazing sunlight. Above was the clean and glorious blue of the
unsullied heavens—below, a dazzling, rolling sea of snow, so
brilliant that it hurt the eye. Was *that* the murky, cheerless
pea soup through which they had just climbed? It was unbe-
lievable; down there lay England—indeed, the whole northern hemisphere—already stiffening in the grip of winter.
And here, scarcely a mile away, it was still summer. When
Alan held his hands in the light streaming through the windows, he could feel the fierce kiss of the sun. It seemed years
since he had last known its benediction.

He let his eyes roam in grateful wonder over this blazing
world, so firm and solid in appearance despite the fact that it
was no more substantial than sunlight and water vapor.
These hills and valleys, which changed their shapes even as
he watched, were grander and more magnificent than any he
had ever seen on the world below. Could even the Himalayas, he wondered, be more awe-inspiring than these mountains that marched across the English countryside? It was
true that they endured for minutes only, before the winds
dispersed and remolded them. Yet even the Himalayas had
been born but yesterday, as the earth measured its life span;
rock and cloud were equally ephemeral beneath the cold
light of eternity.

These thoughts were altogether untypical of Alan, who
had no time for what he considered highbrow philosophy.

But the first impact of this resplendent world above the clouds was so overwhelming that for a moment he found himself, both physically and spiritually, in wholly unfamiliar realms.

The magic slowly died. The mind cannot dwell on the heights forever, and there is nothing that it will not at last accept as commonplace. Within minutes, Alan was sparing only brief glances to the glory around him; all his attention was devoted to the instructions coming over the radio, and the action that Collins was taking on them.

The aircraft, losing height rapidly as Dennis brought it down to the correct level, was being turned into line with the still-distant runway. In little more than a minute, if pilot, Traffic Director, and equipment all did their jobs properly, S Sugar's slowly moving echo would appear on the radar screens of the precision system, and the Approach Controller would take over.

The shining roof of the world reared upward as the plane banked around the sky. Seconds later, it was as if it had never existed; the rain was pelting against the Perspex, the sunless gloom of winter was all around, and Alan's infinite horizons had contracted to mere yards. Despite all that he knew about the skill and science controlling the movements of this aircraft, the sense of being lost was terrifying. The fact that nothing in the skies of the whole world had its position pinpointed so accurately as S Sugar did not help him in the least. *That* was theoretical knowledge; the reality was the wet and swirling fog beyond the windows.

For heaven's sake, Bish, he told himself angrily, stop giving yourself the willies. Everything's under control, and you know it. Nevertheless, he felt a vast sense of relief when he pressed the channel-selector button of the receiver-transmitter set and heard a familiar voice say, "Controller calling S Sugar. I have you on the approach at eight miles. Maintain present height and change course fife degrees left; I say again, fife degrees left."

In his mind's eye, Alan could see the needles creeping across the scales, following the movements of the invisible aircraft. He had become a split personality, his body up here among the clouds, his brain down on the ground in the distant GCD truck. The experience was invaluable; now he knew what the pilots had to cope with, and could understand why there were times when they did not react at once to the Controller's instructions—when, indeed, they sometimes did just the opposite of what they were told.

Five miles from the runway, S Sugar was ordered to begin the normal rate of descent. The pitch of the engines dropped as Dennis throttled them back, but apart from this it was impossible to tell whether the aircraft was moving up or down, right or left. The mist still hid all reference points, and this was not an environment for which man's senses had been designed. No wonder that, in the days before reliable instruments were developed, so many planes and pilots had come to grief.

Only three miles to go, said that calm and confident voice over the RT. (Easy enough to be calm and confident, thought Alan, when you were sitting comfortably on the ground in a warm, snug little room.) At any moment now they should break through the clouds, and the airfield would be dead ahead of them.

Yet nothing was visible but the dirty gray mist flickering past the wings. Alan looked anxiously at the altimeter, and saw with some alarm that they were less than a thousand feet from the ground. The cloud base must have descended with unusual speed while they were disporting themselves in the sun; perhaps by now it had come all the way down to the deck, and they would have to land completely blind. This had been done often enough before, but Alan did not look forward to doing it himself.

"Two miles to go," said the Approach Controller. "You are nicely on track, but a little below the glide path. Reduce rate of descent slightly."

The featureless fog was breaking up around them. Chunks of alternating light and darkness were flashing past as S Sugar dropped down through the ragged foundations of the cloudscape. Misty fields and woods, uncomfortably

close, appeared momentarily, then swept astern. A barrage
of rain drummed fleetingly against fuselage and wings; then
they were through, flying just beneath the raveled tendrils of
cloud through which this aerial ocean was leaking its way
back to earth.

And there, exactly in line with S Sugar's nose, was the
long lane of the runway. As far as the unaided eye could tell,
they were coming precisely down its center, neither to right
nor to left.

"Half a mile from touchdown," said the Controller. "Go
ahead and overshoot."

The huge identification number painted on the runway
whipped beneath the wing as the concrete highway unreeled
below. Dennis was still losing altitude as if he intended to
land, and for a moment Alan wondered if he was going to
attempt it. But when he came in line with the GCD trucks,
he suddenly pulled back the stick, and the dim horizon
dropped swiftly out of sight. Forced back into his seat by the
unexpectedness rather than the violence of the acceleration,
Alan caught only the briefest glimpse of his little electronic
empire before it was snatched away.

"Continue on present course and climb to three thousand
feet," said the Controller. "Switch to Channel A and acknowledge. Over."

He had relinquished them and was handing them back to
the Traffic Director, in a few seconds he would be talking
down F Fox, but Alan would no longer hear his voice. He
would be climbing once more away from rain and cold, up
the invisible highway that led to summer.

CHAPTER 10

IT WAS ONE of those mornings when everything seemed to be running smoothly. The radar signals were coming in at full strength, the aircraft were co-operating nicely, and the talk-downs were taking place with monotonous regularity. There was nothing that Alan could do to help matters; in the event of technical trouble, Mac and Howard were on the spot. He had work back at the hut—unfinished notes, unanswered mail—so he climbed on his bike and stared to cycle home across the airfield.

This was a complicated maneuver, because he could not take a short cut along the runway in use; the great concrete ribbon was out of bounds to cyclists, for at any moment someone might want to land on it. So though there was a magnificent road only fifty yards away, Alan had to push his bike across several hundred feet of soggy grass before he came to one of the other runways. At night, or in heavy fog, it was easy to get lost on the airfield and to cycle around and around its vast concrete maze, unable to find a way out.

The temporary hut, which despite all the promises of the Station Adjutant had now become the unit's permanent liv-

ing quarters, was empty when Alan reached it. This suited
him very well, for privacy was a rare and valued gift, to be
made the most of whenever it came one's way. Alan could
do with it now; he could not put off answering Miss Hadley
any longer. She wrote at least twice a month, and her last
letter had brought disturbing news.

Would things have been different, Alan thought wistfully,
if the *Channel Queen* had come safely back from Dunkirk?
So many of his own boyhood memories were bound up with
her that he could understand the Captain's feelings; he had
known her much longer, and much more intimately.

The *Channel Queen* had been a small ship—1,565 tons,
to be exact—and had passed a quiet, uneventful life until
those last flaming moments when she had met her destiny.
Every summer she had plodded from pier to pier with her
cargo of happy (and sometimes not so happy) trippers. Car-
diff, Weston-super-Mare, Minehead, Lynmouth were her
main ports of call; to Alan, these names had once been as
romantic as Bombay, Valparaiso, Buenos Aires, Mandalay.
. . . On occasion, greatly daring, she would venture as far
afield as Lundy Island, where the Bristol Channel ended and
the awesome Atlantic began. In the thirty years since she
had first kissed the muddy waters of the Clyde, she had
brought pleasure to at least a million people; and in the
three days before she died she had carried ten thousand men
to freedom.

The Captain had cursed her often enough, but she was
part of his life, and his share in her ownership was most of
his worldly wealth. Now she lay—what was left of her—a
rusting hulk off the hostile shores of France, and there were
times when Alan had a superstitious feeling that when she
was at last scattered in meaningless fragments over the sea-
bed, that would be the end for her skipper as well.

Yet the trouble had begun long before Dunkirk; now that
Alan looked back, he realized that the Captain had never
been a very temperate man. There were times, he remembered, when his behavior on the bridge had been distinctly
odd—and there was that mysterious affair of the collision

with the *Pride of Barry.* For several weeks thereafter the Captain had been very subdued, while every few days hard-faced men came to see him and made copious notes. Even if it had all started when Mother died, there must have been a fundamental weakness somewhere; other men had lost their wives or their ships without taking to drink. And now—

"I am sorry to tell you, Alan," said Miss Hadley's prim copperplate, "that your father has been causing us a good deal of anxiety during this last month. Doctor Rogers has given him another severe warning, but it seems to make no difference. I hope that you can come home soon, as I know that will cheer him up and stop him brooding. We all send our love and look forward so much to seeing you again."

It was difficult to answer such a letter; indeed, it was difficult to write anything. There was not a word that Alan could say about the work he was doing; even if security had not been involved, he was moving now in a world that would be totally incomprehensible to the Captain and to the stubborn old lady who had taken charge of him.

Who had, indeed, taken charge of them both. Without her early influence on him, Alan knew, he would never have obtained his commission. She had supervised his studies, and given him the additional coaching that the local grammar school could not provide. She had also given him some degree of poise and self-confidence—though he would never have as much as those who were born to the purple, like Dennis Collins.

Only now, as he moved in wider circles, did he wonder if her influence had been wholly to the good. She had taught him an exaggerated respect for "Society," for the Royal Family *(any* Royal Family), which he knew would amuse his American friends if he were ever foolish enough to reveal it.

And, above all, there had been that time she had caught him with Elsie Evans. They had both been fifteen years old, and though they had not actually been *doing* anything when Miss Hadley returned to the house unexpectedly, it was quite obvious that they soon would have been. . . .

Alan's face still burned at the recollection of that traumatic experience. Miss Hadley had said nothing; she had merely looked at Alan with a disappointed sadness that was more withering than anger. She had not looked at Elsie at all.

When the Captain arrived next day, with the *Channel Queen,* he had spent rather more time than usual with his son, to the embarrassment of both. Alan was not likely to forget that interview; he could still see his father, sitting at his big roll-top desk, fidgeting with the papers stuffed in the pigeon holes. He was wearing his uniform (slightly frayed, overdue for pressing), and he needed a shave—he usually did.

He must have been quite handsome in his youth; sometimes Alan could still glimpse the fading ghost of the man his mother must have loved thirty years ago. If he had paid a little attention to himself, he might still have been distinguished—save for one fatal flaw. The watery eyes would never look at Alan; they always seemed to focus at a point over his shoulder.

They were even more evasive now, as the Captain said: "Alan—I don't think you ought to—ah—see any more of Elsie Evans. She's not—ah—a nice kind of girl for you to know."

"Yes, Father."

A long pause; then, "I don't mean you shouldn't have a girl friend. But it should be someone respectable. Like—ah —Miss Wilkins, for example."

"*Rose Wilkins?*" gasped Alan, in mingled disbelief and horror. Rose was a standing joke among all the local boys, who had christened her Miss Droopy Drawers—though there was no direct evidence that this nickname was well founded. She had a permanently supercilious expression, rather like a camel which had just noticed a bad smell, and seemed to dislike boys in whatever shape or size they came.

There was, however, just one point in Rose's favor; her father was manager of the largest local bank. Elsie's father, on the other hand, ran a fish-and-chip shop down in the harbor. . . .

It was the Captain who was embarrassed now, and Alan who was angry. He saw, with pitiless clarity, the thoughts that were taking shape in his father's mind. Understanding brought not only anger, but a deep and aching grief. Captain Bishop was not in the least interested in his son's happiness (just imagine life with Rose!), still less in his morals. He was thinking of Alan only as a means of improving his own affairs.

Alan turned away from these bitter memories, and painfully ground out his reply to Miss Hadley. It was a short note full of vague generalities, good wishes, and pious admonitions. When he had finished it he became aware of an all-too-familiar smell—the acrid odor of burning insulation. To the end of his days he would associate this smell with the Mark I, but he hardly expected to meet it here in the billet. Getting up from his chair, he quickly tracked it the length of the hut; it came, without question, from Professor Schuster's room.

"Is anyone there?" said Alan, knocking on the door. A cheerful voice answered at once.

"Come on in," said the Professor. Alan took a deep breath and pushed open the door.

"I'm just fixing the radio," explained Professor Schuster, waving a soldering iron with one hand. "I got fed up with all the wisecracks from the controllers."

"Good show, Professor," said Alan. "It's time somebody did it." The fact that the hut radio had been out of action for almost a week had caused a good deal of sarcastic comment from the nontechnical personnel. They did not appreciate that men who spent long hours wrestling with multiplex radar circuits did not feel like starting all over again when they crawled, exhausted, back to rest. "But where's the stink coming from?"

"I hadn't noticed it," confessed Schuster. The remark did not particularly surprise Alan; he himself had sometimes been so intent on repair jobs that he was unaware of the fumes of charred ebonite and burning rubber that eddied around him.

But this stench was not coming from the radio, whose entrails were scattered over the table. Alan's sensitive nose led him at once to a nearby wall plug, and what he discovered there wrenched a cry of anguished rage from his lips. Feeding power into the Professor's soldering iron, and crackling and bulging with the heat it generated in the process, was a piece of Alan's property—the adapter that allowed his 110-volt electric shaver to work on the British 230-volt mains.

With a glare at the guilty scientist, Alan whipped the smoking resistor out of the socket, scorching his fingers as he did so. "Prof!" he cried, as much in utter disbelief as in anger. "How much power does that damned iron of yours take?"

"Er—about a hundred watts."

Tossing the adapter from hand to hand like a hot potato, Alan stared in flabbergasted wrath at Schuster, who now closely resembled a schoolboy caught looking at dirty pictures. This was not the first time that the incompatibility between British mains and American equipment had caused trouble, but nothing quite as ludicrous as this had ever happened before. Now Alan understood Hatton's remarks about the Professor's practical ability, and could appreciate what Howard had meant when he had once remarked, "I can cope with the gremlins *or* the Prof, but not with both at once."

"Professor," said Alan sadly, in the tone of voice one might adopt when speaking to a retarded child, "my shaver takes only twelve watts, and your blasted iron takes ten times as much. It's a wonder the resistance didn't burn out —you practically short-circuited it."

"I didn't think the job would take so long," said the Professor, rather lamely. "I thought I could get away with it. Don't worry—I'll fix you up with another."

Alan was blowing on the hot plastic, which still made crackling noises as it cooled. There was really nothing more to be said, and he had to admit that the situation gave him an enjoyable feeling of superiority. He had caught one of the electronics wizards of the Allied nations doing something that would have shamed any electrician's mate who'd ever heard of Ohm's law.

Alan watched skeptically while the Professor stuffed the chassis of the radio back into its case, tightened a few screws, and switched it on. When, after a long pause, it was obvious that nothing was going to happen, he decided to take over. He guessed that he could fix an eight-valve superhet, even after it had been "repaired" by Professor Schuster, in about ten minutes.

He had had plenty of practice at this sort of thing, both before and after he had joined the Air Force. Fixing a domestic radio was child's play to anyone who had survived the Practical classes at Gatesbury, where the instructors would pull some vital part out of a radar set containing a couple of thousand components—and give you five minutes to find what was wrong.

Almost at once, he spotted the loose connection from the speaker transformer, and crimped it tightly with a pair of pliers. While he waited, with complete confidence, for the set to warm up, he glanced at the papers on Schuster's table, covered with a perfect maze of calculations. Immediately, his smugness evaporated; he would not forget about the soldering iron, but it was no longer quite so significant.

Schuster caught the direction of his gaze.

"I'm designing the Mark II," he explained. "That is, if there's ever going to be a Mark II."

"What's wrong with the Mark I?" Alan asked, almost aggressively.

"It's far too complicated and clumsy, and now I have a lot of better ideas." He paused and sighed. "But I don't know yet if I'll ever have a chance of trying them out."

"Surely by this time we've convinced everybody!" Alan exclaimed. "Why, we must have done five hundred approaches in the last month!"

Schuster smiled, a little grimly.

"I'm afraid, Alan, you underestimate the factors involved —and the inertia of the service mind. But we should get a decision very shortly. My spies tell me that there's an air commodore coming down in a couple of days. If we can convince *him,* that should be the last hurdle."

At that moment, the radio burst into life and drowned all conversation until Alan could switch it off.

"We'll convince him," said Alan confidently. He was quite sure of himself,.for he could not believe that all this skill and devotion and effort could go for nothing.

"Thanks for the vote of confidence," answered the Professor as Alan headed for the door with the radio under his arm. "I appreciate it." Even before Alan had left the room, he was writing again, already unaware of his visitor —soaring away like an eagle into realms where few other men could go.

Yes, that was a good analogy; and Alan was not thinking of Schuster's lameness only when he remembered that eagles are clumsy walkers when they come down to earth.

CHAPTER 11

"BY THE WAY, BISHOP," said Flight Lieutenant Deveraux as they left the Mess together after breakfast, "when did you last take a day off?"

"I haven't a clue," replied Alan. "Not since I came here, I think."

"Well, I've a job that will give you a break. Two jobs, in fact. There's an Air Commodore Burrows arriving at Launceston on the 4:30, and we've got to make a good impression on him."

"Yes, I know," said Alan grimly.

Deveraux looked surprised.

"Your sources of information are better than mine," he grumbled. "I only heard half an hour ago. Anyway, get the best car MT will let you have, and collect him from the station. On the way, call at Filey to drop off that secret equipment that's got to go back to Stores—you know the procedure."

Alan looked forward to the trip; it would be a good thing to get away from the station for a few hours. No matter how enthusiastic one may be, working too long at the same task inevitably produces staleness. During the last few days, he had been aware of a certain loss of zest, not to mention a shortness of temper which had resulted in several minor explosions. He had even been foolish enough to quarrel with Sergeant McGregor over the best way of tuning the precision system, and had been utterly routed.

There was yet another reason why he welcomed a trip to Filey, whose echoes he had often admired on the radar screens. Through the service grapevine he had discovered that one of his earliest RAF friends was Technical Officer there, and this was his first chance of bridging the trivial distance between them.

The harassed Motor Transport Section produced a limousine suitable for air commodores, and a WAAF driver of unusual elegance. She was quite the prettiest and neatest that Alan had seen, and lacked the somewhat tatty, beat-up appearance characteristic of most airmen and airwomen from MT. Unfortunately, the spell was shattered as soon as she opened her mouth and addressed Alan in the purest Cockney; he decided to sit in the back where he could look at her but wouldn't have to talk to her.

They stopped at the Guardroom to collect a Webley pistol, for the equipment he was carrying was so secret that it had to travel under armed escort. That armed escort would be Alan, though he was not sure how long he could protect his wares if suddenly surrounded by German paratroopers.

The SP Sergeant who issued the pistol, and carefully collected the receipt, was very particular about explaining how the safety catch worked; obviously he had grave doubts of this young officer's ability to use so complicated a piece of equipment. Alan felt like remarking casually that he had scored ninety-five out of a possible hundred at target shooting back in his training days. This was perfectly true—but he had done it only once.

As the car drove out of the gates, collecting a snappy salute from the corporal on guard, Alan settled back on the upholstery with a sigh of contentment. It was strange to see the outer world again, after weeks of peering into radar tubes and mazes of wiring. The weather was not as good as he might have wished, but at least it wasn't raining, and though there was ten tenths cloud at the moment, there seemed a fair chance that the sun would break through later in the day.

He stared with interest at the narrow, winding roads, bordered by low walls built from uncemented stones, piled one upon the other. It seemed a bleak, hard countryside, a world away from the friendly, fertile fields that he had known for most of his life. Yet he was scarcely a hundred miles from home; the thought made him realize how much variety England encompassed in so small an area. No wonder the Americans found it fascinating—when they did not find it exasperating.

Past rocky coves, every one of which looked as if it could tell its tale of wrecks and smugglers; past country cottages that still proclaimed Cream Teas, even though the Ministry of Food had banished cream years ago; past the artificial mountains reared to the sky by generations of clay miners; past sleepy fishing villages festooned with nets—so the car wove through the Cornish landscape. Ahead now reared the slender steel masts and the shorter, more massive wooden towers of Filey Chain Home Station, watching the distant skies above France.

Alan presented his credentials at the heavily guarded fence, and was told that he would find F/O Ronson in R Block. This turned out to resemble a large air-raid shelter, half buried in the ground. At his knock on the steel door, a shutter slid aside and a suspicious WAAF asked him the password.

"I haven't the faintest idea," Alan answered, wondering how necessary this cloak-and-dagger atmosphere really was. "Mr. Ronson is expecting me—tell him Flying Officer Bishop is here."

The shutter slammed, but a moment later the door opened and Geoffrey Ronson's well-remembered voice called from the gloom: "Come in, you old bastard. Wipe your feet and leave your sabotage gear outside."

They shook hands vigorously, grinning with mutual pleasure at meeting again. Then Geoff led Alan past the bulky radar receivers (how clumsy and old-fashioned they now looked!) and into his little office.

"Before we start nattering," said Alan, "let me dump the stuff I've brought. You understand how it's got to be handled?"

"Yes—it has to go back to Group with our own secret U/S stores."

Alan winced. By general consent, the unit had dropped the standard RAF abbreviation "U/S" for "unserviceable"; it took too much explaining, and even when explained was liable to hurt sensitive American feelings. But there was no point in going into this with Geoff.

"That's the idea," he said. "As long as I get a receipt saying that I've handed everything over to you, I'm quite happy. Sorry to be a nuisance, but there are no proper channels for this sort of transaction over at our place. Coastal Command Stores can cope with *ordinary* secret equipment, but this is Most Secret."

"I'm intrigued. What's inside?"

"Sorry—I can't tell you. Please sign the receipt like a good chap."

"It isn't that I don't trust you, Bish." Ronson grinned, looking at the packets piled on his desk. "But I want to see what I'm signing for. How do I know there's anything in those boxes except bricks?"

"What a pity," sighed Alan, "that I'm not allowed to let you open them."

"And too bad I'm one of those stubborn types who won't sign for a pig in a poke. It looks as if you've come all this way for nothing. Your MT officer will be annoyed; ours is very sticky about wasting petrol."

"I'm supposed to defend these to the death," mused Alan, "but I'm badly out of practice. I'll probably only shoot you in the leg."

"Fair enough," said Geoffrey. "I could do with some leave." He was already untying the string on the nearest parcel, and a moment later was examining the peculiar object it held.

Scarcely larger than the palm of his hand, it had the approximate shape of an old-fashioned pair of bellows. The flat, circular body was made of black-painted metal, and had cooling fins around its rim. The two "handles" were sealed glass tubes from which dangled flexible copper leads, and the "nozzle" on the opposite side of the round body was also made of glass. It looked simple enough, and was indeed far less complex than many tubes in an ordinary radio set. Yet it was the Allies' greatest single secret—the weapon that was to win the war. For the waves that it alone could generate were to sweep the U-boats from the Atlantic, lead the bombers into the heart of Germany, and trace the final fading image of Hiroshima on the radar screens of the *Enola Gay*.

Geoffrey looked at the tube thoughtfully, hefting it in his hand.

"One resonant cavity magnetron," he announced, like an auctioneer calling the next lot. "Slightly the worse for wear, but still capable of churning out a few kilowatts at ten centimeters." He spoke the "ten" with heavy emphasis, challenging Alan to confirm or deny his guess at the wave length. But Alan was not being helpful.

"You wouldn't get much out of that one," he said. "The envelope's sprung a leak."

"So it has," admitted Geoffrey. "Some careless clot must have bashed it with a hammer."

"I hate to confess it, but that's exactly what happened. We had a spot of bother when we were trying to install it in the transmitter."

"Anyway, I'm disappointed. I've seen ten-centimeter maggies before. What else have you got?" Geoffrey put the tube back into its sponge-rubber nest, and opened another box. This time he gave a slight whistle of surprise.

"Hmm—this is more like it. My guess is—three centimeters? I've heard they've got down to that."

"Don't ask me. I'm not here."

Geoffrey looked closely at the compact little magnetron,

holding the matchbox-sized section of wave guide between thumb and forefinger.

"Cute," he said. "What will they think of next? If I could get one of these across to old Adolf, I ought to get the Iron Cross with knobs on."

Having satisfied his curiosity, he repacked the tube and signed Alan's receipt without bothering to check the contents of the other boxes. Though it was a close fit, he managed to get all the packets into his safe for temporary storage; then they left the office and started on a tour of Geoffrey's empire.

It was an impressive one, for the four gigantic towers dominated the landscape for miles around. As they came to the foot of the transmitter towers, Alan did a swift mental calculation. The biggest antenna in the GCD truck was fourteen feet high, and had always seemed inconveniently large. But the array of aerials now floating above him soared three hundred feet into the sky. . . .

It was suspended, like so much washing beneath a clothesline, from a cable slung between the two slim pencils of steel, each balanced on its point and held vertically by sets of guy wires. As Alan stared up at the fragile latticework, he marveled that any man could work on such a construction project, or climb out like a spider on the rigging to make adjustments to aerials and feeders. But *someone* had to do it; this fact seemed almost as wonderful as radar itself.

Geoffrey was following his gaze; and, with a horrid premonition, Alan knew exactly what he was going to suggest.

"Like to run up it?" he said. "It'll only take about fifteen minutes, and the view is something to remember."

"I'm sure of *that*," said Alan, "but is it safe?"

"Perfectly. You're inside the latticework almost all the way, so you can't fall off. I do it once a week, just for the exercise. It's developed a lot of muscles I never knew I had."

"All right," Alan answered, without enthusiasm. "But you go first."

"Certainly, if that helps. But look up at me—it may make you giddy. Concentrate on the rung in front of your eyes while you're climbing, and forget everything else. Then you can't go wrong."

They scrambled onto the concrete plinth supporting the mast, which was a simple triangular girder, its lower end terminating in a huge ball-and-socket arrangement that allowed it to sway freely in the wind. It was a neat balancing act, but Alan did not permit his mind to dwell upon it in too much detail.

He waited until Geoffrey had got a good start, then began his slow climb up the plain steel ladder inside the mast. Fifty feet from the ground, he decided that there was nothing much to it; the metal latticework surrounding him, open though it was, gave a considerable sense of security. Ignoring his colleague's advice, he glanced downward; he would have to go much farther yet before he felt uncomfortable.

A hundred feet up, they came to the triangular platform that ended one section of the mast, and were able to rest for a few minutes. Alan was not particularly short of breath, but he had noticed an unaccustomed aching in his arms. It had not occurred to him that they do an appreciable fraction of the work when one is climbing an absolutely vertical ladder.

At the end of the second lap his arms were aching quite badly, and he was glad to rest on the two-hundred-foot platform. For the last few minutes he had been following Geoffrey's advice, and pretending that nothing existed except the metal framework immediately surrounding him.

The last lap was a distinct ordeal; his forearms were now hurting abominably—though this was largely his own fault, for he was clinging to the ladder with quite unnecessary devotion. It seemed a long time before the third and final platform appeared above him, and he knew that he was now three hundred feet above the ground. But—*where was Geoffrey?*

The shock of seeing no one on the little platform jolted him badly; the explanation was almost worse. Geoffrey had not bothered to mention one trifling fact; the final twenty feet of the ascent were on the *outside* of the mast. . . .

His friend's voice, muffled through the steel above him, shamed Alan into continuing his journey. If Geoffrey could do it, so could he. With this thought to encourage him, he wriggled through the framework of the mast and began, very carefully, to climb the last section of the steel ladder. There was absolutely nothing between him and the ground, three hundred feet below; though metal hoops had been fixed around the ladder, they were about three feet apart, so there was plenty of room to slide through them if one slipped and fell backward.

Alan found Geoffrey standing, with perhaps unnecessary bravado, on the sloping roof of the squat pyramid that crowned the pylon. One arm was wrapped casually around the central lightning conductor, but that was his only concession to the force of gravity.

It seemed to Alan, when he had recovered most of his breath and some of his composure, that he was clinging to a tiny raft adrift in the sky. There was no way of ignoring the fact that it was swaying to and fro in leisurely undulations; best to accept it and file it quickly away as an interesting piece of local color. And an even more intriguing phenomenon, to be looked at firmly or not at all, was the behavior of the great steel cable fastened to the uppermost point of the mast.

Springing from immediately beneath their feet, it leaped out into the abyss, swooping down and away in a long, vertiginous catenary. For a hundred yards it descended in that hypnotic curve, drawing the eye after and luring the body to follow. Then it began to climb until it was back once more at the height from which it had started, and had merged into the distant summit of the other pylon. Its slow oscillations, taking minutes to complete, had the quality of movements seen in a dream. The fact that he could reach out and touch the cable, at the very point where it started its journey, Alan found peculiarly disturbing; it somehow linked him with empty space.

Yet, of course, it was not empty, for the curtain of the

transmitter array hung suspended from the great cable, sharing its slow undulations. One below the other, like the rungs of a giant ladder, the massive copper tubes of the antennas hung in space, each hurling its quota of power toward Europe.

"It's a pity the weather isn't clearer," said Geoffrey, raising his voice above the moaning of the wind through the girders and rigging. "On a really fine day you can see more than twenty miles, way past Land's End."

That was easy to believe; as it was, when Alan felt confident enough to run his eyes around the horizon, he discovered that there was sea both to the north and to the south. He could tell at a glance that he was on the last tapering tongue of England as it jutted out into the Atlantic, and somehow this added to his sense of instability.

"I've seen all I want to," he said, and did not wait for Geoffrey to answer as he lowered himself gingerly over the edge of the platform. There was a horrible, sweat-triggering moment before his foot found the first rung; he did not really breathe again until he had wormed his way back into the interior of the mast and was surrounded by its reassuring steelwork.

The descent was harder than the climb, because he dared not look down and his already tired arms clutched the ladder with redoubled anxiety as his feet searched for the rungs beneath him. Each hundred-foot section seemed twice as long as the one before, but at last—and quite unexpectedly —Alan realized that the ladder had come to its end. He stared with disbelief at the ground only a yard away, then clambered through the base of the girder and jumped down onto the grass. It appeared to be rocking slowly to and fro, like the deck of a ship; he had to close his eyes for a few seconds before the world came to rest.

"That's quite enough for one day," he told Geoffrey, who joined him a moment later. "I'm glad that all *my* gear is a reasonable size, and that I don't have to be a steeple jack to inspect it."

"At any rate, it keeps me fit. Old Father Kruschen would approve."

They both laughed at the shared memory of the days when they were still raw, untrained airmen. "Old Father Kruschen," who might indeed have served as model for the energetic grandfather of the health-salts advertisement, was an elderly, gray-haired dynamo who came to the Thomas Coram Technical Institute twice a week and gave the boys their PT exercises. There he would stand, tying himself in knots or waving his limbs like a semaphore, while boys a third his age sagged and wilted all around him. If they could not duplicate his contortions, he would walk along the writhing ranks, and, with a well-placed push or tug, snap muscles and sinews into positions Nature never intended. It was agreeable to think that others were now going through the mill; but Alan had to admit that he had never felt healthier before or since.

Swapping reminiscences, they walked back to the Mess together; by the time they had finished lunch, they had re-called scores of faces, relived a dozen forgotten incidents. Once again they were trying to keep awake on lonely guard duties in the endless hours before the dawn; once more they fought old battles with warrant officers and flight sergeants, attended camp concerts and cinema shows, dodged church parades, anxiously awaited exam results, celebrated promo-tions with riotous parties in the NAAFI. . . .

All these things they had shared; but as they talked to-gether a strange sadness came over them. In the very act of recollection, they realized how much their lives had now diverged, and what little chance there was that they would ever again be part of so closely knit a team. There was some-thing unique about the camaraderie of those early days, when the whole squad had been as intimate as a single fam-ily. They had all been carefree boys then; now he and Geof-frey were responsible men, guarding property worth millions, on which their country's very existence depended.

It was a somber thought, and cast a shadow over them as

they said good-by at the security fence. If one looked too long into the past, it seemed to Alan, the result was always sadness. But now it was time to look in the other direction; for what happened in the next few hours might determine not only his own future, but that of GCD.

❋ CHAPTER 12

AIR COMMODORE BURROWS did not seem to be in a very good mood; perhaps the fact that the train was an hour late had something to do with it. As the car drew out of town and started the climb toward Bodmin Moor, Alan did a little discreet angling to discover his attitude, if any, toward GCD.

He had extracted only a few monosyllables from his passenger when, on a desolate stretch of moor miles from anywhere, there was a sudden sharp explosion, and the car swerved violently to the side of the road. It came to rest almost in a ditch, but luckily still on an even keel—apart from the list due to the flattened tire.

They climbed out and inspected the damage. The Air Commodore said nothing, but he appeared to be thinking a good deal. Alan felt both embarrassed and annoyed. Though the accident was completely beyond his control, this was not the way to impress an important visitor. To make matters worse, he could hardly tear a strip off the driver; she looked as if she would burst into tears if he tried anything of the sort.

He walked around the car kicking the three sound tires, to prove that he was in command of the situation. They seemed fully inflated, and the treads were good, which left him with no obvious grounds for criticism. "I'm terribly sorry about this, sir," he said to the Air Commodore. "I'll lodge a complaint with the MT Officer when we get back to the station. He promised me his best car because I explained how important your visit was."

Having, he hoped, simultaneously flattered his passenger and dissociated himself from the debacle, Alan felt a little better. But this did not help them to get moving again, and he had never changed a flat tire in his life. Well, he'd better have a bash at it.

The Cockney vision, however, had other ideas. She was already throwing jacks and wrenches out of the trunk and was wrestling competently with the spare wheel. Conscious of the Air Commodore's coldly sarcastic eye, Alan hurried forward to give what help he could.

For a moment it looked as if the driver was going to refuse his assistance. Her hesitation had nothing to do with considerations of rank, but was due to an accurate estimate of Alan's usefulness. However, before she could object, he had heaved the spare wheel out on the grass (too bad about his uniform, but war was hell) and had taken charge of the proceedings.

On the whole, he did not delay the job by more than a few minutes. It would have taken an acute observer to notice that he was always one jump behind, and that the driver was really leading the way. Air Commodore Burrows was, unfortunately, an acute observer.

Twenty minutes later they were on the road again. Alan was covered with mud, but the little WAAF was still spick and span. If there was any light conversation during the rest of the journey, he did not remember it.

When they arrived at the Mess, the Air Commodore would not trust Alan with his baggage, but insisted on lifting it out of the car himself. He did, however, unbend a trifle as they parted.

"Tell the MT Officer," he said, "that his young lady did a good job."

"Certainly, sir," replied Alan, "and I'll look forward to showing you round the unit in the morning."

That was a thundering lie, and they both knew it.

"I sometimes wonder," Alan remarked to Deveraux the next morning, "whether we're supposed to be training crews or running a publicity campaign."

Deveraux cracked a glacial smile.

"Both," he said. "Unless we get the right sort of publicity, and in the right places, there'll be no point in training anybody."

"Have you learned anything about our visitor?"

"Enough to worry me. He's the C-in-C's right-hand man on landing aids, and what he says will have a lot of influence."

Alan found it surprising that anyone should have much influence with the legendary head of Bomber Command, who had organized more destruction than Attila and Genghis Khan combined.

Deveraux glanced at his watch.

"I'll be bringing the Air Commodore out in thirty minutes, so make sure that the trucks are properly lined up, then get 'D' Flight off the ground. By the way, what's the Met forecast?"

"Not too bright. There's a front going through later this morning, and the weather may turn bad about noon, with heavy rain squalls."

"Well, as long as it holds off until we can have a few good runs, that's all that matters. Oh—one other thing. Get the covers off the antennas, so I can show the Air Commodore how they work. It's always a good idea to blind the opposition with Science."

When Alan reached the trucks, which were positioned along side Runway 320, he found that the setting-up procedure was already far advanced. He waited until the Corporal mechanic had made the final adjustment, then took over.

Only a few weeks ago, the mass of switches, controls, and meters in front of him had been utterly meaningless; now he knew the functions of every one of them, and could find them blindfolded.

Alan studied the screens intently, identifying the pattern of echoes and making a few turns with the tracking wheels. That blob there on the right—it was a radar reflector he had placed himself, three hundred feet from the runway. He cranked the pointer across to it; where did the meter say it was? Two hundred and ninety feet right—only ten feet out. Fair enough.

"OK," he said to the Corporal, who had been hovering anxiously in the background. "Let the operators in, and tell 'D' Flight to get airborne."

As the mechanic cranked the field telephone to Flying Control, the truck was invaded. First came the three WAAF trackers; though they had brought their knitting, this was not necessarily a vote of no confidence in the serviceability of the equipment. Even on the best of days, there were long waiting periods between approaches when there was nothing else for them to do.

Next entered the Traffic Directors, both of them sergeants with control-tower training, and then the Flight Lieutenant who was to do the actual talking down. The team was complete.

It was always fascinating to see how swiftly these six individuals, so different in training, rank, and outlook, merged into one entity—the crew. And the crew itself, by some higher symbiosis, then became part of the complex machine it was tending, yet without any loss of human dignity. There was nothing here of the degrading, mindless repetition that Chaplin had satirized in "Modern Times." For this work was not mechanical; it demanded great skill and understanding. No two approaches were ever the same, and all involved in the operation, from tracker to controller, had to be ready at an instant's notice to deal with unexpected developments.

The tense silence of the darkened truck was broken by

the roar of C Charlie getting airborne. A minute later the aircraft's echo emerged from the amorphous blobs of light at the centers of the radar search screens, as it climbed away from the airfield. "I've got him," said the Traffic Director. Then he pressed his transmitter key and articulated carefully: "Sheepdog calling C Charlie. Continue on course three two zero and climb to two thousand feet." Sheepdog was the unit's current call sign; it was changed every few days for security reasons, though it seemed to Alan that any bright German signals officer listening to the talk between ground and aircraft could deduce exactly what was happening, and could even estimate the accuracy of the system. But unless Jerry had developed excellent microwave radar himself, he would find it hard to guess how it was done.

This was now being explained to Air Commodore Burrows, who was standing in front of the transmitter truck, watching the impressive behavior of the antennas. The wood-and-canvas covers that protected them from the weather and from prying eyes had been removed, and they were thrashing back and forth in the clear light of day.

The Air Commodore had seen hundreds of radar and radio antennas, but these were quite the oddest he had ever met. Long wooden troughs, their curves coated with reflecting tin foil, they looked like overgrown electric fires. The azimuth array was rocking from right to left like a spectator at a tennis match, while its tall, thin companion, the elevation array, was nodding up and down from earth to sky as its invisible beam searched the heavens. Over in the control van the lines of light on the display tubes were moving in exact synchronism with them, reproducing in miniature the strange world they saw—a world that knew neither night nor day, in which cloud and fog had no existence.

Deveraux finished his little lecture on the antennas, explaining how they scanned the skies with the narrowest beams yet made by man. Then he led the Air Commodore away from the thrashing antennas and the roaring diesel, into the cloistered calm of the control van.

The blackout curtains, their hems lined with lead, swung

sluggishly aside, then parted to let them through. There was barely room to stand between the wall and the three WAAF trackers crouched over their sloping display panels, but Deveraux was able to crane over the girls' shoulders and point out the features of the display without interfering with operations.

They had come at just the right moment, as an aircraft began its approach. There it was—a sharply defined blob of light at the limit of the tube. It was moving even as they watched; with every sweep of the scan it edged a fraction of an inch closer to the glowing maze that marked the airfield. The successive images formed a fading comet tail behind it, drawing the path it was following down the sky.

Now the creeping echo was only eight miles away. Sometimes it drifted to the left, sometimes to the right, as the pilot changed course according to the Controller's instructions. And all the while the three WAAF trackers held it transfixed with their shining electronic needles, kept in place by imperceptible movements of their wrists on the handwheels. They seemed quite unaware of the visitors peering over their shoulders; nothing existed in their spheres of consciousness save the echoes crawling toward the end of the runway. Though this was merely a training approach, carried out in broad daylight and good weather conditions by a pilot who could see exactly where he was, the operators could not have been more intent had they been landing a damaged aircraft in thick fog. They took pride in their work, and realized its importance; one day, men's lives might be in their hands, and when that time came, they would be ready.

With an abrupt clicking of relays, the radar images suddenly exploded, like pictures painted on the face of an inflating balloon. The final, critical two miles had expanded fivefold, filling the space on the screen originally occupied by ten. Now the last stages of the approach could be watched on a greatly exaggerated scale, so that the slightest deviations from the glide path were clearly visible. On this magnified view, the echoes hopped forward perceptibly between each sweep of the antennas. When the Air Commodore glanced at the elevation display, he could see the echo losing height at what appeared to be a most alarming speed. But the meters indicated that it was still above the glide path, so he must have been misled by the great enlargement of the picture.

And then, during the last stages of the approach, he noticed a curious phenomenon. At the very bottom of the screen, a ghost echo was matching the movements of the aircraft down the sky. As that descended, so this was creeping *upward,* apparently from below the level of the ground. The two echoes formed a pair of mirror images, and the Air Commodore realized that he was seeing with his own eyes something that, until now, had been only theoretical knowledge to him. He was watching the earth itself act as a radio mirror.

It was quite a good one, at this glancing angle. The reflected underground image was almost as bright as the direct one crawling down the glide path, and as they came closer and closer together he saw that this was not merely a pretty proof of the laws of radio propagation. It was also extremely useful, for it showed very precisely the exact position of the ground, as the line bisecting the two images. When these coalesced, the aircraft would have landed.

But it had no intention of landing on this approach. In the distance the Controller's voice was saying: "You are now a thousand feet from the end of the runway. Overshoot and change to Channel B." On the screen, at the same moment, the swiftly moving echo seemed to pull up from the ground; in a matter of seconds it had passed off the edge of the screen, into the blind region behind the precision system's limited field of view. Simultaneously there was a faintly audible roar beyond the walls of the truck as the plane climbed away from the airfield and prepared to go around again.

"Well, sir?" said Deveraux, a little too anxiously.

"Interesting," was the noncommittal reply. "But can you do it every time?" The Air Commodore waved around the truck, pointing to the banked racks of equipment. "And all

this—how serviceable is it? There are far too many operators, and as a pilot I'm not happy about putting myself in
the hands of someone sitting safe and snug on the ground."

"This is only the prototype," explained Deveraux patiently. "Professor Schuster's designed an operational model
that will be much simpler and more reliable, and won't require so large a crew. As for the pilot's viewpoint—well,
they all seem to like it. I suggest you go up presently and try
for yourself."

"I mean to," said the Air Commodore grimly. "I've seen
far too many systems that worked beautifully with pilots
that were used to them, but were no good with anyone else.
But I'll watch a few more approaches first."

He spent another hour inside the control van, and the
dozen approaches he saw were uniformly successful. One by
one, B Baker, C Charlie, and S Sugar bisected the runway
with monotonous precision.

The thirteenth approach was just starting when the telephone to Flying Control rang like the voice of doom. Deveraux answered it, and put the receiver back with an
expression of annoyance. Through long experience, everyone in the truck knew what had happened.

"Runway change," he announced. "The wind's swung
round—we've got to move to 270." He turned to the Air
Commodore.

"As a matter of fact, sir, this is rather handy. If you like,
we'll land one of our aircraft and drive you round to 'D'
Flight. By the time you're airborne, we'll be operating on
the new runway." He gave a slightly deprecatory, think-
nothing-of-it kind of cough. "And it will give us a chance,"
he added, "to show you just how quickly we can move to a
new site when we have to."

He did not guess how much the unit's luck had changed
with the changing wind.

CHAPTER 13

RUNWAY 270 WAS a particularly easy one to operate from; Alan had lined up the equipment on it dozens of times, and knew its radar pattern by heart. There were the great amoeba-like blobs of Numbers Three and Four hangars; there were the smaller blips of the Liberators parked in the dispersal sites—and there were the radar reflectors he had carefully set up to identify the line of the runway.

It had taken them only twenty minutes to move to the Dew position and to get the equipment lined up again. S for Sugar, now piloted by Air Commodore Burrows, was already airborne and was being vectored around the sky by the Traffic Director; in another five minutes, the Air Commodore would be doing his first GCD approach. Everything looked perfect; the signals were coming in nicely, and Flight Lieutenant Arnold Evans, who was handling the talk-down, was the best controller in the business next to Dr. Wendt. As long as the Mark I behaved itself, and the Air Commodore did exactly what the Controller told him, they would have nothing to worry about.

"He's on the cross-wind leg," the Traffic Director called

to the girls in the back room. "You should be seeing him in a couple of minutes."

"I've got him!" cried the elevation tracker. "Nine miles out!"

Alan peered over the girl's shoulder. Yes, there was a nice fat echo, at just the right altitude. A moment later it appeared on the azimuth display as well; even at this distance, it was already well lined up with the runway. This would be a piece of cake.

"I'll take him now," said the Controller, when the echo had approached to within six miles. He switched on his transmitter and began the familiar routine: "Sheepdog calling S Sugar. Continue on course two seven zero. Are you receiving me? Over."

"Receiving you loud and clear," said the Air Commodore's voice. Did it sound a little baffled? Alan could not be sure; but nothing could go wrong now—it was a beautiful line-up.

The Controller had an absurdly easy job; though the aircraft was a little slow at responding to orders, for the last three miles it needed no corrections at all. To Alan, watching both displays at once—he was quite good at this by now—the echo seemed almost glued to the glide path.

"You are now a thousand feet from the end of the runway," said the Controller, giving his final instruction. "Go ahead and overshoot."

But the echo did nothing of the sort. Instead of climbing away into the sky once more, it got closer and closer to the ground. Well, that was the pilot's own affair, for he was flying visually now and could see exactly what he was doing. But it was a little surprising, and Alan passed the news on to the now-relaxed Controller.

"I think he's landing on this approach. Was he cleared with Flying Control?"

F/Lt. Evans sounded annoyed and surprised.

"No—he wasn't. He should have known better than that. Maybe he's had engine trouble."

"Well, he's on the deck now. Quite a smooth touchdown, by the look of it."

The descending blip had merged into the ground echoes and was trundling swiftly along the runway; in a few seconds it would come abreast of the trucks and would disappear from the radar displays as it entered the blind zone behind the antennas.

The Controller reached toward his mike and pressed the transmit key. Unless the aircraft had developed a fault, there was no reason why the pilot, whatever his rank, should disobey standard operating procedures. F/Lt. Evans had never reprimanded an Air Commodore, and rather looked forward to the experience.

"Sheepdog calling S Sugar," he said. "Are you receiving me? Why have you landed? Over."

There was a considerable delay before the reply sounded in his earphones. When it came, it was surprisingly faint; and even over the low-fidelity RT circuit, it crackled with indignation.

"I don't know what you think you're doing," spluttered the distant and furious voice of Air Commodore Burrows, "but at the moment I am about five miles out to sea, somewhere over the Channel. And if I'd kept the rate of descent you gave me, by this time I'd be in the drink. I was only a hundred feet from the water when I broke off. I am returning to the airfield and will request permission to land visually. Over and OUT."

That last explosive syllable was still echoing in the Controller's ears when the control van reverberated to the roar of great engines. As the heavy bomber that had just landed —without the slightest assistance from GCD—went taxiing past them, one needed little knowledge of aircraft to appreciate that no modest twin-engined Anson created *that* amount of noise.

In the silence that followed, the elevation tracker made what was widely acclaimed as the most superfluous remark of the day.

"You know, sir," she said to the still-stricken Alan, "I *did* think it was rather a big echo for S Sugar."

The post-mortem took place in Professor Schuster's little office; though the atmosphere was one of extreme gloom, there were no recriminations. With heroic self-restraint, none of the Americans said: "If only we had been doing the controlling . . . !" But that had been against the ground rules; a major purpose of the demonstration had been to prove that GCD did *not* need a team of Ph.D.s to run it.

It was perfectly obvious what had happened, and a quick check with Flying Control had confirmed the instant diagnosis of everyone who had been working in the truck. Somewhere on its circuit around the sky, S Sugar had passed within a mile or so of a Liberator coming home after a mission, and the two echoes had been confused. Thinking they were following S Sugar, the operators had started tracking the wrong aircraft. As the Liberator had been making a normal landing in good visibility, it was scarcely surprising that the radar had reported an excellent approach. And so poor S Sugar, left to his own devices in quite another part of the sky, was being solemnly assured that he was nicely on the runway, only half a mile from touchdown—while all the while the indignant and astonished pilot stared at the open sea. . . .

Wearing the wool-lined flying jacket that was his all-purpose protection against British weather and British heating systems, Professor Schuster sat quietly at his desk while Deveraux poured the sad story into his ears. He showed no signs of worry, disappointment, or anger; indeed, he might have been listening to one of his students explaining how a physics experiment had gone wrong. Which, in a sense, was not far from the truth.

"If there's a weakness in the system," he said, "it's just as well that we've discovered it—though I wish we could have done it some other time. What we're up against is a simple technical problem; therefore, it must have a simple technical solution."

Schuster pulled across a large writing pad and began to cover it with neat sketches.

"The weak point is *here,* just before the final approach starts. The Traffic Director has an aircraft on his display and is bringing it into line with the runway. The girls in the back room are looking at their screens, and they see an echo approaching. How can they be sure it's the same one? Ninety-nine times out of a hundred it will be; today, unfortunately, it wasn't."

"You know," said Hatton, "I thought of this a long time ago, but decided that the risk was too small to bother about. Well, I was wrong; the statistics have caught up with us."

"If you don't like the odds in a game," said Benny, "there's one way of improving them. You can mark the cards."

"That's the answer," exclaimed Dr. Wendt. "We have to put a label on the echo we're interested in. Anything will do —a pointing arrow, a little circle, X marks the spot. Just as long as it distinguishes *our* aircraft from any others that are stooging around."

"Don't we already have enough electronic markers cluttering up the picture?" grumbled Deveraux.

"It need only be there for a few seconds—just long enough for the search system to hand over to approach. Then it can be switched off again."

"Benny's right," said the Professor. His pencil was already flying over the paper, filling it with little squares and oblongs, and connecting one to the other.

"This should do the trick," he said, half to himself. "Trigger from scope central, variable gate, clipper, mixer, cathode follower—there you are, Howard—you can work out the details."

"I wish someone would please translate," complained F/Lt. Evans, who had contrived to push his way in from the back. "Will it stop me making a fool myself by talking air commodores into the drink?"

"You'll see what it does when we've fixed it up," Schuster

replied. "And I'm afraid, Arnie that there's no circuit yet invented that can stop a man making a fool of himself."

He happened to catch Alan's eye at that moment, and he had the grace to blush.

The electronics engineer, thought Alan, as he helped Howard assemble the bits and pieces, had a much easier life than the mechanical engineer. He, poor fellow, had to make accurate drawings, send them off to a workshop, and wait days or weeks before the hardware came back.

How much simpler it was in this business! You sketched out a circuit, grabbed the necessary resistors, capacitors, and tubes from Stores, and then wired them up for yourself. The first model was usually a mess, and it seldom worked, but it took only minutes to change components and try again. The cathode-ray oscilloscope—that essential tool without which the radar technician would be completely blind—showed exactly what your brain child was doing; you could see on the screen what happened when you adjusted the controls, and could tell at a glance whether you were making things better or worse.

"That's the lot," said Howard, ticking off the last item on his shopping list. "Mind you, I don't know where we're going to put the thing even when we've got it working. There's no room left in any of the racks."

"We could tuck it under the controller's desk."

"And get a rocket from him when it takes off his knee-cap? Not if I can help it. We'll manage somehow—even if we have to squeeze it under the floor boards."

Howard was always an optimist; many times, when the radar images had suddenly faded from the screens, his cry: "Don't worry—I'll fix it in a minute!" had helped to sustain morale. Though he frankly admitted that he was the worst mathematician ever to graduate from MIT, he was brilliant at practical circuitry; he knew exactly what was happening throughout the miles of wire that made up the Mark I's intricate nervous system, and understood precisely what each of its five hundred tubes was doing. His compatriots referred to him as the "rambling wreck"—a phrase that puzzled the British. Eventually Pat explained that a rambling wreck was a product of Georgia Tech—"an obscure Southern educational institution where Howard was incarcerated before he escaped to MIT. He still has the marks of the chains."

The little workshop-*cum*-store in which most of the GCD repairs and modifications were carried out was deserted at the moment; there were no wireless mechs surreptitiously building private radios or filing down homemade cigarette lighters. Alan and Howard had it to themselves, and as they waited for the soldering irons to warm up, Alan broached the subject that had been puzzling him more and more deeply ever since he joined the unit.

"Howard," he said, "what makes the Prof tick? I just don't understand him."

"How d'you mean?"

"Well, the other day he practically burned out my little shaver resistor by trying to run a soldering iron from it. I can tell you, it shook me rigid."

"I bet it shook the Prof, too, when you caught him at it."

"Not particularly; he just apologized and promised to let me have a new element—which he hasn't done yet."

"Don't worry; he will."

"I'm not worried about *that*. What puzzles me is how a man who invented GCD can be so impractical—yet at the same time can do the sort of job he did when he sketched out this circuit for us this afternoon. He *did* invent GCD, didn't he?"

"He invented it," said Howard firmly. "Doc Wendt designed it, and we built it. Of course, it wasn't as simple as that, but that's the general idea." He cleaned the bit of the iron with a few strokes of a file, and lightly touched it with a stick of solder. Like a film of mercury, the molten metal spread in a glistening mirror over the hot copper.

"Let's have that board. . . . Have you screwed on the tube bases? Fine—I think we'll start at this end."

It is always a pleasure to watch any craftsman at work,

even if you do not understand his trade. Though Alan rather fancied himself a practical man, he had to admit he was not in Howard's class. The circuit began to grow like a piece of abstract sculpture under his skilled fingers; he seemed to know where everything went, without glancing at the diagram. And as Howard worked, he talked in his soft Southern accent, not unlike Alan's own.

"There's only one man on this team," drawled Howard, "who can really give you the low-down on the Prof, and that's Benny. They're both mathematicians; the rest of us are hairy engineers, dragging our knuckles on the sidewalk. Of course, the really *pure* mathematicians would tell you that Prof Schuster is only a mathematical physicist, but I don't think we need worry about the distinction. Until the war, all his work was purely theoretical—atomic physics—nothing of any practical importance. Let me have that twenty-K pot, will you? Thanks.

"Then Radiation Lab grabbed him, soon after Pearl Harbor. One of our first big jobs there was developing an anti-aircraft radar that would automatically follow an aircraft, so that the pilot couldn't escape from the beam no matter how he twisted and turned. Well, we built it, and one day the Prof was watching it in action when he said to himself, "If radar can follow an airplane *that* accurately in order to shoot it down, why can't it do something useful, like landing it in bad weather?" Seems an obvious idea, doesn't it? But it took the Prof to think of it first.

"So he talked Radiation Lab into making a test. It worked and that led to the Mark I. Right from the beginning we only regarded this as an experimental unit, to test the basic principle. But then along came Ted Hatton and kidnapped us all. We sent the Mark I across on an aircraft carrier, with an armed escort and classified Top Secret—"

"Yes," said Alan. "I heard how it was stuffed with Scotch and nylons."

"Oh, you knew that, did you? When we heard it had dodged the U-boats, we flew over by Clipper to join it. Bob Hope and his troupe were on board, and when we arrived at

Shannon there was such a reception for *us* that Bob said, 'I guess we should have made a bigger fuss over you guys.' Maybe one day we'll be able to tell him what it was all about. And that's how we got here. Any other questions?"

"I don't think so—for the moment, anyway."

The picture was starting to come into focus, though there was much that was still unclear. But for the first time, Alan was beginning to appreciate the difference between a man like Professor Schuster and one like Dr. Wendt.

The Doctor was enormously versatile; there was no technical task he could not carry out brilliantly. Alan could follow every detail of his performance, and be duly impressed by it, for Wendt operated in a world that he could understand completely.

Schuster's world, on the other hand, was one that Alan could scarcely glimpse, much less enter. Most of the things that Wendt could accomplish, Schuster could probably do after a fashion, if the need was great enough. But he could not be bothered; there were more important things to concern his mind. Only in one of his off moments, when he was trying to relax, would he start playing around with actual hardware in a halfhearted fashion—with the disastrous results that Alan had witnessed.

Dr. Wendt was a highly capable engineer who would always be a leader of his profession, but Professor Schuster would be a Nobel prize-winner in the 1950's. All that separated them was the yawning, immeasurable gulf between superb talent and simple genius.

CHAPTER 14

TROUBLES NEVER COME singly, thought Schuster, as he read the priority signal for the third time.

"What do *you* think it means?" asked Dr. Wendt anxiously. "Surely Burrows can't have torpedoed us as quickly as this!"

Schuster glanced at the time of dispatch on the signal form, and shook his head.

"If he has, he's a fast mover. Still, it's a good idea to go to TRE; we may be able to do a little fence-mending. If Big Chief will back us up, we can trump our Air Commodore friend with a few generals."

Dr. Wendt's cigarette holder, which had been at a very depressed angle, crept up a few degrees. "Dennis is going to be angry with us," he remarked, "if we ask for an aircraft over the weekend. 'D' Flight's gotten used to working a five-day war."

"Too bad for 'D' Flight," said the Professor grimly. "Unless we're at TRE before nightfall, heads are going to roll."

To do the Flight justice, it was ready. There were grumbles, of course, about weekend leaves. Yes, said pilot and navigator testily, we *know* there's a war on—but this is a training unit, so why the panic?

Schuster wished that he knew, as he watched St. Erryn fall behind. As soon as they were airborne, he took over the controls. He was too important now to fly solo, and had been expressly forbidden to do so, but before the war, flying had been his chief relaxation. When his hands were on the wheel, and his fingers were sensing the tug and pull of the air's invisible forces, he felt completely happy. Riding a spirited horse must be like this—but horseback riding was too dangerous for his frail body; so instead, he had half a thousand horses at his finger tips.

He knew perfectly well why he needed this form of recreation, and felt no bitterness against the infantile paralysis that had closed all other sports to him. That was the luck of the draw, and there were many compensations. He could never have become what he was without the long years when he had lain in bed or bath, always reading, reading, reading. (How many books he had ruined in the salt water of the hydrotherapy rooms! Well, it was worth it; books were meant to be used.)

Three thousand feet below, something strange caught his eye. A circle of stone columns, dull gray in the somber light of this cloudy afternoon, stood in lonely isolation on an open plain.

"What the devil's *that*?" Schuster asked the pilot, jabbing his thumb toward the ground.

"Stonehenge, of course," came the prompt reply. "I guess you haven't got anything as old as *that*."

Schuster was impressed; he banked the aircraft in a great circle, picking out the pattern of the immense slabs and wondering how they had been reared into position. In the face of such antiquity, his own problems seemed suddenly transient and trivial. A thousand years from now, these monoliths would still be defying the elements, while the only record of his existence would be a few articles in moldering scientific journals.

No—that was not true. Already he had made his mark

upon history—upon *real* history, not the blinkered, myopic narrative that records only the doings of generals and politicians. He was a part, and no small part, of the forces that were shaping the future.

A staff car was waiting at the airfield, and a few minutes later they were driving into the small provincial town that, if Hitler had only known what it housed, would have been one of the *Luftwaffe's* prime targets.

From the outside, Malvern College still looked like a typical English public school; but none of its old pupils or masters would have now recognized the interior. The classrooms and halls were crowded with weird equipment, most of it either unfinished or else in the process of demolition. Wires, meters, cathode-ray tubes, electric motors, sprawled over benches and tables. Silent men stood in little groups around blackboards covered with the hieroglyphics of radar, contemplating miracles yet unborn. Models of experimental antennas spun and rocked and wobbled with peculiar motions. Less identifiable devices did even odder things, watched by their anxious inventors. Air Force squadron leaders, Royal Navy commanders, U.S. Eighth Air Force generals, pipe-smoking civilians, and Royal Engineer lieutenants argued technicalities with a complete disregard of service and rank.

Schuster had been to the Telecommunications Research Establishment dozens of times, but the place never ceased to fascinate him. TRE was a unique institution, and the Germans would never have been able to understand it. What would they have thought of its famous Sunday Soviets, where the problems of the week were thrashed out in discussions so democratic that the humblest lab technician had no scruples in telling a Nobel laureate that he was talking nonsense? In Germany, it would take weeks for the diffident correction to reach the Herr Doktor Professor; here, the feedback was almost instantaneous.

Generations of boys had trembled outside the heavy oak door that now carried the sign RADIATION LAB—LIAISON. Schuster knocked, heard a familiar voice reply, and went in.

Dean Walters looked perfectly at home in a headmaster's study, as indeed he should. In his time, he had administered two of America's greatest universities, but now his responsibilities were somewhat heavier. Though he had made only one important discovery—and that twenty years ago—he was known to every scientist in the United States. According to legend, the reverse was also true.

"Nice to see you—Carl, Alex," he said. "And I'm sorry to pull you in at such short notice . . . especially at the moment."

"So you've already heard how we laid an egg in front of Bomber Burrows?" said Schuster, without surprise. He had long since ceased to be astonished by the efficiency of Big Chief's spy system. Thanks to his network of loyal colleagues and ex-students, he knew everything that was happening along every sector of the scientific front line. He was *supposed* to, of course; but he usually knew well before the official reports reached him.

Dean Walters gave a long puff with the famous pipe that was responsible for his nickname.

"Yes, I've heard," he said slowly. "But it's not about GCD that I called you. You won't like this, but something bigger's come up—much bigger. You're both going back to the States as soon as you can pack your things."

There was a long pause. Then Schuster gave a sigh and answered. "Well, I was expecting it. But I'd hoped that we could get GCD accepted before they grabbed us."

"Who's 'they'?" asked Wendt.

"Use your head, Alex," replied Schuster. "There's only one thing bigger than radar, and you know what *that* is."

Big Chief said nothing, though a whole series of smoke signals went up from his pipe.

"But what about GCD?" demanded Wendt, angry and upset. "If we leave now, we may lose everything. Anyway, I know damn little about uranium isotopes, and care less."

"Then you're going to learn a hell of a lot, and very quickly," said Dean Walters sharply. "As for GCD, Carl's work is effectively done; we can't waste him any longer as a sort of Fuller Brush man trying to sell his product to the services. Hatton and the boys can carry on without either of you. Isn't that true?"

"Yes," admitted Schuster a little reluctantly. "But the Mark II—the production model . . ."

"All the fundamental ideas are in that report you gave me; from now on it's a matter of straightforward engineering. And you can still keep an eye on the project when you get to Los Al—to the States."

"That's just it," said Schuster unhappily. "Will there *be* a project if you pull us out? Can you do anything to head off Burrows? I can just imagine what he's saying right now, back at Bomber Command."

"I'm doing my damnedest," said Walters. "But at the moment we're having a little fight of our own with the bomber boys. We've just put up some new proposals for navigation aids, pointing out the miserable accuracy of their present aiming techniques. And do you know what the C-in-C answered?"

"I can guess," said Schuster.

"He said: 'Tell TRE to mind its own ruddy business.' Well, blast his eyes, we're doing just that."

There was a brief, indignant silence; then Dr. Wendt remarked, to no one in particular: "I wonder what he'll do with the bomb, when he gets it?"

"I still hope," said Schuster, "that the filthy thing won't work. But if it does—what's it going to do with *us*?"

CHAPTER 15

"THAT'S THE LOT," said Howard decisively, switching off the oscilloscope and unplugging the soldering iron. "We'll start fixing it into the truck tomorrow."

"But we can't—the operators will need it. We'll have to wait until Saturday."

"Where *I* come from," said Howard, "Saturday usually follows Friday. This happens to be Friday—all day."

"Oh," said Alan, counting on his fingers. "I seem to have lost a day somewhere."

"You take things too darn seriously. If you carry on like this, you'll soon be ulcer fodder. Why not relax once in a while?"

"When and how?" demanded Alan, reasonably enough. The camp cinema, installed in a drafty hangar with excruciating acoustics, was showing an antique comedy which might have racked up one laugh per reel when it was made, but had not improved with age. There had been a variety show last week over which it was best to draw a veil of oblivion. A Mess dance had been planned by the Entertainments Committee at the end of the month, despite the damage done at the previous one, when painstaking experiments had refuted the popular theory that beer improved the tone of a grand piano.

Of course, there were the nearby towns, the closest of them ten miles away at the end of an erratic bus service that ceased operating at 9:00 P.M. Alan could still recall Pat Connor's summary of the local urban scene: "The first time I've ever come across a cemetery with traffic lights." Yes, it was hard work relaxing; so much so that it was really less trouble to stick to the job.

Howard glanced at his watch and did some mental calculations. "Maybe I can help out," he said thoughtfully. "Pat was supposed to be coming with me tonight, but he's got a heavy date somewhere else. Can you meet me after dinner— around 8:30?"

"I suppose so," said Alan, without much enthusiasm. "What are you planning?"

"Never mind; I can promise you it'll be interesting." There was a twinkle in Howard's eye, but a good-natured one.

"OK," said Alan, capitulating abruptly. After this day's alarms and excursions, he felt that he had earned a break. "But what about transport?"

"We can use our bikes; it's not very far."

That made it a little mysterious. Within comfortable cycling distance of the airfield there was nothing except a few lonely farmhouses and a couple of villages. That any of these could provide entertainment or relaxation on a winter evening was quite beyond the bounds of possibility. But the Americans seemed good at making local contacts, and enjoyed them more than their RAF colleagues, who saw no great novelty in such functions as tea at the vicarage.

Alan was no wiser when they rode out through the main gate. Luckily, the rain that had been threatening all day had not put in an appearance, and it was pleasant and relaxing to bowl along the narrow country lanes. An almost-full moon, breaking occasionally through the clouds, gave enough light for comfortable vision. The bicycle lamps, in accordance with blackout regulations, had been dimmed and hooded so effectively that one could just manage to read print with them a yard away; they provided warning for oncoming vehicles, but that was about all.

A mile from the airfield, Alan was already lost, and let Howard cycle confidently ahead. The road ran downhill between bleak walls of mortarless stone, which looked sinister and sepulchral in the pale moonlight.

"I hope you know where the heck you're going," he shouted to Howard's back, a dozen feet ahead of him. The only reply was a chuckle floating down the breeze.

They had traveled about three miles, Alan estimated, when a faint light appeared, like a will-o'-the-wisp, at an indefinite distance ahead. Somebody's blackout was not as efficient as the law required—but in this remote corner of England, where the sound of a bomb dropped in anger had not been heard for at least two years, the air-raid wardens were inclined to be easygoing.

A few minutes later the ghostly shapes of cottages loomed up out of the moonlight; they were entering one of those microscopic hamlets that were often much easier to find on the Ordnance Survey maps than in reality. They went through it, bells tinkling furiously to warn any belated pedestrians, before Alan had quite realized that they were not going to stop; he had half assumed that Howard had found a favorite pub here.

A few hundred yards beyond the sleeping village, Howard swerved off into a small driveway. "Here we are," he said. " 'Wit's End'—at least, that's what Pat calls it."

The house ahead was a good deal better-kept and more modern than those of the village; of medium-size, with two stories, it was just the sort of home that a successful businessman might have built during the years before the war. The style was that aptly known as Stockbroker Tudor.

Howard dismounted and knocked in a masterful manner on the front door. It was opened almost at once by a large lady whose face Alan could not see in the scarcely relieved shadows. She was obviously expecting them and greeted

Howard like a long-lost son, planting a resounding kiss on his cheek.

"How sweet of you to come, Howard! It's been such a long time, we thought you'd forgotten us. Bring your friend in and let me see him."

Alan had already received one surprise. His still unknown hostess did not speak in the West Country dialect he had expected, but in an accent that clearly came from somewhere in central Europe.

Howard closed the front door, and the hall lights clicked on.

"Alan, meet Olga Buckingham. Olga, this is Alan Bishop."

Alan blinked a little at the "Buckingham," which went with neither Olga's accent nor her appearance. She was a handsome woman in her late forties, with dark eyes and hair, and a slightly Oriental cast of features. In her youth she must have been extremely beautiful; now slightly overdressed and overjeweled (surely those stones in her rings couldn't be genuine?), she looked like a Russian who had come down in the world, but not very far.

"Oh—a flyer!" she gushed, as soon as she saw Alan's uniform. "And so young, too!" Alan colored and looked at Howard for moral support; finding none, he decided not to shatter Olga's illusions about his status in the Royal Air Force. Fortunately her attention was soon diverted to the large parcel that Howard had been carrying on the back of his bicycle, and which he was now unwrapping with care. Alan was not surprised to find that it contained a bottle of Haig & Haig and several pairs of nylons.

This gift was received with the greatest delight, Olga at once calling out, "Lucille! Elise! Look what Howard has brought for us!"

Alan was still trying to identify Olga's accent when a door burst open and he had his second surprise of the evening. Two vivacious young ladies, who at first glance appeared to be about eighteen years old, immediately hurled themselves upon Howard with glad cries. They devoted about five seconds to him, and considerably longer to the nylons, which seemed to give them even greater pleasure. By the time they had worked around to Alan and had been introduced by Olga as "My nieces—they're staying with me until they can go back to France," he had come to some startling and indeed downright fantastic conclusions.

Seen at close quarters, the "nieces" (Alan was already mentally referring to them in quotation marks) were nearer twenty-five than eighteen. Lucille was a somewhat improbable blonde, Elise an apparently natural brunette, and both were very pretty. They spoke excellent English, though with a slight accent, which, unlike Olga's, was clearly French. So *that* part of the introduction might be perfectly true.

What Alan found hard to believe was that his rapidly solidifying suspicion (or hope, if he were a little more honest with himself) could possibly be justified. The setup looked convincing; but *here,* in the remote and almost inaccessible wilds of Cornwall, two hundred miles from the happy hunting grounds of New Bond Street or Piccadilly? That was absolutely absurd. . . .

He was still trying to get oriented when they walked into the tastefully decorated lounge. No plush *fin de siècle* decadence here, but a perfectly up-to-date room in clean modern style. (And why not? Alan asked himself. What did he expect—gilt mirrors and red-velvet curtains?)

Olga settled luxuriously in an armchair: Howard and Elise, with a kind of automatic reflex, homed on one settee, leaving Alan and Lucille the other. There was a prolonged silence while everybody waited for someone else to speak. Then Howard tried to break the ice with the popular catch phrase "Read any good books lately?" He was the only one of the Americans who listened regularly to the broadcasts from that mythical RAF station Much-Binding-in-the-Marsh, and had not only mastered many of its jokes, but had also picked up some of its dialogue.

It worked, though not in the way he had expected. Apparently the girls were not familiar with Much-Binding, for Elise answered in all seriousness, "We never seem to have any time for reading," whereupon Lucille instantly broke into a fit of giggles. This spread rapidly around the room, order being restored only by the arrival of a maid with a tray of drinks.

The maid was the first fully conventional item on the evening's program; she was obviously a local girl, not another exotic import. Alan wondered what she thought of the ménage, but a glance at her placid—indeed bovine—countenance told him that there was no need to worry. Olga clearly knew how to choose her staff.

"Your very good health, ladies," said Howard, in what he fondly believed was a British accent. (The British were usually the last to recognize it.) "And how are you today, Joan?"

Joan gave him an adoring simper and answered, "I be fine, Mister Howard," as she refilled his glass. It occurred to Alan that there was a touching domesticity about the whole scene. Howard seemed utterly relaxed and at ease, like a busy wage earner who had come home to his family after a hard day at the office. This was a Howard he had certainly never suspected. There seemed to be a lot of other things he had never suspected, too.

"You can leave the tray here, Joan," said Olga, rousing herself from the armchair and walking toward the massive phonograph that occupied most of one wall. She fiddled with the controls for a minute; there was the "plop" of a descending record and a brief sibiliation of needle scratch, and the room resonated softly to the "Warsaw Concerto."

The background music had the probably calculated effect of inhibiting general conversation and leaving each couple to its own resources. Howard was already chatting with Elise, while Olga surveyed the scene with a general air of benevolence. Alan had no choice but to try his luck with Lucille, who so far had not spoken a single word to him.

It was difficult to know a safe gambit, but "How long have you been in England?" seemed fairly foolproof. It led him by short, easy stages to the discovery that she had been in the country since 1940, that she liked England very much

but that she was homesick for Paris, where her parents were
(she hoped) still living. By this time Alan was beginning to
feel very sorry for her, though perhaps the excellent whisky
(so much better than any they ever saw in the Mess) may
have had something to do with the remarkable speed with
which he became sympathetic. In a very few minutes the
space separating them on the sofa had shortened to the vanishing point. When Alan looked up some time later, he discovered that Olga had tactfully left and that he had been
equally unaware of the discreet departure of Howard and
Elise. It was all so smooth, so pleasantly inevitable, that
when he stopped to realize what was happening, it was almost too late.

"What's the matter, Alain?" queried Lucille anxiously, as
he edged out of her clutches and straightened his tie. (His
hair would have to wait—there was nothing he could do
about it now.)

Like a trapped animal, Alan swept the room with his
gaze, wondering through which of the doors Howard and
Elise had vanished.

"Someone may come in," he answered lamely.

The limpid blue eyes staring into his were extraordinarily
innocent, almost childlike in their candor. That was confusing; it did not agree with the sophistication of her neatly
painted lips and penciled eyebrows, nor with the heady fra-
grance of her perfume, the range of which was sufficient to
reach his end of the sofa.

"That's all right," Lucille reassured Alan. "No one will
bother us in my room."

Alan shot to his feet and started to orbit the sofa. It was a
highly eccentric orbit; some of its perturbations were due to
the whisky, but most of them sprang from profounder psychological causes. Though he would have hated to admit it,
he was still, at twenty-three, as near a virgin as made very
little practical difference. Not counting the near miss with
Elsie Evans, his total sexual experience added up to a couple
of inconclusive fumblings with another of the neighborhood
girls, a highly refined encounter with the clergyman who

had (very briefly) run the local scout troop, and a more satisfactory contact with a lady who had been smuggled into the Thomas Coram Technical Institute one night by his enterprising classmates. That, however, was more of a catharsis than a rapture.

He had sometimes wondered, listening to his companions' accounts of their exploits, whether he was really undersexed or whether it was merely lack of opportunity, combined with excess of scruples. There was no lack of opportunity now; then what was the trouble? Could it, said a faint voice from the subconscious, all go back to his interrupted rendezvous with Elsie Evans, and the memory of Miss Hadley's icy disapproval?

Lucille watched these gyrations with calm confidence. She had seen them so often before, and they always ended the same way. Soothing the qualms of inhibited Englishmen was a specialty of the house, and the effort was often surprisingly worth while.

It took Alan, as she had calculated, about two minutes to spiral back to the sofa. In that span of time he had suppressed any scruples, and decided that pleasure took precedence over prophylactics. The house was very quiet, apart from the subdued background of the phonograph, when they went hand in hand into Lucille's room. They might have been alone in the building, though Alan was acutely conscious that they were not.

The huge, square bed was resilient, Lucille even more so. Matters were proceeding, though not too quickly, to a satisfactory climax when Alan was thrown off his stride by the classic interruption. The doorbell rang.

"Don't worry, Alain," whispered Lucille, playing a xylophone solo on his vertebrae. "Olga will answer it. I expect it's that nasty old air-raid warden. This is the only house he bothers about."

Alan could well understand that, but it did not help to restore the *status quo*. He lay in the warm darkness, straining his ears through the night, now only half aware of the skillfully passionate little creature upon whom, only seconds ago, all his senses had been concentrated. The phonograph had by now run out of ammunition, so he could hear the door opening and Olga saying, her voice edged with annoyance, "You should have telephoned us."

"We tried," came the answer, "but the line was out of order. So we thought we'd just drop around."

"And what's more," said a second voice, "If I find anyone else here, I'll knock his bloody head off."

"Oh my God!" gasped Alan, disentangling himself in one swift movement and bounding out of the bed. It was not the implied menace of the words that upset him, though they were alarming enough. What had started him frantically grabbing his scattered uniform was the fact that the voice, slightly disguised by alcohol, was without question that of his tough and exceedingly pugnacious colleague Sergeant McGregor.

CHAPTER 16

ONE CAN NEVER tell when the most peculiar skills and talents may suddenly prove useful. When he had been under training, Alan had learned how to dress and undress in two minutes flat; little more time was allowed between lectures and PT drill. Now he beat even his best record, and was fully presentable, if disheveled, while Olga was still arguing with her visitors in the hall.

"Is there a back way out?" he asked anxiously.

"Why are you making such a fuss? There's nothing to worry about. Olga can handle Mac."

"It's all too complicated to explain now," said Alan. He did not doubt Olga's ability to cope with most situations, but he had seen McGregor when he was drunk and knew that he could be a very awkward customer. The house was getting much too crowded.

They tiptoed out through the kitchen, where they found Howard and Elise taking a fond farewell. Howard was already dressed for the road, and his cheerful, relaxed expression only made Alan's own frustration more acute. As soon as Howard saw his face, he gave a quite unsympathetic smirk. "It serves you right," he said. "You shouldn't have wasted so much time." Alan did not deign to reply; he was too busy trying to file as many memories as possible for future reference.

He had never felt quite so foolishly conspiratorial in his life as they pedaled softly away into the moonlight. Not until they had passed through the sleeping village did he call over his shoulder to Howard: "Thanks for a *very* interesting evening. But there are a lot of things I'd still like to know—"

"So would I," said Howard. "What was all the panic about? I thought you and Mac were good friends."

"That has nothing to do with it," Alan answered, a little testily. "It's—er—a matter of discipline. It would have made me the laughingstock of the unit. You civilians have nothing to worry about, but officers and men aren't supposed to mix off duty. Especially in a place like *that*. And besides, Mac might have lost his temper; he can get nasty when he has a few under the belt."

"And you were afraid he would have beaten you up?"

"He might have behaved," said Alan with dignity, "in a way that would have made our future relations difficult." He added, in a pensive afterthought, "I once saw him throw a man through a NAAFI window."

"Sorry—I didn't hear that," said Howard, who seemed to have difficulty in keeping up with him.

"Oh, never mind. I'd like to know what an establishment like Olga's is doing here in the middle of nowhere."

"You call this nowhere?" said Howard. "There are ten thousand men within a five-mile radius. Besides St. Erryn, there's that big experimental airfield over at Davistowe."

"I hadn't looked at it from that point of view," Alan admitted.

"Don't go so fast—I can't keep up."

"Where does she come from, anyway? And is Buckingham *really* her name?"

"I think so. When she was young, she married an Englishman—not for long, I gather—so that she could get a

British passport. She had quite a place in Paris, and left it when the Germans got too troublesome. Then she was bombed out of London, and now she's waiting for things to quiet down so that she can go back. Elise says that she came here because there used to be a 'Croix de Lorraine' squadron at Davistowe."

"Huh—the Free French," grunted Alan. Then he realized that the adjective was not completely accurate. "Can I settle up with you for the whisky and nylons?"

"Of course not," Howard answered, to his slight relief. "It was my idea—and anyway, I gather you didn't have much luck."

"That," grumbled Alan, "was entirely Mac's fault. And how does he know about the place? For that matter, how did *you* find it?"

"Top secret. Radiation Lab doesn't disclose all its techniques."

"Oh, come off it!"

"Well, the 'D' Flight officers told us; they inherited Olga from the Frenchmen. But we've been asked not to advertise —Olga's in retirement and doesn't want a beaten track to her door. You were lucky that Lucille took a fancy to you."

Alan did not answer: he needed time to think. A new and highly disturbing element had come into his life. He did not know whether to be grateful to Howard or angry with him —but it made no difference either way.

He was not quite ready to admit it, for the inhibitions of his upbringing were still powerful. But sooner or later he was going to see Lucille again—and next time he'd make damned sure that Mac did not come barging in at the crucial moment.

It was a subdued and thoughtful little group that gathered at the trucks the next morning. Only Howard was fitfully cheerful; Sergeant McGregor appeared to have a slight hangover and clearly resented being dragged out to the airfield on a Saturday morning, while Alan had a somewhat anxious expression and kept glancing apprehensively at his

NCO. He had not slept at all well, and his dreams had been highly frustrating.

Mac tramped morosely into the transmitter truck, from which bad language emerged in an unbroken stream for a good five minutes before the diesel coughed into life. The petrol-driven starter engine was on strike, and Mac was compelled to swing the massive motor by hand. This was not an easy job at the best of times, and was certainly not recommended immediately after a hectic night. Then the regulator began to misbehave, the voltage swinging wildly between 90 and 140 until Mac hammered the recalcitrant unit into submission. When the lights had stopped flickering and the generator had accepted the fact that it, too, had to work on a weekend, Alan switched on the electronic circuits and waited for them to warm up. His own warming-up period still showed no signs of coming to an end.

After an hour's work with hack saws, soldering irons, screw drivers and electric drills, the new circuit was tucked into an out-of-the-way corner of the van, and its wiring added to the maze that already existed. The actual test was a considerable anticlimax; when Howard threw the switch, all that happened was that a faint dotted line appeared simultaneously on all the radar indicators. He turned the control knob, and the line glided smoothly across the screens, a movable signpost that could be set on any target at the touch of a finger. Now, no matter how many aircraft there were on the screens, the trackers would know which to start following, and which to ignore.

"Well, that's that," said Howard, in a rather self-satisfied voice. "What shall we call it?"

"Oh, what about—er—identification marker?"

"Too much of a mouthful. You want something short and snappy. I have it—target indicator!"

"Well, that's a bit better," admitted Alan, who was sending the dotted line scurrying back and forth across the azimuth display. Filey Station's little group of four tightly bunched echoes made a good target; he could place the indicator on each in turn without confusing it with its neighbors. Which of these echoes, Alan wondered, was the tower he had climbed with Geoffrey?

He was still amusing himself with the new control when a faint, luminous mist appeared at the extreme edge of the tube, ten miles away. A heavy rainstorm was approaching, and with surprising speed. The rain was moving forward in parallel bands, quite sharply defined, so that the radar screens looked as if they had been smeared with streaks of luminous paint.

"I'd hate to be up in *that*," said Alan thoughtfully. "Let's get back to our billets before it hits us."

"I agree," answered Howard. "Looks like a regular cloudburst. I'll tell Mac to close down." He was about to call the transmitter truck when the field telephone to Flying Control startled them by its sudden urgency.

"What the heck!" said Howard. "We're not supposed to be here. Someone must have got the wrong number; I shouldn't answer."

"It may be important," Alan reprimanded him as he lifted the receiver. "GCD truck here; who's calling?"

The next few minutes were highly frustrating to Howard, who could hear only one end of the conversation. It consisted mostly of, "I see. . . . Yes, of course . . . I'm afraid that's impossible. . . . But there are only three of us here. . . . No, they all have the weekend off—there's probably not one on the station. . . . Well, you can try. . . . Of *course* we close down on weekends—this is a training unit, not an operational one. . . . It's no good blaming *me*. . . . Oh . . . I see. . . . Well, in that case . . . How long did you say? . . . Let me talk it over. . . ."

He put down the phone and turned to the exasperated Rawlings.

"Flying Control has an emergency on their hands. There's an aircraft trying to land over a Davistowe—it's been caught by this storm—seems it was on its way there from somewhere else. They want to know if we can bring it in."

"Can't it use Standard Beam Approach?"

"No. It's an experimental prototype and only carries VHF radio."

"Then someone ought to be shot."

"It was making a delivery flight and the weather forecast was good, so I guess it seemed safe enough. But what are we going to do?"

"There's damall we *can* do. We've no trackers and no controllers."

"Flying Control is trying to round some up, but I doubt if they'll find any on the station. And the pilot only has fifteen minutes of fuel left."

"Then he'll just have to bail out. I presume he *has* a parachute?"

"I didn't ask," Alan replied, too worried to notice the sarcasm. "But it's a very valuable aircraft, and they don't want to lose it. Besides, what a boost it would be for us if . . ."

"I know what you're thinking, and it's impossible. There are only three of us here—just enough to do the tracking, though I don't suppose Mac has ever tried his hand at it. That leaves no one to do the talking down, even if we knew how to."

Alan was perfectly well aware of this, but it did not affect his belief that something could be done. A few minutes ago he had felt a sense of helpless frustration—the Flying Control Officer had been quite unnecessarily rude—yet now he was swinging to the opposite extreme. He had been presented with an exciting challenge and had already seen one way of answering it. There was no time to analyze the motives behind his actions, but his two recent, though totally different, debacles undoubtedly spurred him on. Now was an opportunity to redeem himself, and GCD, at one swoop.

He picked up the telephone and spoke to the impatient Flying Control Officer.

"We'll do our best," he said. "Try to locate one of our controllers while we get lined up. While you rush him out here, we'll contact the aircraft and vector him into position. What's his call sign and frequency?"

"Z Zebra; he's using your Channel D."

Thank God for that, thought Alan. If their press-button radio transmitters had not been set up on the right frequency, they would have been completely helpless. It would have involved too great a time lag to relay all instructions via Flying Control; at least they could talk to Z Zebra directly.

Once he had made up his mind, he moved swiftly. "Howard," he snapped, "get the precision system calibrated as quickly as you can; it won't have drifted much since last time. Mac"—this into the intercom—"see that your side's OK and come over here. The transmitter truck will have to run itself—we want you as a tracker. I'll explain when you get here. Just make sure that everything's tuned up and hope for the best. Check the search system first—we've got to locate an aircraft."

That was not going to be easy with all this rain cluttering up the screens. As Alan peered into the hundred-mile-wide plan-position-indicator display, he was faced with a hopeless confusion of echoes from ground and sky. To find a lost aircraft among them seemed impossible; luckily a now-less-acidulous Flying Control Officer was able to give him an approximate fix, so he knew which area of the tube to examine.

Twenty miles away to the northeast, on bearing 040, he found the faint, solitary echo whose comet tail betrayed its movement. Was it the right aircraft? Well, there was probably no one else in the sky at the moment, and he'd soon know.

He pressed button D on the channel-selector switch. In a few seconds, he'd find out if there was any hope.

"Hello, Z Zebra," he said. "This is Ranger. We are going to vector you toward St. Erryn. Can you hear me? Over." One was not supposed to mention the name of the airfield (as if the Germans did not know it was there!), but this was no time to worry about correct radio procedure and the feelings of the Station Signals Officer.

The ether was silent, apart from the louder-than-usual

background caused by the static of the approaching storm. Perhaps Z Zebra had been transmitting and hadn't heard the message. Alan tried again.

He had wasted thirty precious seconds, and worked himself into quite a state, when he realized he'd pushed the transmit-receive key in the wrong direction. Well, he'd known experienced controllers to do the same thing, and he'd never handled this job before. No need to panic, F/O Bishop, he told himself firmly. But no more mistakes, *please.*

It was just as well for his morale—not to mention Z Zebra's—that contact was established immediately. The delay might even have been useful, for it had given him extra time to size up the situation on the radar display, and to decide the best course to give the aircraft. If he could get it roughly lined up by the time a controller arrived, that would be half the battle.

"Hearing you loud and clear," said Z Zebra. "Awaiting your instructions. Over."

The pilot sounded remarkably calm, considering the circumstances. But then, test pilots had to be calm in emergencies, and perhaps this one had an exaggerated impression of the help that was now being offered to him.

Alan's problem was to get the aircraft orbiting in a convenient spot from which it could be whistled down to the approach with the minimum of delay—*when* the still-hypothetical controller turned up to do the job. Mac, who had just arrived from the other truck, said that the station P.A. system was bawling its head off in an attempt to locate any GCD controllers, trained or untrained, who hadn't taken a weekend pass. He also remarked that it was a filthy day outside, that he'd got soaked crossing the forty feet between trucks, and what the hell was all the flap about?

Howard told him while he checked the calibration of the precision system. Mac, who would try his hand at anything, was quite confident that he could follow a radar echo at least as well as the girls who had been practicing for weeks. Though it had never been attempted, it was theoretically possible for two people to do the work of the three trackers.

Mac could handle azimuth while Howard coped with range and—most crucial of all—elevation.

There were only ten minutes left when Alan, with as much luck as judgment, got Z Zebra approximately lined up on the runway, some fifteen miles out. The aircraft was orbiting in tight circles at three thousand feet, its pilot doubtless very conscious of his fuel gauge and wondering what was happening on the ground.

In between reassuring messages, Alan was watching the clock and waiting desperately for the news that a controller had been located. As soon as one was found, it would take at least two minutes to rush him out to the GCD site, and he would have only a single opportunity. Z Zebra would not have enough fuel to go around again if the first approach failed.

Up there in the stormy sky, fuel was dripping inexorably from almost-empty tanks. Soon the engine—or engines, no one had told him which—would cough into silence, and then would follow the long, whistling dive to the ground. The pilot would probably get out in safety, but how much of the taxpayers' money would go up in smoke, and how big would be the setback to the country's research-and-development program?

It was too dangerous to wait any longer; the half-hoped-for, half-feared decision that had been hovering in Alan's mind from the very beginning must now be made. And after that, there could be no going back—either for himself or for Z Zebra.

He had never talked down an aircraft, even on a practice run. Well, now was the time to learn.

CHAPTER 17

"RANGER TO ZEBRA," said Alan into the mike. "I am now bringing you on to the approach. Cease orbiting and change course to zero two zero; I say again, zero two zero."

"Wilco," acknowledged Z Zebra. Perhaps it was imagination on Alan's part, but he thought he could sense the relief in the pilot's voice. He only hoped it was justified.

Almost at once, the distant echo on the search screen broke away from the circle in which it had been wheeling for the last few minutes. Now it was heading for the airfield, flying on the same bearing as the runway in use. It seemed an impossibly tiny target to hit from such a distance—a strip of concrete fifty yards wide, more than ten miles away. . . .

The problem, of course, was not really quite as bad as that. As long as he funneled the aircraft into the twenty-degree-wide field of view of the precision system, the first part of the job was done. Admittedly it was the easier part, but unless it was successfully accomplished, there was no hope of proceeding any further.

"He's twelve miles out," Alan warned the waiting trackers. "You should pick him up in a minute."

"Are you going to try to land him?" said Howard in a shocked voice.

"Have you any other suggestions?" asked Alan. "He has about five minutes' gas left."

There was no reply from the back room. For a moment Alan wondered if Howard would volunteer to take over the job, and relegate him to the humble role of tracker. But Howard had never landed an aircraft either, and wisely stayed where he was.

Alan gave Z Zebra one more course correction when he appeared to be drifting to the left, and rather belatedly told him to reduce height to fifteen hundred feet. A few seconds later there were simultaneous shouts from Mac and Howard.

"We've got him! Too high, and well off to the left."

"OK. Start feeding me information."

As reluctantly as a man lowering himself into an electric chair, Alan moved the short distance from the director's position to the approach controller's seat. He swiveled around until he faced the meter panel; scores of times he had sat here, checking the readings on the handmade scales while one of his mechanics adjusted the calibration. But he had never dreamed that the time would come when he would have to use these meter readings and convert them into instructions to a pilot. It was not his job, he had never learned it, and it seemed highly unfair that he should have to do it. He did not even know the precise meaning of some of the controller's patter: "Check gyro," for example, was a mystic incantation whose exact purpose he had never bothered to ascertain. As to allowing for drift and suchlike navigational minutiae—well, he might be able to do it with paper and pencil; but certainly not in his head.

This spasm of annoyance lasted no longer than the moment it took Alan to settle himself comfortably before the controller's panel. By the time he had checked the readings on the range, elevation, and azimuth meters he had already

arrived at a less egocentric view; the person he should be
sorry for, he told himself, was the unfortunate pilot wandering around up there in the clouds.

"Z Zebra," he said, his voice as full of confidence as he
could make it, "I have you on approach control. Change
course ten degrees right; I say again, ten degrees right.
Maintain height at fifteen hundred feet. How do you receive
me? Over."

"Receiving you loud and clear," answered the pilot.
"Changing course ten degrees right. Over."

Somewhat late in the day, it occurred to Alan that he
should have warned the pilot what to expect. He must be
completely mystified, unless he had already heard of GCD.
But there had been no time for any explanations, and perhaps it was just as well.

That ten degrees right was not sufficient, Alan saw at
once. He gave an extra five, then told Z Zebra to leave his
receiver on and not to acknowledge further instructions.
From now on, Alan would be doing all the talking.

He was no longer aware of time or space, except as seen
through the three meters that occupied his entire field of
consciousness. Even his own identity had ceased to exist; he
had merged himself into all the controllers he had ever seen
sitting in front of this panel, and was using all the skills he
had unwittingly absorbed as he watched them work. He had
almost forgotten that these moving pointers wrote the fate
of a valuable aircraft and a still more valuable man. It was
better to think of this purely as a kind of game, like getting a
dart into the bull's eye. But perhaps golf was a closer analogy—and he had to hole in one. . . .

In the back room, Howard and Mac had also submerged
their personalities into the machine. Mac's task was rela-
tively simple, since he was Tracking only in azimuth, but
Howard had become a veritable one-man band. Not only
was he tracking simultaneously in range and elevation, using
one hand for each control, but he was also monitoring the
whole approach, prepared to warn Alan if anything went
seriously wrong. He had the gravest doubts about the entire

proceedings, and thought that Alan was a fool to attempt such a feat. Yet at the same time he could see no alternative, and wondered if he lacked guts because he hadn't volunteered for the job.

The echo was six miles away when Alan got it reasonably lined up with the runway, though it was still much too high. A few seconds later it flew into one of the bands of rain that had been the cause of all the trouble, and they caught only glimpses of it through the sparkling fog. They were tracking by guess for half a mile, but Howard thought it as well not to let Alan know. If he realized that his information was dubious, it might ruin his confidence. Luckily, when the aircraft emerged from the obscuring haze, it had drifted less than a hundred feet from the assumed position, and the back room corrected the error so smoothly that even an experienced controller would never have known.

It seemed to Alan that the plane was coming in unusually fast, even for a fighter; the range meter was clocking off the miles at a startling rate. Five miles from touchdown, the aircraft entered the glide path; at this speed of approach, the normal five-hundred-feet-a-minute rate of descent would be nothing like enough. With a silent prayer, Alan radioed: "Reduce height at a thousand feet a minute."

That would bring him down to the ground in ninety seconds. It was a horrifying thought, but little more time was available. Z Zebra was no leisurely Anson or Oxford, stooging gently down the sky at a modest two miles a minute.

"You are four miles from touchdown," said Alan. "Check wheels and flaps."

Perhaps he'd said that before, but it was a good idea to play safe.

"You are getting a little low. Reduce rate of descent to fife hundred feet a minute."

Howard, who had been watching the plunging echo on the elevation screen, breathed a sigh of relief when he heard this order.

"Now change course fife degrees left; I say again, fife degrees left."

Was five degrees enough? The azimuth meter said he was two hundred feet off to the right. But too large a correction would do more harm than good; it took time for an aircraft to respond, and more time for it to straighten out again. Only experience could give the controller that delicacy of touch that allowed him to judge whether ten degrees was too much, or five degrees too little.

Yes, the needle was swinging back toward zero—the aircraft was edging in to the line of the runway. He must be stopped well before he got there, to prevent overshooting to the left. I'll wait until he gets within fifty feet, thought Alan, and straighten him out then. With any luck, he'll be bang on by the time he's responded.

But what about height? Alan's eyes flickered toward the elevation meter. Getting a bit high again—time to do something about it. . . .

"Increase rate of descent slightly. You have three miles to go. Now you are lined up with the runway. Change course three degrees right; I say again, three degrees right."

That should hold him; it had darn well better—there would only be time for a couple more corrections.

"Maintain present rate of descent. Two miles to go. Now you are nicely lined up."

That was a little premature, but it would be true in about ten seconds. But would it stay that way?

"One and a half miles to go." My God, thought Alan, he's coming in fast! Or is there something wrong with my sense of time? At moments like this, I always thought things seemed to happen slowly. . . .

"One mile to go. Increase rate of descent slightly. You are getting a little high. Half a mile to go. The runway is slightly to your right. Go ahead and land visually."

There was nothing more that he could do. Either the pilot had seen the runway and would be able to land or else he would have to climb away and bail out. The third possibility—that he had been talked into the ground—did not bear thinking about.

Alan felt utterly drained of strength. He slumped in the

controller's seat, staring at the now-motionless needles on the meter panel. He would never again be able to look at them with the detachment of the technician who was not required to act on their information.

Then he heard Howard's voice call, as if from a great distance: "He's down! We've lost the echo!"

Down, but where—and how? There was only one way to find out. Radar could not help them now.

Mac and Howard were already outside the truck, racing toward the runway. As Alan joined them in the pouring rain, he was acting more through reflex than reason. He was not even sure what he expected to see or hear: at best, the roar of engines overshooting the airfield; at worst, a column of smoke slowly ascending into the sodden sky.

What was upon them within seconds could never have been expected. It broke through the veil of rain that concealed the runway like a curtain. It was down, moving fast —but not too fast for safety. And ahead of it, battering their deafened and incredulous ears, was a sound such as they had never heard before in all their lives. Instead of the familiar deep-throated roar of piston engines, there came a screaming banshee wail, like the voice of a million demons escaping from hell. It tore at their eardrums and set their teeth on edge, leaving them stunned yet at the same moment exhilarated by the sheer impact of overwhelming power. As the low, squat aircraft, half shrouded in flying spray, hurtled down the runway and disappeared once more into the mist, they felt the fiery breath of its passage lick across their faces. They had a clear view of it for perhaps two seconds, but the awesome shriek of its engines lasted for minutes, fading away into the distance and presently swooping down octave by octave as the spinning turbines idled to rest.

Oblivious to the pouring rain, even forgetful of what they had just achieved, Alan and his companions remained staring along the empty runway. In that moment they knew that the age of the propeller was coming to its end. The sound still echoing in their memories was the voice of the future.

CHAPTER 18

"IT'S A POOR SHOW," grumbled Alan, "that we can't even see the ruddy kite we landed." With Howard and Deveraux, he was walking away from the locked and guarded hangar that now housed the shrieking apparition of the previous night. Two service policemen with conspicuous holsters and unfriendly expressions were parading in front of the great steel doors, turning away all unauthorized visitors.

The events of yesterday already had a misty, dreamlike quality about them. At first, Alan had gone into a state of shock at the realization of what he had done—and of what *might* have happened had he been a little less lucky. But there was no need to dwell on that; he had made his gamble, and he had won.

How much he had won only time would show. Certainly he must have struck a resounding blow for GCD, and given its critics something to think about. As Deveraux remarked, rubbing his long fingers together with satisfaction, "Even if Bomber Command takes a dim view of us, the fighter boys will be on our side now they know we can land a jet!"

Alan felt like adding that he was not sure that he could do it again; but at least he would be prepared to try, and twenty-four hours ago that would have been inconceivable.

Something had happened to him during those hectic minutes in the control van. His view of himself had changed, and so had the attitude of his companions toward him. In the past, they had always treated him with friendly tolerance, but now they looked at him with both surprise and respect. The experience was very satisfactory.

"By the way," said Deveraux, "I've put through your leave application, but I can only let you have a week. The Station Adj will have your warrants and ration cards ready first thing tomorrow."

"Oh—thanks," said Alan, almost absent-mindedly. A week was quite long enough, for the visit was one of duty as much as pleasure. Miss Hadley's last letter had been unusually insistent and had reported with some exasperation that the Captain had met with a slight accident. It was not the first time that had happened, and Alan could guess the cause. While in bed, his father would have a chance of sobering up, at least.

He felt ashamed of the thought, but it was no use ignoring facts. Yet what was he going to say to the Captain when he did get home? They had few subjects of conversation in common, and any mention of his work would have to wait until after the war. Even if the Official Secrets Act had not existed, the problem of communication would remain. Scarcely a single person he knew, among all the friends and acquaintances of his youth, could understand what he was doing now. As Schuster moved in a world beyond Alan's knowledge, so he himself moved in a world that would have baffled his father.

Yet Captain Bishop was a highly intelligent man, with a good understanding of machinery. How often Alan had seen him watching the great connecting rods and crankshafts of the *Channel Queen* going through their leisurely, silken-smooth revolutions, while he discussed some technical point with the engineer! It was incredible, the gulf that separated the massive machines he had once admired so much from the equipment he was operating now. With the dawn of electronics, something new had come into the world—something for which the word "machine" was totally inadequate. For here were no gears and cranks and wheels; only silent, motionless lumps of glass and metal through which pulsed, at lightning speed, images too swift for human eyes, sounds too shrill for human ears.

"Hello," said Deveraux. "That looks like S Sugar. The Prof must be back."

They watched as the Anson swept down the runway and taxied over to "D" Flight. By the time they had arrived at the hut, Professor Schuster and Dr. Wendt were already hard at work, rapidly dumping their property in three separate heaps on the wooden floor.

"Oh, no!" said Alan, with sudden apprehension.

"Oh, yes," answered Dr. Wendt. "I'm off to *be* the Wizard—the Wonderful Wizard of Oz. This pile is secret waste —to be burned by the Station Security Officer. The middle one is for the poor of the unit. The third we're taking with us."

The third pile was a very small one. More interesting was the second, which contained numerous cans of Spam and other monosyllabic American meat products, boxes of sugar, jars of jam, books—and an opened bottle of Scotch, already a third gone.

"My God," said Howard, looking from the bottle to the two scientists, "you only got here five minutes ago."

"We'd been saving this," answered Schuster, "until they told us to start building the Mark II. I'm afraid we've had to jump the gun—but I don't think it will be too long now." He took Alan's hand, and pumped it vigorously. "Thanks— Alan—we'll get all the propaganda mileage we can out of your effort."

"It was all luck," mumbled Alan, somewhat embarrassed.

"The sort of luck that comes to people who deserve it—

which is us," said Wendt. Then he looked puzzled. "Which *are* us? Oh, the hell with it."

"Anyway," said Schuster, "I've a little present for you." He reached into his flying jacket, and handed Alan an electric-shaver resistor. "Sorry it isn't a new one," he apologized. "I had to borrow it from a pal at TRE. It will last you until the war's over."

"Which," said Dr. Wendt, "may be sooner than you think." He caught a disapproving glance from Schuster and added hastily: "If you really want to know, we're going back to MIT to build a rocket that will home on Hitler's mustache. Our secret agents have got a clipping at last, and we know its resonant frequency."

Nobody laughed; despite all the forced gaiety, the atmosphere of gloom was too intense. It had lightened just a little by the time the Scotch was finished; but it came down again with a bang when S Sugar made a final farewell pass along the runway, and climbed away into the clouds.

Now that he, too, was preparing to leave, Alan was quite anxious to get away. He had screwed himself up to face his family responsibilities, and had even begun to look on them as an interesting challenge. This self-confidence was something new to him; it remained to be seen how long it would last. Certainly it was with almost a jaunty step that he entered the Assistant Adjutant's office and asked that pale young man for his travel documents.

His step was not quite so jaunty when he emerged a few minutes later. The Assistant Adj, on the other hand, was a good deal more cheerful. Like many other people on the station, he slightly resented the glamour that surrounded the GCD unit, the special treatment it was given, and the administrative complications it caused. Now he had an opportunity of getting a little of his own back. He did not wish Alan any personal harm—indeed, he liked him—but it gave him a rarely experienced sense of power to announce that all leaves had been canceled.

"Terribly sorry, old boy," he said. "It's a Group order—

nothing to do with us. There's a big defense flap coming up, and everybody on the station has to take part in it. No exceptions allowed."

"We'll see about that," Alan muttered darkly, and went storming off, after delivering a sloppy salute. Grabbing his bicycle from the rack beside the Orderly Room, he headed out to the perimeter track in search of Deveraux. On occasions like this, Dev usually knew what strings to pull and what priorities and regulations, fictitious or otherwise, to invoke. So indignant was Alan, and so intent upon his own affairs, that he pedaled furiously under the low-slung wing of a parked Liberator about two seconds before its engines coughed into life. The shaken ground crew watched him depart into the distance completely unaware of how narrowly he had missed the huge blades as they started to turn.

By the time he had reached "D" Flight's office, halfway around the airfield, he had cooled down considerably. The news had arrived there before him, and nobody else was particularly upset at being confined to camp. Alan was the only one who had planned to go on leave, and all the sympathy he got was expressed in the wry phrase "You've had it, chum."

Even Deveraux, with the best will in the world, could think of no way out.

"It's only forty-eight hours, after all," he said. "If it was really urgent, you could put in for compassionate leave. But surely there's nothing that couldn't wait for two days?"

"I suppose so," said Alan reluctantly. "But you know how it is, when you've got everything ready."

"Cheer up, Bish," chortled one of the pilots, clapping him on the shoulder. "Worse things happened in the RAF, even in peacetime. I've heard of blokes being recalled on the first morning of the honeymoon. On the way to the church, in fact."

"Talking of passionate leaves," said Dennis Collins, "have you heard about the airman who asked his CO for a forty-eight because his wife was going to have a baby?"

"No. What happened?"

"Well, when he came back, the CO said, 'Is it a boy or a girl?' And the chap looked at him as if he were daft and answered: 'Don't be silly, sir—it takes *months.*'"

Alan did not join in the general laughter; he did not believe in encouraging Dennis. Moreover, his thoughts were elsewhere. One of Benny Schwartz's mottoes, which he was fond of bringing forth in moments of crisis, was "Co-operate with the inevitable."

He couldn't go home for two days, but at least he could spend this evening out of camp. And he was sure it would not be necessary to twist Howard's arm too hard to get Olga Buckingham's phone number.

CHAPTER 19

"NOW WHY, ALAIN," said Lucille, "did you leave in such a hurry? I was very angry with you."

"The place was getting too crowded," replied Alan a little testily. He had no wish to go into *that;* it reflected on his manhood in more ways than one. He was not sure what he would do if McGregor put in another unwelcome appearance, but this time he had safeguarded himself. As Mac's superior officer, he had taken an unfair advantage of his NCO. Mac was now on duty, changing a magnetron that had shown signs of going soft. Alan knew just how long the job would take, even if everything went smoothly—which it probably wouldn't.

It was a dirty trick to play, since the suspect tube would certainly have lasted for several more runs. But what was the point of being an officer if you couldn't enjoy it now and then? And Alan was certainly enjoying it now.

Lucille's body was small but perfect—and she knew exactly how to use it. For several minutes Alan was too busy to think about rivals or competitors, but presently a nagging worry entered his mind. He propped himself up on one arm

and looked down into the shadows. All he could see of
Lucille's face, in this delightful dimness, was the faint glitter
of her eyes staring up into his. Any emotion they held failed
to bridge the few inches of darkness between them.

"Tell me, Lucille," he said thoughtfully, stroking her
long flaxen hair. "Do you like Sergeant McGregor?"

"I thought you didn't want to talk about him."

Alan needed no light to see the little pout of annoyance
on her face; the words conveyed it perfectly.

"I was just wondering," said Alan, and lapsed into silence.

Lucille sighed; she had been through all this so many
times before. These immature boys (after all, she was two
years older than Alan by the calendar—and at least twenty
years older in terms of experience) soon became possessive
and demanding. They behaved as if you belonged to them;
and Lucille had no intention of belonging to anyone.

She had no illusions about romantic love. Insofar as she
had any goals, they were pleasure and security—not necessarily in that order. Lucille had spent most of her life in a
rapidly disintegrating Europe, had known air raids, hunger,
and Nazi occupation. She would be quite content, she often
told herself, to settle down as the respectable, thoroughly
married wife of some solid citizen in a French provincial
town where nothing ever happened.

A good many minutes later, Alan made a circuitous return to the subject. He was not sure that he wanted to know
the answer, but he hated to be left in suspense.

"I suppose you know quite a few of the chaps from the
station," he said, with all the disinterest he could muster.

"Oh, thousands," answered Lucille. "Of course, I can't
remember them all."

Serves you right, Alan told himself.

"You're a little liar," he answered, only half playfully.
"Ouch! That hurt!"

"It was supposed to," said Lucille sweetly, retracting her
claws. "But let's not quarrel."

"It wasn't quarreling. When can I see you again? It will

have to be the week after next. I've got seven days' leave coming up."

Lucille mentally flicked the pages of her diary, but it was difficult to make plans *that* far ahead.

"I'll send you a message," she said.

"How?" Alan asked.

"Umm—no, not by Mac—oh, through Howard, or maybe Dennis."

"Dennis who?" growled Alan, with a horrid suspicion. Lucille, who could detect emotional nuances a mile away, knew at once that she had hit a sensitive spot.

"Why, Dennis Collins, of course. He's in your Flight, isn't he? *I* think he's cute," she added, with quite unnecessary emphasis.

The explosion she had hoped for did not materialize. Instead, Alan lay for a moment muttering like a partly extinct volcano, which, indeed, he now resembled in several respects. Then he snorted: *"That* stuck-up twerp! What can you see—"

Perhaps fortunately, he was interrupted by a discreet knock on the door.

"Come in," called Lucille. Alan, feeling slightly sheepish —though far less so than he would have believed possible a few days ago—retreated under the counterpane as the lights went on and Joan advanced toward the bed behind a loaded tray.

"I've brought the things you asked for, Miss Lucille," she said, without looking at Alan.

"Put it down there," ordered Lucille. She turned to Alan and shook him briskly. "It's a long ride back to camp," she said, "and it's nearly freezing outside. Stop sulking and eat this, like a good boy."

Alan looked at the tray, and the last vestiges of romance evaporated from the evening. Lucille, he decided, was a very practical young lady, and she had certainly acquired some English customs.

"Don't get any crumbs in the bedclothes," she ordered.

He waited until Joan had retired; then, with an appetite

that surprised him but not Lucille, he started on the Oval-
tine and muffins.

The last time Alan had entered this assembly hall, it had
been for the screening of a gruesome and cautionary film
which had kept the entire station continent for almost forty-
eight hours. This occasion was slightly different, but the
audience was the same. Every officer and airman not on
essential duty was present, listening with various degrees of
attention to the short, stout Squadron Leader on the platform.

Alan had never envied the Station Security Officer his
task. He had come into contact with S/Ldr. Strickland on
not more than half a dozen occasions, when it was necessary
to arrange an armed guard for the GCD trucks or to transmit secret documents to Group Headquarters. One meeting,
however, had been considerably less formal. Alan had a
vague memory of helping to hold the Squadron Leader
down after an unusually rowdy Mess Dance, while some of
his fellow officers snipped off his tie with a pair of scissors.
They had collected quite a number of ties that evening, including the CO's.

"Men," began the Security Officer, in a voice that
boomed metallically through the speakers hanging from the
bare girders. "In total war, one must be totally prepared. If
Jerry drops a parachute brigade on this airfield, every one of
us—clerks, cooks, aircrew, signals staff, fitters—must be
prepared to fight. The RAF Regiment, of course, will do its
job, but in the event of a major attack, *you* are needed.

"The Air Officer Commanding has, therefore, given orders for the defense exercise, beginning 0001 hours tonight.
For the next forty-eight hours, everyone will be confined to
camp, and the station will be in a state of alert." ("A state of
panic," muttered an irreverent interrupter standing beside
Alan. Glancing out of the corner of his eye, he saw that the
cynic was a much-decorated bomber-navigator.)

"You will all be given instructions as to the roles you
have to play, and will be issued weapons from the Armory.

Detailed defense plans have been drawn up, and your flight commanders will assign you to your posts in due course. That is all. Thank you."

A few hours later, the plan of operations was brought around to "D" Flight by an RAF Regiment Sergeant, who clearly had little use for effete radar personnel. The only person toward whom he showed any respect was Mac. Alan later discovered that they had once had a glorious fight that had half wrecked the Sergeants' Mess. Mac had lost, but his opponent had had to work unusually hard for victory.

Spreading out a large-scale map of the airfield, the visitor indicated the positions the defenders would occupy. The plan had one redeeming feature; the GCD personnel had been given a familiar section of the airfield, not far from the "D" Flight hut itself. Operating so close to home would give them a comfortable, if spurious, feeling of security.

An attacking force would have to approach across open ground for several hundred yards before it came to the barbed-wire fence surrounding the airfield. This was not much of an obstacle; there were at least a dozen unofficial exits through it, which had been made by airmen—and airwomen—anxious to go on leave without passing the scrutiny of the Guardroom. These weak points were now being energetically dealt with by the RAF Regiment, but even when it had done its best, the wire could offer little more than token resistance. This was not surprising, since its main function was to keep the runways clear of stray cows, not determined Nazi paratroopers.

"Surely," said Alan, "the enemy wouldn't attack from *this* direction? Real paratroops would land on the airfield, inside our defenses."

The RAF Regiment Sergeant, who knew that his job was hopeless but was bravely determined to make the best of it, looked Alan straight in the eye.

"The airfield, sir, is—ah—presumed to be covered with pointed stakes at intervals of twenty feet. That will discourage the paratroops."

"It would certainly discourage me," grumbled one of the

pilots. "If you've got to do *that* sort of thing to an airfield to defend it, wouldn't it be simpler to abandon it without a fight?"

"I have a still better idea," said Pat. "If you guys really were armed, you'd kill far more of each other than the enemy. So why not use passive resistance? Several thousand unco-operative prisoners would foul up an attack more thoroughly than anything else you could possibly do. Look what happened in India when Gandhi got organized."

This suggestion, equally insulting to the Royal Air Force and the British Empire, was received with the frigid silence it merited. But not so the proposal put forward a few hours later by Benny Schwartz.

"Why," said Benny, "should we sit out there all night in the cold and wet when we can use the precision system to do our watching for us? It's an ideal setup—open ground with no obstacles to confuse the radar picture. We should be able to spot anything moving across it."

"Do you mean to say," asked one of the pilots a little incredulously, "that radar can detect human beings? I thought it only worked on metal."

"Phooey. In the right circumstances, it can pick up almost anything. Besides, the targets we're after will be loaded with guns and tin helmets."

"It's worth trying," said Alan. "We could do a test this afternoon, when the day's program is finished." He looked at Deveraux for approval, but the Flight Lieutenant appeared to be wrestling with his conscience.

"I'm not sure that it would be playing the game," he objected. "After all, the whole purpose of the exercise is to test our defenses."

"Well? If we show that GCD can be made part of the defense system, won't *that* be a valuable contribution to the station's security?"

Deveraux thought it over. It hardly seemed cricket, but it would be a most interesting experiment. . . .

"Oh, very well," he said at last. "But not a word to anyone outside the unit. If it doesn't work we'll look fools—and if it *does,* we'll get a rocket from the Security Officer for messing up his plans."

"We may get worse than that from the Regiment," said Sergeant McGregor thoughtfully, "if they hear what we're up to." He flexed his biceps, and a slow smile spread across his face. "Maybe," he added hopefully, "we'll see some *real* fighting, after all."

CHAPTER 20

THE TEST WAS carried out at four in the afternoon, during the last hours of daylight. The operators had finished their training schedule and the aircraft had landed, but there was still enough light to see what was happening around the airfield.

With some difficulty, the GCD trucks were maneuvered into their unorthodox positions, with the scanners aimed down the gentle slope up which the expected attack would come. As Benny had forecast, the picture on the precision screens was a clear and simple one. There in the foreground, only a few hundred feet away, was a brilliant line of glowing blobs that marked the barbed-wire fence. Beyond that, there was nothing for almost a mile.

The next step was to send out men carrying rifles and wearing steel helmets. The results were encouraging; the echoes that crawled slowly across the face of the radar screen were somewhat anemic, but they could be easily seen. Benny's plan was vindicated; sitting here in warmth and comfort, sustained by occasional cups of cocoa, the defenders could pass the night in complete confidence that nothing

could penetrate their radar picket without detection. It was
still advisable to have men out in the forward foxholes
equipped with field telephones, but their task would be enormously simplified. They would no longer warn the rear
when the enemy approached—the rear would warn them.

Meanwhile, life went on, though with annoying interrup-
tions. All officers were issued service pistols (though not,
fortunately, with ammunition) and had to carry them day
and night. Practice alerts were sounded at inconvenient moments, resulting in frantic rushing back and forth by the
station personnel, while umpires stood around with stop
watches, calculating how long it took for the defenders to
locate and occupy their positions. Several small battles developed between rival groups trying to take over the same
slit trench or pillbox, but casualties were light.

The biggest problem about the whole operation was getting sufficient sleep. In such a small group as the GCD unit,
it was not easy to arrange a twenty-four-hour roster; there
were simply not enough people to go around. The final result was that the officers and senior NCOs got what sleep
they could by cat-napping on temporary bunks. Catering
and sanitary arrangements were primitive, but these hard-
ships could be endured for a couple of days.

Alan was dreaming as peacefully as the scratchy blankets
permitted when a rough hand shook him awake. For a moment he could not imagine where he was; then it all came
back to him and he heaved himself wearily out of the bunk.
"What time is it?" he yawned. The earlier it was, the better
chance he would have of getting back to bed again.

"Three-thirty," answered Sergeant McGregor, dashing
his hopes. "We think there's something happening out there.
Come and have a look before we wake up everyone else."

Still half asleep, Alan stumbled out into the night. It was
completely dark; thick clouds hid the stars, and the only
light was the feeble glow from the Sergeant's shielded torch.
The cinder path underfoot was a better guide, since it
crunched beneath his feet, and the comforting, deep-

throated roar of the transmitter truck's diesel told him that he was heading in the right direction.

The control van loomed up before them, a deeper darkness, except where a thin thread of light leaked out beneath an ill-fitting door. As Sergeant McGregor rapped sharply on the side, the sliver of light winked out and the door opened. The only illumination inside was the familiar green glow of the radar screens. It seemed surprisingly brilliant to Alan's night-adapted eyes, but he knew that it would not carry very far when the blackout curtain swung aside.

He was completely awake when he slid into the azimuth tracker's seat and studied the mottled rectangle of light that the radar trace was perpetually repainting. No-man's-land was no longer completely empty; it now held three brilliant blobs of light, marking the positions of the forward outposts with their field telephones. They had made themselves conspicuous in the radar void by hoisting corner reflectors— small metal pyramids, open at the base, which behaved in the radar beam exactly like cats' eyes in the headlights of a car. Though only eighteen inches on a side, they gave as big an echo as that of a four-engine bomber, and were normally used to mark out the line of the runways on the radar screens.

Not far from the outermost reflector was an altogether different kind of echo—a ghostly amoeba that shortened range with almost imperceptible slowness. It was pulsing as it moved; sometimes it faded out completely, then flashed up again with redoubled brilliance.

Alan had seen this phenomenon before; he was watching not one echo, but a group of them, almost superimposed. At a guess, he would say that there were between five and ten men moving in a tight bunch—and they were not far from the luminous blob of Outpost Number Three.

"Hello, Number Three," said Alan softly into the field telephone. "Keep a good watch—they're only about two hundred feet north of you."

"Ok, sir," said a faint and nervous voice which he recognized, with difficulty, as that of Corporal Hart, a competent but rather conceited young mech. Doubtless Sergeant Mc-Gregor was responsible for his present lonely eminence.

"Any sign of them now?" asked Alan anxiously a few minutes later. The slowly moving echoes had now almost reached the reflector, and were beginning to merge into it.

"No, sir," came the answer. "Everything's quiet."

Alan, who judged that the separation was now less than thirty feet, found this hard to believe.

"They're almost on top of you. Surely you can hear something . . . Corporal Hart!"

"Glug—ouch—gulp," said the field telephone. Then it went dead.

"So," remarked McGregor, with considerable satisfaction, "they got him."

"Looks as if they've got the marker, too," said Alan, for the glowing blob of light had suddenly vanished. Equally abruptly, it returned.

"I know what's happening," exclaimed McGregor. "The silly clots have grabbed it as a souvenir. Wonder what they think it is?"

It was true; the brilliant echo was bobbing slowly across the screen—probably, Alan realized, carried with great willingness by a captive Corporal Hart. This made it really too easy; the attackers were like blind men marching into the beam of a searchlight—and, for good measure, waving a large mirror to make themselves more conspicuous.

"They'll be at the wire within ten minutes," said Alan. "Time to alert Dev's Daredevils."

Flight Lieutenant Deveraux, with a motley group of defenders armed with blank cartridges and thunder flashes, was now camped out for the night on the left flank, sheltered inside a bell tent that smelled as if it had not been aired since the Boer War. He was in a drowsy stupor midway between sleep and waking when the field telephone jarred him into complete alertness, and he received Alan's news with much relief. It looked as if the unit was going to do something useful after all.

"That's fine," he said enthusiastically. "I'll alert my men

and let them know what's happening. You say the enemy will be here in ten minutes?"

"That's only an estimate. They may slow down, for they won't know how many other outposts we have."

"Well, I'll give them five. Let me know at once if you have any other information."

"Mac's watching the screen," said Alan. "He'll keep feeding range to you." That wouldn't be difficult, he thought, with a target moving at about a hundredth of the normal speed.

Since there was nothing else that he could contribute to the impending battle, Alan decided that he might as well have a good view of it. The roof of the transmitter truck, almost ten feet from the ground, provided a fine vantage point—though a somewhat precarious one on a pitch-dark night when a single false step might take one over the unguarded edge.

He braced himself against the plywood cylinder of the search antenna housing, and peered in the general direction of the expected attack. It was cold and windy up here, and the slats beneath his feet vibrated in sympathy with the roaring diesel immediately below. Lacking all visual references, he could easily imagine that he was no longer on dry land, but aboard the pitching deck of a ship fighting its way through a stormy night.

Suddenly, it was night no longer. A blinding flare erupted above the sleeping landscape, revealing every detail with a harsh clarity that seemed fiercer than daylight. It was beautifully timed; the attackers were caught completely by surprise, exposed in the open about a hundred feet from the barbed wire.

Within seconds, all hell broke loose as the defenders expended their ammunition at the maximum possible rate. The air was rent by concussions and curses, and the acrid smell of gunpowder came floating down the wind. It had been a long time since Alan had seen such a fireworks display, and childhood memories of forgotten Guy Fawkes nights came back to him across the years. He was fully awake now and thoroughly enjoying himself.

But it was soon over. Authoritative shouts and torch-wavings slowly restored order, and the barrage of thunder flashes died reluctantly away to sporadic explosions, then to silence. By the time Alan had climbed down from the roof of the truck, the battle had ended. Annihilated a dozen times over, the attacking forces had made their peace and were trudging toward the Flight HQ, where the WAAF operators were already preparing extra mugs of cocoa for victors and vanquished alike.

When Alan and Sergeant McGregor arrived, a three-cornered argument was in progress, involving Deveraux, the RAF Regiment Flying Officer who had led the attack, and a lieutenant from the local Army liaison group who had accompanied it as umpire. The latter two were very puzzled men, and Devereaux was not giving them much help. "We got *all* your scouts," they complained. "How did you know where we were?"

"I'm afraid I can't discuss that," Deveraux answered.

"But I've got to write a report!" protested the umpire.

"Well, you can say that the defense was effective and we weren't taken by surprise. What more do you want?"

"I believe," said the patrol leader, as if the idea had only just occurred to him, "that you were using that gadget of yours."

"Indeed?" Deveraux replied politely. "I didn't know it was against the rules. Have some more cocoa."

When Alan left, in the hope of making up some lost sleep, they were still at it. He had a good deal of sympathy for the frustrated soldiers, now that he understood their problems better and appreciated the risks they ran. Perhaps it *had* been unfair, but the whole operation was symbolic of modern war. Skill and courage and resolution were no longer enough; the time was fast approaching when only machines could fight machines.

CHAPTER 21

"I HOPE YOU make it this time," said Deveraux, as Alan piled his luggage into the little Fordson truck.

"So do I. If there's another cancellation, I'll get a persecution complex. Once I'm past the main gate, you won't see me for smoke."

He was to remember that rash remark a few minutes later. They had barely checked out of the Guardroom, and the station entrance was still in sight, when one of the service policemen rushed out into the road and began to wave furiously at the truck.

"Oh, no—not *again*!" Alan cried in silent anguish. Then he did something that would have been quite inconceivable a few months ago. He turned his back and hoped fervently that the driver would not spot the commotion in her rear-view mirror.

He did not breathe easily until the train had pulled out of the station. Now he was safe; no one could catch him until he reached Lyncombe, so even if the worst came to the worst, he would be able to spend a few hours at home. This had suddenly become very important to him; after the upheavals—mental and physical—of the last few weeks, he needed to establish contact with some fixed reference point, even though he knew well enough that there would be problems waiting for him as soon as he set foot indoors. What was going to happen about Father? Miss Hadley could not cope with him much longer, and the rest of the family had shown little inclination to help, beyond giving good advice and expressing pious distress.

He was still worrying about this when the hypnotic rhythm of the rails, and the peaceful seclusion of the empty first-class carriage, lulled him into a slumber from which he did not wake until the train stopped at Exeter. For once his luck was in; there was a connection in less than an hour, so he would be able to finish the journey in daylight and thus avoid the dismal boredom of rail travel by night in a blacked-out, inadequately heated carriage.

And so it was still daytime when the gray waters of the Bristol Channel came in sight, and the ancient locomotive gasped and clanked to rest. He refused any help from the woman porter who opened the carriage door, not merely because he objected to wasting money—though that was a consideration—but because he would feel both a fool and a cad to let a lady old enough to be his mother carry his luggage. It was not at all clear whether she appreciated or respected his scruples.

Nor did he take a taxi; it was only a couple of hundred yards to the house, and the brief walk through familiar surroundings would help him reorientate himself. He was just in time for tea, and if he knew Miss Hadley, she would already be preparing it, now that she had heard the train pulling into the station.

The narrow, gabled house with its two bay windows, its diminutive lawn, and its air of genteel neglect was exactly as he had always known it to be. Simultaneously, it depressed him with its tawdriness and warmed his heart with its comforting familiarity. He tried to put aside the fear that a message recalling him to the station would be lying in ambush in the hall.

As he had guessed, Miss Hadley was waiting for him; she must have been watching through the lace curtains as he bounded up the steps. Before she could greet him with her usual "Welcome home, Alan!" he had bussed her on her wrinkled cheeks; then he held her gently at arm's length and said smilingly, "You look fine. How's the Captain?"

Her eyes opened in surprise, and her hand flew to her lips.

"Oh," she gasped, the words coming out before she had time to think. "So you never got my telegram."

Even before she finished speaking, Alan knew why the guard had tried to intercept him at the main gate. And he knew that all his worries about his father were ended.

In all the world, there is no sound more devastatingly final than the thud of earth upon a coffin lid. Yet it would be hypocrisy to pretend that he knew much grief, as the solemn farce in the graveyard drew to its end. If Alan felt any emotion in his present state of numbed shock, it was resentment that society insisted upon this final insult to the defenseless dead. Did old Parson Williams who had not exchanged a civil word with the Captain for the last twenty years, really believe what he had just said about "this fine, upstanding citizen whom we can ill afford to lose in the prime of life" ? And these lugubrious uncles and aunts and cousins, half of them totally unknown to him—were their expressions of regret more than skin deep? In the final analysis, there were only two people who would miss Captain Bishop, and none who would weep for him. Nor was there cause for tears, Alan told himself. His father had escaped from a life that had no purpose for him; all he had lost was a difficult and unhappy old age.

The mourners were drifting away. After their brief reunion in the face of death, few would meet again before the next tolling of the bell. The family was scattering once more to the ends of England. Presently the last handshake had been given, the last whispered condolence delivered. Alan and Miss Hadley stood close beneath the worn sandstone arch of St. Matthews, still suspended in the timeless void between life and death.

It was Miss Hadley who moved first, the ferrule of her stick rapping briskly on the flagstones as she walked toward the waiting car. "Come along, Alan," she said. "It's all over; let's go home."

Suddenly, that was the last thing Alan wanted to do. He had to get away from the house, with all its associations of failure, its memories of past scenes and crises, its reminders of problems still to be faced. In that moment, he saw Miss Hadley as she really was—the eternal governess, good-hearted and well-intentioned, deriving her only satisfaction from molding the lives of others. Since his boyhood he had looked up to her with awe and admiration, wondering at her knowledge of the world and its peoples; but now he knew a world far wider than hers.

He loved and respected Miss Hadley, but he saw her now with pity in the lonely evening of her life, one of her wards already gone and the other fast slipping beyond her reach. A wave of tenderness swept over him as he helped her into the car and realized how old and frail she had become.

"Please go on without me," he answered. "I'm sorry, but I feel restless—I'll be back later."

He waited until the car had gone out of sight, then started to walk slowly up the narrow, winding road that led away from the center of the town. There was no goal that he had in mind; indeed, he was almost unconscious of direction. He was driven by a blind urge to get away from people, to find some place where he could be alone with his thoughts.

Around him now were the alleys and byways through which he had played as a child. Some of these streets were still cobbled, for this part of the town was very old and had scarcely changed in a century. The houses were low and mean; if it had not been for the war, they would have been pulled down years ago. But Alan was glad to see them; they were reassuring and familiar. Many of his friends had been born here, though Miss Hadley, with her acute awareness of

class distinctions, had often objected to some of the associates he had picked up in this neighborhood. Tony Shelton,
for instance—he had lived in that red-tiled cottage across
the way. Tony had taught Alan how to swim, something his
father had neglected to do. Other tuition had been less innocent, but that did not matter now—for the grave of Warrant
Officer Shelton, DFM, was only a few yards from Captain
Bishop's.

The Old Town was behind him; he was out in the open
space of Terrace Gardens, with its coyly contrived paths
zigzagging up the steep face of the hill. Once, this little park
had seemed a vast wonderland where wild beasts and savage
men might lurk. Indeed, it had held one terrifying menace—
the blue-uniformed park attendant, whose job it was to keep
small boys off the flower beds and out of the trees. At that
memory, Alan came to a sudden halt—for there, spiking his
ten-millionth piece of litter, was the man himself. There was
no doubt of his identity, for Alan could never forget the face
which had launched so many imprecations at him in the
past. Yet it seemed incredible that this harmless old man
could be one of his childhood ogres; it was still more incredible that he nodded affably at Alan, and continued his endless task, without a flicker of recognition.

Above the park, standing in their own wide grounds and
protected by forbidding walls, were the houses of the
wealthy. This was a region through which Alan had always
passed with respectful awe, never imagining the possibility
of social contacts with it. For here lived the Member of
Parliament for the county, the Mayor, retired officers who
liked to spend their declining years beside the sea, and the
greater part of the town's doctors, lawyers, and other professional men. It was a little world in itself, keeping its distance
with an air of conscious superiority, like a duchess drawing
aside her skirts.

Now the grand houses were all below him, as he continued his ascent of the hill. For a while he lost sight of the
town completely as he passed through the wide belt of trees
just below the summit; they were bare and cheerless in their

winter garb, perfectly fitting his mood. Rain was still dripping from their branches, which strained toward the sodden clouds like skeleton arms.

He went on tirelessly, sparing only a glance at the sinister pile of masonry that had so fascinated him as a boy—the ruined Folly that Sir Roderick Bampton had built when Lyncombe was only a tiny fishing village. If half the tales about Sir Roderick's orgies were true, these lichen-scabbed ruins would indeed be haunted, as many people still believed. Alan laughed at such superstitions; but he would not have cared to spend a night here alone.

At last the road leveled out on the open moor, a gently undulating expanse of gorse and heather—the land the red deer still ruled, because man had not bothered to assert his sovereignty. Here on the border between the tame and the wild, Alan finally came to a halt, resting against an ancient iron gate which was all that was left of some forgotten attempt to fence in the moors. Hanging between its two stone pillars, its hinges frozen by rust a generation ago, it was the very symbol of futility.

From this viewpoint, the whole town lay spread beneath him, as if in an aerial photograph. On the far right was the harbor, with the fishing boats bobbing at anchor or drawn up on the sand. It grieved him to see that the pier from which the *Channel Queen* had set out on her great adventures had been sliced ruthlessly in two, to make it useless to invaders. The gaudy pavilion, which had housed so many concert parties, could no longer be reached; it lay unattainably offshore, a disintegrating island of rusty steel, tattered canvas, and peeling paint. The slot machines earned no money now, the cry of the ice-cream vendor was silenced. Only the sea gulls remained.

Alan knew every street and alley in the map spread before him, for once this had been his entire universe. Now it seemed very small, and its smallness was not merely physical. He had outgrown his home; the ties that bound him to it were dissolving. There was no longer any place where he really belonged.

Yet everyone expected that he would come back after the war, and he had not had the courage to disillusion them. Mr. Morris had waved his old job in front of him, pointing out—truthfully enough—how valuable Alan's electronics experience would be when he returned to the shop, and even hinting at an eventual partnership. Once this would have been the height of his ambitions; now the idea of spending the rest of his life repairing radios and TV sets hardly appealed to him. He had higher aspirations; but as yet he did not know what they were.

Abruptly, his thoughts switched to another track. At the funeral he had caught several frankly appraising glances from young ladies who had been in pigtails and school uniforms when he saw them last. Even Elsie Evans had been there, looking so plump and frowsy that Alan shuddered at the narrowness of his escape. Rose Wilkins, alias Miss Droopy Drawers, had also changed, but considerably for the better. She was not a pretty girl, and never would be, but the resemblance to a camel was quite gone. It was amazing what a difference a few years could make; the idea of Rose as a wife, though not wildly attractive, was no longer utterly ridiculous. . . .

Alan wondered, with a certain smugness, what the solemn young ladies at the funeral would think if they knew about Lucille. He also realized that it was quite impossible to picture Lucille in any scene of wedded bliss. Alan had made the important, though hardly original, discovery that womankind may be divided into the two great categories of wives and mistresses; and never the twain must meet.

Yes, he had cerainly changed since last he stood upon this hill. Miss Hadley had noticed it when she remarked, soon after they had met: "You're different, Alan—you seem much older." And he had lied to her even through his smile, when he said: "*You* haven't altered a bit."

Whatever change he was undergoing, it was not yet complete—of that he felt certain. For the strongest of his links with the past had now been snapped.

More than his father had been buried today; the falling

earth had covered his childhood. He could never escape from its influence, for it had shaped his character irrevocably, as it shapes that of all human beings. But it would no longer dominate him. For the first time in his life, he was a free man.

CHAPTER 22

WHEN ALAN RETURNED to St. Erryn, at the end of that nightmare week, he found himself in a new world. The long campaign was over; they had won. Though he would never know how much he had contributed to that victory, he could claim at least one battle as his own.

Every Command in the Royal Air Force wanted GCD, and of course they wanted it yesterday. With this capitulation, the still-wavering U.S. Air Force had also made up its mind. Not to be outdone, the Navy had ordered a unit—to be modified for landings on the pitching, heaving deck of a carrier.

"We started to think about its circuits," said Pat, "but had to give up—we got too seasick. I'm afraid the Navy will have to wait; it will be tough enough producing a landbased Mark II in the time we've promised. But we'll do it—and it'll make the poor old Mark I look like a pile of homemade junk."

In spite of all this optimism, and the sense of achievement which now gave the entire unit a warm glow of satisfaction, it was an unsettling period. It was also a time of transition and farewell. In a couple of days, Pat, Howard, and Benny would be gone to work on the Mark II. No one could imagine the place without them, and several red-eyed WAAF operators were clearly unable to resign themselves to the prospect. Even the two girls currently at daggers drawn over Pat Connor now seemed reconciled in mutual misery.

There were farewell parties at all levels—in the Officers' Mess, the Sergeants' Mess, the NAAFI. For the last time Benny coaxed the "Moonlight Sonata" from the battered piano in the anteroom; for the last time Pat recited "The Good Ship *Venus*" and, by popular demand, what was generally considered to be his masterpiece—the pathetic "Farewell to his Slide Rule" of Dr. Wolfgang Wunderbar, a scarred and monocled *Luftwaffe* scientist whom Goering had ordered to produce a death-ray by Tuesday afternoon, or else. . . .

The day the Americans finally left was memorable in more ways than one. Until now, "D" Flight operations had been remarkably smooth; sometimes the aircraft (like the Mark I) were not serviceable when expected, but when they did get into the sky they usually behaved themselves. In particular, there had not been a single crash. That afternoon the record was broken; and Alan had a grandstand view.

He was standing with Howard beside T6, drinking some coffee that the operators had just brewed; at least they claimed it was coffee, and it was certainly not tea. S Sugar had just overflown the runway on a practice approach, and had begun to climb away into the west. As it was passing over the perimeter track, barely clear of the airfield, the starboard engine cut out.

Thereafter, everything seemed to happen with incredible slowness. The Anson should have been able to maintain height on the port engine alone, but that also appeared to be giving trouble. The pilot had no hope of getting back to the airfield; the aircraft's nose went down, and it started to swing to the right like a crippled bird.

Alan watched in frozen horror as S Sugar slid down the sky. It could not have taken more than thirty seconds to reach the ground, but it seemed an eternity. Even when it disappeared below the trees, the aircraft was still under partial control; the pilot was fighting to the last as he spiraled back to earth.

Though Alan was quite unaware that Howard had moved, he was already in the cab of T6, starting the motor.

"Snap out of it, Alan!" Howard shouted. "Let's get moving!" People were pouring out of the two trucks, but Howard did not wait to pick any of them up; he was already tearing down the runway. From the other side of the airfield there came the clanging of bells as ambulances and firefighting equipment headed for the main gate.

"Did you see where he came down?" asked Howard as they shot past the Guardroom.

"I'd say take the first right, down that lane," said Alan. "He must be near that farm where the Mess buys its eggs."

"That's what I thought. By the way, who's flying S Sugar?"

Alan took so long to reply that Howard looked at him sharply and was about to repeat the question.

"I've just remembered," Alan said. "It's Dennis Collins."

He had paused because he was thoroughly ashamed of himself. Clear and vivid into his mind had flashed an undeniably attractive picture—of himself gently breaking the sad news to Lucille. . . .

The discreditable fantasy vanished as quickly as it had come, leaving a brief afterglow of guilt. The guilt might have lasted a little longer had Alan not spotted S Sugar at that same instant.

So had Howard. He turned the truck off the road, and swung it skillfully through the huge gap in the barbed-wire fence. They bumped across a pasture—the ambulance, Alan noted with admiration, had already got here—and braked to a halt at a respectful distance from the downed aircraft. A very respectful distance.

It was the biggest mess he had ever seen, but not at all the sort of mess he had expected. S Sugar appeared practically undamaged—what one could see of it. Dennis Collins was

GLIDE PATH 169

still inside, not having yet figured out a safe way of emerging. All around him, distributed impartially over much of the surrounding landscape, were the remains of what must have been a really enormous dunghill.

Howard gazed at the spectacle in awe. Then he remarked solemnly: "I'd no idea, Alan, that mechanized farming had reached such an advanced stage in your country."

Those were almost the last words—apart from a tender farewell message to Elise—that they exchanged before Howard boarded the Liberator that would take the now-depleted team back to the States. As the thin white wings dwindled into the sky, Alan felt not only a sense of personal loss, but a sense of mild panic.

They were on their own now; when things went wrong—as they would—there'd be no Prof or Doc or Howard or Pat or Benny to whom they could run for help. It was the end of an era, in more ways than one. The sales campaign, as it had often been sarcastically called, was over; now they had to deliver the goods.

The changes started to take place almost at once. The first, received with mixed feelings, was the move to permanent quarters. For months all the officers of the unit had been living in the same large wooden hut. It was a comfortable hut, and the only hardship involved was the lack of privacy. But now they would live behind bricks and mortar, two to a room, in the Officers' Quarters of the Mess.

The old hut was taken over by the pupils who were now arriving in increasing numbers. More controllers, more operators, more radar mechanics—more of everything was on the way. The process of empire-building had begun, and with it the process of myth-making. From now on, all those involved in GCD could be divided into two groups—the old-timers, who remembered the pioneering days and were always talking about them, and the newcomers, who took it all with a grain of salt.

Reinforcements had also appeared for Alan and Deveraux, in the shape of a new radar officer. To Alan's surprise and pleasure, this turned out to be his first Gatesbury instructor, Sergeant—now Flying Officer—Lebrun, RCAF. Having to teach his old teacher gave Alan considerable satisfaction.

Lebrun was to take over the synthetic trainers, which would soon make life much easier and would multiply the rate of instruction. They would enable several crews to practice at once, without the use of the Mark I itself. Each trainer had an exact replica of the controller's panel, with its meters reporting the approaching aircraft's deviation from the glide path. But there would be no real aircraft flying expensively around the sky—only black boxes, full of electronic equipment, that would feed the appropriate signals to the meters. And so fledgling controllers could practice without using the Mark I or risking "D" Flight's aircraft—not to mention its pilots.

As for the Mark I itself, it, too, seemed to have settled down to the new routine; the mechanics were now so skilled at spotting incipient faults even before they appeared that there was very little time off the air. The equipment had reached a kind of serviceability plateau, and would probably remain there until some final and catastrophic breakdown developed. In human terms—and such terms were only too often applied to it—the Mark I had not attained a healthy maturity. But no one knew whether the senile decay of old age was months, or only weeks, ahead.

Meanwhile, the war went on—so far beyond the horizon that it might have been on another world. Every evening at nine most of the officers would gather around the radio in the anteroom, listening to the names that were passing into history—Stalingrad, El Alamein, Anzio. . . . Sometimes, as he listened to the reports from these distant battlefields, Alan would feel a vague sense of dissatisfaction at his own peaceful war record, and this had been underlined when he went through his father's effects. There were souvenirs of 1914–18 that he had never known about—faded medal ribbons, still more faded photographs of antiquated ships and uncomfortably posed groups of sailors in old-fashioned uniforms. And, still bright and new, was the George Medal the Captain had won at Dunkirk.

He had been proud of that medal, small compensation though it was for his ship. It had been pinned up inside his battered rolltop desk, where it would be before his eyes every day. Just beneath it was a photo of the *Channel Queen;* to Alan, the juxtaposition was almost heartbreaking.

When he had been taking down that photo, to put it in his picture album, Miss Hadley had made a curious remark.

"You know, Alan," she said, "that was the trouble with the Captain. He was more fond of things than of people."

"But you can lose people," Alan countered, "just as easily as you can lose things."

"No—that's not true. When material possessions are gone, there's nothing left—there's just a vacuum. People are different. You never really lose those you once loved, no matter what happens. They're always part of your mind, waiting to be called up whenever they're needed. Even if they've died or become strangers."

It was an odd thing to say, and one of the first times that Miss Hadley had ever revealed her deeper emotions. She must have had a cheerless life, thought Alan, though it was typical of that led by generations of lady's companions and governesses, trapped in the genteel limbo between domestic service and "society." But at least she would have no material worries in future; the house was Alan's (surprisingly, it was not heavily mortgaged), and now that fewer rooms were needed, they had been able to let the ground floor for a satisfactory rent. Miss Hadley would be an efficient concierge and, with the tiny income she drew from some investments, she would be quite comfortable. That was another problem settled—unless he married and brought home a wife.

He did not think of this possibility very often, but before he had met Lucille he had not thought of it at all. With her he had achieved domesticity without responsibility, and there was a good deal to be said for that, especially in time of war. But one day, surely, he would need something more permanent.

The first time he had cycled to Olga's by himself, after Howard had gone, he had felt a brief return of his old nervousness. Matters were not helped when Sergeant McGregor brazenly asked him to deliver a parcel to Olga, with apologies for his own absence. Their little game of hide-and-seek had quickly petered out, for this was not the kind of secret that could survive in such a close-knit world.

Alan was very anxious to give Lucille the first account of Flight Lieutenant Collins's ignominious descent into the manure heap. It would, he calculated, take that overrated gentleman down a few pegs, and perhaps make Lucille a little less enthusiastic about him. ("Cute," indeed! That adjective still rankled.)

His description of the event was not exactly untruthful, but it failed to mention such important matters as Collins's skillful handling of the aircraft. It also gave the impression that it was Dennis, not S Sugar, that "D" Flight had spent several days scraping down; in reality, Dennis had sacrificed nothing more than a pair of shoes, and had reported to the Mess half an hour later in a perfectly acceptable condition—though that, of course, had not stopped everyone from going through ostentatious checks of wind direction when he appeared.

One would not have gathered any of this from Alan's distinctly biased report, and when he had finished he did not feel quite as pleased with himself as he had expected. Lucille had sat and watched him with her big blue eyes, making no comment and not appearing to be particularly interested, though he knew perfectly well that she was. After a while, he was glad to change the subject, and bring up his other big piece of news.

"I'm going away for—oh, several weeks," he said, with all the tragic emphasis he could put into it. "I won't be able to come and see you for quite a while."

Lucille seemed to be bearing up under the shock remarkably well.

"You're not being posted?"

"Oh, no, nothing like that; I'll be coming back again. It's a trip right round the country—and what's more, they're giving me an aircraft of my own."

"Will you be flying it yourself?" asked Lucille.

She knew a lot better than that, and Alan looked at her sharply. But if she was pulling his leg, she gave no sign of it.

"No; I'll have a pilot and navigator."

"Dennis, perhaps?"

Alan swallowed hard. There was in fact some danger of this, and the idea of a month with Dennis did not appeal. On the other hand, it would be one way of keeping him away from Lucille. . . .

"No," he said firmly. "*Not* Dennis. And I'm sorry—I can't tell you any more."

Perhaps he had said too much already; there were times when he had wondered about Olga and her nieces. Their establishment was almost too much like a textbook example of the best way to coax information from young and inexperienced officers. Often he had joked with Howard about this, and their private nickname for Olga was "the beautiful spy."

Was it possible that the matter was more than a joke? The thought occasionally passed through Alan's mind, causing him momentary discomfort. Then he reassured himself with the reflection that at least *he* had given no secrets away. Even if Olga was up to no good from the security point of view, she'd got nothing out of him. He was the one who had derived all the benefit at a very modest cost (so far, about ten pounds on blackmarket petrol, chocolates, and cigarettes, as well as sundry liquors and nylons for which Howard refused to accept any payment). Olga and the girls seemed to have plenty of money and no interest in acquiring more, which was a little odd. But when Alan had diffidently raised the subject, Lucille had answered, "You're helping us to get home. This is *our* war effort." She had sounded perfectly sincere; it was one of the few times that Alan had known her to be completely serious.

Anyway, there was one thing that settled the matter. No one with a name like Olga could possibly be a spy in real life. . . .

The argument, unfortunately, was not quite as convincing as Alan hoped.

CHAPTER 23

ALAN'S AIRBORNE Grand Tour of the British Isles was the bright idea of someone at Group Headquarters—probably of Wing Commander Stevens, who had selected him for this job at that crucial interview so many lifetimes ago. He was to visit a dozen airfields, strategically placed through the United Kingdom, and draw up the necessary plans for installing GCD.

His pilot was not Dennis Collins, he was relieved to discover, but an amiable young New Zealand Flying Officer. For navigator, he had an intense Scots sergeant, who was loaded down with tables, maps, and calculating instruments. They seemed a competent pair, not likely to land him in Germany by accident.

The trip lasted a month, and took them the length and breadth of the British Isles. At each airfield, Alan would report to the Commanding officer, give him a pep talk on GCD, and then go into a huddle with the Senior Flying Control Officer over a set of airfield maps. From these he could tell, very roughly, where a GCD unit might best be sited; then it was a matter of getting into a car and looking at the actual locations, to see if there were any unexpected snags.

The work became easier as he grew more experienced, and toward the end of the tour he needed only a day to complete his report on an airfield's suitability. Inevitably, after a while one RAF station merged into another, and sometimes he had to think twice to remember where he was. But there were a few episodes in his circumnavigation of Britain that he would never forget.

There was the airfield that had a railway line crossing the main runway, and operated through a kind of nonaggression pact between the Flying Control Tower and the nearest stationmaster. When a train was scheduled to go through, no aircraft were allowed to interfere, and vice versa. It was a hell of a way to run a railroad—or an airfield—but it seemed to work. And it was, of course, in Ireland. Alan wished he could have told Pat Connor about it.

It was here that he had his first glimpse, for longer than he could easily remember, of a country not at war. Just over the road was the Irish Free State, and if he had brought his civilian clothes with him, he could have walked across into that unknown country. It was hard to believe that only a hundred miles away the Swastika was flying above the German Embassy in Dublin, while British sailors were dying to keep the republic supplied with essential foods. Alan felt that he should be indignant about this, but like most Englishmen he found it impossible either to dislike the Irish or to take them quite seriously.

Back in England, he caught up with the war when he spent his second night in the control tower of a Bomber Command station, and watched the Lancasters disappear with their deadly loads toward the heart of Germany. Once again he listened while, from some distant holocaust, the radio brought its meaningless code messages, whether of triumph or disaster he could not tell. Then the real waiting began. That night, out of the twenty-five bombers that had left, only nineteen returned.

These hours beneath the operations board had an unsettling effect upon Alan, and destroyed some of the satisfaction he had derived from his tour. They reawakened his slumbering self-doubts; when he sat among the bomber crews in the anteroom, he felt almost ashamed of himself. This was real bravery—to go out night after night into the hostile darkness, knowing that sooner or later the odds would turn against you, and to be reminded always of that fact by the empty seat, the absent friend.

It was not that he had any romantic ideas about war—no one but a fool had, in this age—or that he had any grave doubts about his courage. But it had never been put to the test, and no man knows himself until he has faced death. That was not a thought that Alan had ever consciously formulated, but deep down in his soul he was dimly aware of it.

He had proved his *moral* courage, when he had landed that Meteor. But that was not enough; for the life he risked then had not been his own.

St. Erryn was not the same when Alan returned; something even more secret, and much more spectacular, than GCD had descended on the station. There had been rumors for weeks, and now the evidence was plain for all to see.

"Just look what they've done to our airfield," lamented Sergeant McGregor as he and Alan stood at the intersection of Runways 320 and 270. "Who'd have thought even Works and Bricks could make a mess like this in such a short time?"

It was indeed an impressive shambles, and it was quite hard to believe that despite it all the airfield was still in full working order. Stretching the entire length of Runway 320, on each side of the broad concrete strip, were rows of pipes supported a foot from the ground. It looked as if the plumbing of an oil refinery had been laid along the runway. At regular intervals the piping doubled back on itself to form sections like giant trombones, and at other strategic spots were huge valves and control wheels. All that was needed to complete the picture were the derricks.

"So this is FIDO," mused Alan. *"How* much gas does it burn?"

"A nice round hundred thousand gallons an hour, so they tell me. There'll be riots if the motorists ever hear about it, with their basic ration of four gallons a month."

"And does it really clear away the fog?"

"We don't know yet," McGregor answered skeptically. "I'll believe that when I see it. But there's a dummy run at 1500 hours this afternoon; that should be worth watching."

He fell momentarily silent as C Charlie appeared over the end of the airfield and came roaring down the runway.

"You see some lousy approaches these days," he grumbled. "These new controllers couldn't talk a bike into a barn."

"I thought," said Alan, "that they'd all passed on synthetic trainers before they tried the real thing."

"Sure they have. Otherwise I suppose they'd never hit the airfield."

The criticism was hardly justified; the new boys were doing quite well, but as one of the original GCD team, Mac would never admit that anyone not trained by Wendt and Schuster could be any good.

At three o'clock Alan was standing on the roof of the transmitter truck—the same vantage point from which he had watched the rout of the RAF Regiment. Almost the whole of Runway 320 could be seen at a glance; the Fog, Intensive, Dispersal Of, burners formed a double line on either side of it. All told, the total length of the installation was at least three miles.

A mile away, over by the fuel-storage tanks whose building Alan had watched with such unsatisfied curiosity during the past few months, a great gout of black smoke billowed up into the sky. Beneath it was a lurid yellow flame, which raced along the line of pipes faster than a man could run. Within seconds, a wall of fire had extended the whole length of the runway, while above it, rolling thunderheads of oily smoke drifted across the airfield. The nearest of the burners was more than a hundred feet away, but even at this dis-

tance the roar of the yard-high flames was impressive, and
Alan could feel the heat against his face.

The smoke seemed to be getting worse, and it was coming
closer. Presently he began to cough in the oleaginous clouds,
which were rapidly reducing visibility to zero. Up here on
top of the truck it was not merely unpleasant—it was becoming alarming. Fog *dispersal,* my foot! thought Alan, as
he retreated down the ladder in search of breathable air.

Slowly, and none too soon, conditions improved, the
FIDO experts were getting their voracious monster under
control. The roar of the flames became still more deep-
throated as the pumps increased their pressure. Now that
the system had warmed up, the fuel was burning cleanly as
vapor, not smokily as liquid. The whole operation reminded
Alan of his attempts, in his scouting days, to get balky
Primus stoves working. The principle was exactly the same,
but the scale was slightly larger.

And now, apart from a stubborn section over there on
the far side of the airfield, the parallel walls of fire were
almost smokeless—roaring jets like those from a gas burner,
but taller than a man and thousands of feet in length. The
entire landscape, on this winter afternoon, quivered with
heat. Was it imagination, or were the clouds themselves being driven upward by the columns of rising air?

Before Alan could be certain, the test was concluded. The
breath from the fiery furnace no longer beat upon his face;
the fuel pumps slackened their efforts, and the quadruple
walls of flame shrank swiftly to the ground. A few streamers
of smoke drifted downwind as the burners gave their final
coughs and gasps; then it was all over.

It had been quite a show—as indeed it should be, at
twenty thousand pounds an hour. And this was in the daytime, with the sun to provide competition. A night test,
thought Alan, should be quite spectacular—but could it really disperse fog? Like Mac, he'd believe it when he saw it.

During his absence, his responsibilities had increased
alarmingly. He would soon be in charge of the unit, for
Deveraux was about to leave. It was universally agreed that

his was the cushiest posting in the entire history of the Royal Air Force; for he was going, of all places, to Hollywood.

It was here that the Mark II production line was set up, presumably among movie studios and orange groves. Reports of progress came from time to time, either on the official level through Group Headquarters, or in more guarded fashion through private correspondence. Several of the WAAFs, who received a good deal of American mail, seemed quite well-informed, and when Alan wanted news of his ex-colleagues, he could usually get it from them.

But no one could tell him anything about Professor Schuster. It was incredible, but he now appeared to have no connection with GCD, and Alan's tentative queries all drew a blank. Then, right out of the blue, a large parcel arrived.

It contained half a dozen fat books, which had obviously been chosen with care. One was Terman's *Radio Engineering,* which Alan knew well and was delighted to have. The others were of a more general nature—*Mathematics for Engineering Students* was typical—and it was quite apparent what the Professor had done. Alan could almost hear him saying: "This is the road ahead, if you want to follow it. The choice is yours."

He wrote a short but heartfelt letter of thanks to the APO number that was the only address he could find on the package; but there was never any reply.

"That was quite a fire you had up at the aerodrome the other day," said Lucille as she reclined lazily on the couch in a negligee so diaphanous that one had to look hard to make sure it was really there. "I hope it didn't do too much damage. They say the fire brigades were coming all the way from Exeter."

That last remark was perfectly true. Owing to some administrative oversight, half the fire engines in the West Country had converged upon St. Erryn during the FIDO tests, and had been dispersed again only with the greatest difficulty. It was hard to convince anyone that matters were completely under control when thousands of acres were apparently involved in a major volcanic eruption.

"Oh, it wasn't as bad as it looked," Alan answered reassuringly. "Just a drop of petrol going up—no damage at all."

Lucille's comment was a perfectly natural one, yet it set him wondering. But when he looked into those limpid blue eyes, he found it impossible to believe any harm of her. She was playful and mischievous, and loved to tease him (especially about Dennis); but he would swear that she was what she seemed to be, and nothing more. So was Elise, who had taken a whole week to recover from Howard's departure.

Now Olga, perhaps . . . He had never really liked her; she had always seemed too flamboyant and gushing, greeting everyone with the same synthetic friendliness. Elise and Lucille were chic, but Olga was invariably overdressed and overjeweled. She was also overfed, and had a sleek and prosperous look that somehow jarred on one in wartime.

But he was imagining things, and jumping to wholly unwarranted conclusions. The truth of the matter was that he had scarcely given Olga a thought. What was more, he had never considered Lucille as a real person, with hopes and fears and ambitions. She had been no more than a delightful plaything, toward whom he would always feel gratitude—and nothing else. If he had believed otherwise, he had been fooling himself.

Yet was it as simple as that? If so, why did he feel jealous of Dennis? He really had nothing against the fellow; Collins could help neither his mannerisms nor his good looks, and if Lucille preferred him, that was her affair. It was foolish to get hot under the collar about it.

He suspected, rather uncomfortably, that he was jealous not of Dennis, but of all that he stood for. And even jealousy was the wrong word—envy would be better. For behind Dennis he could always see that bomber operations board, with its blank spaces and all that they symbolized.

Flight Lieutenant Collins stood for a world that he could not enter. but why did he resent that? Alan knew very little about psychology, least of all his own. His only contact with that elusive science had been through some eyebrow-raising books that Benny had been reading, and which he had borrowed briefly.

It had to be some complex or other, and it probably stemmed from his childhood. (After all, what didn't?) He was very near the truth, but he would never reach it, for it was one of those obvious facts that the mind carefully focuses upon its blind spots.

There was a striking resemblance between Dennis Collins and the young Captain Bishop; anyone but Alan would have seen it at once.

It was almost midnight, and time to get back to camp. As Alan buttoned up his shirt, there was a knock on the door.

"Come in, Joan," Alan called.

But it was not Joan with the usual nightcap. It was Elise, looking quite as attractive as Lucille, and less disheveled.

"Thanks, sweetheart," said Alan, taking his steaming cup. "Where's Joan? I haven't seen her all evening."

"She's left," said Elise. "She had a row with Olga. We're running the house now, until we can get someone new."

"Well, it'll be good practice for you," said Alan. "One day you'll have a place of your own."

He was still trying to picture what sort of place it would be when they let him out into the night. Whistling happily, he cycled away up the hill; and his departure was duly noted by a patient observer in the shadows.

CHAPTER 24

SQUADRON LEADER STRICKLAND, Station Security Officer, felt very annoyed with the world. For the sixth time he read the police report on his desk, wondering what he had better do about it. The situation was an extremely delicate one, and action could not be delayed any longer.

He walked over to his heavily barred window, and stared out into the night. It had been a filthy day, and it was rapidly growing worse. A light fog had shrouded the airfield since noon, and during the last few hours it had turned into a fine drizzle—not exactly rain, but a steady precipitation that seemed wetter than ordinary water. Even driving a car was difficult, for visibility was less than ten feet. All operations had been canceled; not even the sea gulls could get airborne in this weather.

He turned his back on the dismal prospect, and picked up the direct telephone to the Guardroom. "Sergeant Jenkins?" he said. "Would you send someone to find Flying Officer Bishop? He'll be in the Mess anteroom, unless he's working over at the GCD unit. Tell him that he's wanted urgently, and bring him straight here."

Well, that was that. When he had hung up, Strickland ran through Bishop's file again. It was absurdly clean; he was a highly conscientious and hard-working officer who had been "mentioned in dispatches" only a few weeks ago, and was now due for promotion to Flight Lieutenant. He had done an outstanding job in connection with the Meteor he'd landed, and he appeared to have no political affiliations of any kind. Strickland wished that his own record were as spotless.

Jenkins seemed to be taking a long time to locate Bishop, and the Squadron Leader was about to call back when the phone rang. He picked up the receiver, and listened to the Guardroom's report with mounting incredulity.

"I can't believe it!" he said, glancing at the wet and Stygian gloom beyond the windows. "Not on a night like *this*!"

"That's how it is, sir," replied the Sergeant. "They're moving out now. I've just checked with the Flight Commander."

"I'll call you later. They must be absolutely crazy!"

He could hardly have guessed how completely Alan would have agreed with him.

It had started off as just another demonstration, but had somehow got out of control. Originally, the plan had been to see how well FIDO and GCD worked together, for the two systems were complementary, rather than competitive. GCD could bring an aircraft onto the runway, but the pilot had to depend on his own eyesight for the last seconds of the landing, and FIDO would be able to help him there.

A demonstration as spectacular as this one promised to be had attracted an unusually large collection of VIPs. Signals specialists ranged all the way up to group captains; Fighter and Bomber Commands were represented by air vice marshals, no less; while the Petroleum Warfare Department was led by a world-famous scientist who had chain-smoked his way past so many million-gallon gas tanks that his associates had acquired permanent gray hairs.

For good measure, three U.S. Air Force generals had arrived at the last moment in a B-26, which had made a hair-raising landing just before the fog closed in completely. The aircraft had come in on the Beam Approach Beacon System —and the pilot had homed on BABS all too thoroughly. For the B-26, in a slightly bent condition, was now entangled in the beacon antennas off the end of the runway, while its passengers sat in the anteroom in a very pensive mood, reading old issues of *Punch* with baffled concentration. It would take several days to get the beacon working again, and still longer to straighten out the B-26.

Owing to the appalling weather, the day's normal training program had been abandoned, and there seemed little chance that the spectators would see anything at all for at least twenty-four hours. Late in the afternoon, however, a mildly encouraging forecast came through from the Meteorological Section, and though it needed the eye of faith to see any improvement in the weather, there was nothing to lose by getting the trucks into position. If the FIDO boys decided to light the wick, Alan decided, then GCD would be ready for them.

Even in good visibility, driving around the airfield was now a hazardous undertaking, for the massive pipelines supplying the FIDO burners were a barrier that could be penetrated at only a few points. To find these narrow gaps, when the driver of the transmitter truck could not even see the ground clearly from his cab, needed a more accurate radar than any yet invented. Alan solved this navigational problem by standing on the running board and shouting directions to Mac. It took twenty minutes to make the journey from hangar to runway—a trip that normally took five.

The raw, wet day merged imperceptibly into a raw, wet night. The massive GCD trucks and their retinue of transport vehicles formed a tiny, isolated enclave in a world of slowly moving fog—a fog that was saturated with water, yet seemed unable to make the transition to honest-to-goodness rain. It was hard to believe that anything else existed beyond the impenetrable wall of mist. Alan was reminded of a description of the planet Venus he had read in one of those farfetched science-fiction magazines that Howard used to patronize. He would much rather be on Venus, he decided; apparently it was a good deal warmer there.

It was shortly to become a good deal warmer here. Alan was pointing out the various landmarks on the radar screens to the three American generals when the field telephone started to ring.

"Excuse me," he said to his distinguished pupils, picking up the receiver. "Flying Control have a message for us." When he hung up a few seconds later, he had a slightly surprised expression.

"They're going to light FIDO," he reported. "It seems that this is just the sort of weather they've been waiting for. I suppose if it can work in this, it can work in anything."

"Tell me, Mr. Bishop," said one of the generals in an honest spirit of curiosity, "are your London fogs as bad as *this*?"

Alan had never been in a really bad London fog, so was not in a position to answer. But he felt it necessary to uphold the reputation of his country.

"Oh, much worse, sir," he answered with relish. "After all, you can see at least two yards in this one."

"Migawd," muttered the general, and subsided thoughtfully.

"I think it would be a good idea," continued Alan, "to go outside and watch them light up—that is, if you don't mind getting wet."

"I can't get any wetter without becoming amphibious," said another of the generals, who didn't look a day over twenty-five and was covered with combat decorations. Buttoning up raincoats, the party squelched out to the dripping concrete. It was the first time, thought Alan, that he had ever seen generals wearing galoshes.

The bulk of the transmitter truck, looming above them in the humid night, gave some protection from the elements. They sheltered against the antenna housing, and stared toward the invisible runway a hundred yards away, and the first row of burners at just half that distance.

It seemed as if the sun were rising in the wrong quarter of the sky. The pulsing, yellow light spanned the entire field of vision, and the mouting roar of the flames, muffled though it was by the rain and fog, was something that could be felt as well as heard. The wall of fire was too far away in the mist for them to make out the individual jets; all that could be seen was the ill-defined curtain of light that marked its presence.

When the second line of burners ignited, it took the visitors completely by surprise. They had lost their orientation in the darkness, and had forgotten that the outer burners were behind them—and much closer than those in front. There was a sudden "woomph!" and within seconds the trucks were sandwiched between two sheets of fire. Both sides of the sky were burning; the ground shook with the sheer force of the pounding flames. The night was no longer cold and clammy; it was uncomfortably warm even at this point, eighty feet from the nearest burner.

One of the generals leaned across to Alan and shouted, raising his voice above the roar: "I've just worked it out from the fuel figures you gave me—this thing is generating ten million horsepower of pure heat!"

Alan had never thought of it that way and couldn't check the calculation in his head. But it seemed a likely figure; it was certainly easy to believe it when one stood in the midst of the man-made inferno and felt its fury beating upon one's face.

"If you want to follow me," he shouted to his awestruck audience, "we'll see what effect it's had over at the runway."

No one seemed in a hurry to accompany him toward what looked like instant immolation, but Alan had been well briefed and knew that it was not so dangerous as it looked. There were gaps in the fiery fence where the pipeline went underground, and if one did not linger to admire the view, it was possible to run the gantlet in complete safety.

As the little party moved in Indian file through the luminescent mist, the roar of the approaching flames grew steadily louder and the diffused glare of light began to concentrate at ground level. They were less than forty feet away when the narrow gateway in the wall of fire became visible for the first time, and now that he had fixed his position accurately, Alan broke into a jog trot. He did not look back to see if his charges were still with him; he was quite certain that none of them would be left behind.

The hissing roar rose to a crescendo; the heat from the blazing jets battered for a moment with terrifying violence against his exposed skin. Then he was through, and the fire and fury subsided behind him. The open runway was ahead.

Mopping their brows, and looking slightly singed, the generals joined Alan on the vast acreage of concrete. And there they fell silent, beholding a miracle.

Like most miracles, it was a very simple one. Overhead, the stars were shining.

On either side the fog still rolled, moving sluggishly through the night. But here, in a narrow band scarcely more than a hundred yards wide, a swath had been cut clear from ground level up to the open sky. As long as the burners pumped their millions of calories into the night, Runway 320—perhaps alone in the whole of England—would have good weather. Alan was witnessing the crude beginnings of meteorological engineering, and the sight was unforgettably impressive.

"It's magnificent," muttered one awe-struck watcher. "But is it *practical?*"

Alan was about to point out that if FIDO saved a single bomber, it would have paid for many hours of continuous operation when one of his radar mechanics emerged from the surrounding fog, gave a startled look at the strip of starry sky overhead, and then homed on the group of spectators. He seemed in a hurry, and this usually meant bad news.

"Excuse me," said Alan, and went to meet the airman. "What's the trouble, Hart?"

"They'd like you to go over to 'D' Flight, sir. Mr. Collins wants to take off as soon as you say it's OK."

Shaken to the core by this unlikely news, Alan stared at the familiar face of Corporal Hart as if he were seeing him for the first time in his life.

"Are you sure?" he gasped.

"Yes, sir. The Station Commander's over there, too. They said something about this being too good a chance to miss."

As Alan shepherded his charges back to the trucks, he wondered what on earth Dennis thought he was doing. True, he was the blind-flying expert—but on a night like this one would almost need instruments calibrated in Braille.

Parking the generals in the control van, where they wouldn't catch cold and could follow any further developments, Alan grabbed his bike and headed for "D" Flight. In this weather, that was much the quickest form of locomotion; there was no peering through misty windshields.

There was quite a crowd at "D" Flight when he arrived after taking a short cut along the flame-fringed runway. Not only the Station Commander, but the Senior Flying Control Officer was there—also the Met Officer, with his synoptic charts and his habitual worried look. Alan's intended opening—"Whose crazy idea is it to take off in *this* muck?"—accordingly died unuttered on his lips.

"Glad you found your way, Bishop," boomed the Station Commander. "Good thing you've got radar on that bike of yours, haw haw. Well, are you all set to go?"

"Er—yes, sir. The GCD's lined up on the runway. But we didn't think anyone would be flying in *this.*"

"Well, it is a bit dicey, but Collins here wants to be the first man to make a GCD—FIDO landing, and he's sure there'll be no trouble. And if we miss tonight, heaven knows when we'll have another chance like this."·

"I understand that, sir. But you realize that this is an experimental unit, and it's nearly on its last legs. We can never be sure of staying on the air. Mr. Collins knows that as well as anybody."

"But it's been working fine all week," interrupted Dennis.

"All the more reason," Alan answered with the wisdom of bitter experience, "for thinking that it's too good to last. If anything goes wrong when you're up there, how will you get down? Remember, the Yanks have just written off our beacon."

"I'm pretty sure I can home on the FIDO glare. Anyway, Flying Control can give me an alternate airfield that isn't closed in. All we want to know is whether you can organize *your* side of the business."

Alan did not like the tone in which this was said, and could not resist snapping back: "Barring breakdown, of course we can; the trucks are ready to operate now. Anyway, it's your neck."

Dennis gave him a peculiarly humorless smile.

"That's the other matter we wanted to speak to you about. The Group Captain thinks we ought to have an expert observer up with me. I'll be too busy, of course, to do everything, and I pointed out that you were absolutely the best man for the job—you know the system and the runway layout. And he agrees with me—don't you, sir?"

"Certainly, certainly," said the CO.

Alan was speechless, completely taken off guard. His mind whirled in all directions like a crazy compass needle, trying to think of reasons why he could not possibly, conceivably accept Dennis's kind offer—for that it was Collins's idea he had no doubt. The obvious reply—that he had to stay to supervise the equipment—Dennis could demolish in a moment. Sergeant McGregor and Corporal Hart between them knew at least as much about the Mark I as did Alan.

He might think of other excuses, even plausible ones, which the Station Commander would accept. But this was no longer a matter of logic or even common sense. It was a private affair, between Dennis and himself—an inescapable challenge to his own pride and self-respect. Well, he had been hankering for such a challenge; now it had come.

And suddenly, with a flash of insight, he knew exactly

what had led to this. He should never have told Lucille, with such obvious relish, the story of Flight Lieutenant Collins's crash landing in the dung heap. It had been a cheap victory—until this presentation of the final bill.

"I'm ready," he said. "Will someone get me a chute?"

✳ CHAPTER 25

THE RUNWAY WAS a road to nowhere, fading into the mist a few hundred feet beyond the Perspex windows. On a night like this, thought Alan, one needed radar not merely to land, but to take off. As long as he lived he would remember this moment, with the Anson quivering eagerly on the wet concrete, the roar of its motors merging with the roar of the flames, as they carved their narrow zone of visibility through the fog. *As long as he lived. . . .*

Precisely. Even now, while they were still taxiing slowly to the center of the runway, there was time to call the whole thing off. But he knew that this was so impossible that it was not worth a second thought. There was no question of bravery—only the fear of being marked down as a coward for the rest of his career. How many heroes, he wondered, had in reality been driven by this same impulse? There could be no such thing as an act of pure, unadulterated bravery when the world was watching.

He wondered if Dennis was as unconcerned and self-assured as he appeared to be. Of course, he had plenty to occupy him; the pure mechanics of taking off in these conditions, and then following his radioed instructions, would keep him from worrying too much about what happened next. It was Alan who had merely to observe—and to think.

The roar of the engines deepened as the aircraft started to move down the fire-girt valley through the fog. The gentle pressure of acceleration thrust Alan back into his seat, and he felt the floor tilt beneath him as the tail lifted from the ground. Faster, faster the Anson rushed through the burning night (did Dennis know how much runway was left?) until the sudden change in the quality of the vibration told Alan what he could not otherwise have known. They were airborne, lifting up into the sodden, lightless sky.

And in that moment, as they left the ground and the undercarriage began whining up into the fuselage, Alan's fears fell away with the earth beneath. There was no going back now; he was committed.

It was easy to understand how, in the days before blind-flying instruments were invented, pilots in fog had become hopelessly confused and had even flown upside down. There was no real sensation of motion; they were sitting in a dimly lit, resonating void that had no contact with any other world. The Perspex windows might not have been there for all the help they gave; all that could be seen through them was the fitful glare of the exhausts, and the more distant twinkle of the navigation lights on the wing-tips. Sometimes even these were lost as the aircraft plunged into a thicker stratum of fog.

Yet another world did exist; if they were not aware of it, it was conscious of them. The calm and omniscient voice over the VHF radio sounded in Alan's ears.

"Longstop calling C Charlie. I have you in view. Continue course on three two zero and climb to three thousand feet."

"Wilco," Dennis answered. Then he switched over to the intercom. "How are you feeling?" he asked his passenger, in a friendly voice.

"Fine," replied Alan, mildly astonished to realize that this was perfectly true. Now that he was airborne, apprehension had given way to an unmistakable zest; he was actually glad to be up here, on this filthy night, proving his confidence in the system more unarguably than could be done in a hundred years of fair-weather flying.

The rate-of-climb indicator dropped back to zero as the aircraft leveled out at three thousand feet. Only a few seconds later came the next order from the Traffic Director, turning them ninety degrees to the left. Alan guessed that the Controller wanted to bring them around the sky and on to the approach with as little waste of time as possible. He heartily approved of this, though the fact that every three minutes saved would reduce the cost of feeding FIDO by a thousand pounds did not even enter his calculations.

The steady roar of the Cheetah engines, drawing them on through the trackless night, was wonderfully reassuring. There was something safe and dependable about an Anson, even if it was no beauty and seemed to be composed mostly of straight lines and flat surfaces. It would still be plodding through the sky years after the Spitfire, with its lovely, sweeping curves, had passed into history.

Course 050—the last lap before they were vectored on to the approach. They had gone right around the sky, tracing out three sides of a huge square, and would soon be making a final right-angle turn as they headed in to the runway. It was a little peculiar, come to think of it, that if you subtracted ninety from 050 you got 320; compass bearings seemed simple enough except when you had to work them out in your head. No wonder that pilots under stress made foolish mistakes that sent them flying off on a reciprocal, in exactly the opposite direction to the one they really wanted.

No such errors could happen here; too many people were monitoring the performance. Yet it was with a considerable sense of relief that Alan heard a new voice say: "Approach Controller here. I have you at six miles." The first part of the task was over, and they were safely inside the narrow field of view of the precision system, heading in toward the runway.

He remembered the first time he had flown on an approach. Well, there was no hope now of watching the runway magically aligning itself with the nose of the aircraft from three or four miles away. They would probably not even see the runway until they were over it—or until they felt the bump and knew that they were on the ground. Yet though he realized how foolish it was, he could not stop himself from pressing against the clammy Perspex, half hoping that he could already see some sign of the double walls of fire that would guide them through the fog. But the sense of sight was now utterly useless; their only link with the ground was that quietly confident voice over the radio.

"Four and a half miles to go," said the Controller. "Maintain present course and start to reduce height at fife hundred feet a minute."

The vibration of the aircraft slackened as the motors were throttled back, and the Anson began to fall down the gentle slope that, in just three minutes' time, should bring them over the end of the runway. Everything was going according to plan—the virtual absence of cross wind made it almost too easy—yet there was a mounting tension in the pit of Alan's stomach. He wished that, like Dennis, he had something to occupy his mind as the ground came steadily, invisibly closer. All the obstacles around the airfield became suddenly exaggerated in his imagination; it seemed that trees and hangars and radio masts and power lines were rearing up to scrape them from the sky. . . .

What was Dennis thinking? He stole a glance at his companion, but that placid, too-handsome profile betrayed absolutely no trace of emotion. To Flight Lieutenant Collins, DFC, this was just another routine piece of bus driving. Such calm confidence was reassuring, yet at the same time Alan found it vaguely irritating.

"Three miles to go. You are getting a little high. Increase rate of descent."

All one's natural instincts revolted at the thought of descending even more swiftly than before into this swirling chaos. It was easy for the Controller to give the order, as he watched his elevation needle climb above the glide path;

Alan had seen him do it a hundred times. He had never realized how much confidence was required on the part of the pilot to obey this order without hesitation.

"Two miles to go. Check wheels down."

On the usual training approaches, that order was given but not acted upon, because the aircraft would be overshooting without attempting to land. Dennis must by now have made more approaches with his undercarriage up than with it down, which was a bad habit to acquire. Even the best pilots sometimes forgot this important trifle, despite the automatic warnings that were supposed to bring it to their attention.

"You are a little to the left of the runway. Change course three degrees right; I say again, three degrees right. One and a half miles to go."

Three degrees was the smallest correction that could reasonably be given; it was a final nudge to get the aircraft exactly lined up. Alan had a comforting mental picture of the azimuth-error needle creeping slowly back to its central zero position as they came precisely on course.

From now on, things would happen quickly; every second would count. Only one mile to go—they must be less than five hundred feet above the runway. In half a minute they would be upon it, descending into that sea of fire like a moth into a candle flame. And still there was no vestige of light from the all-encompassing darkness.

"Three quarters of a mile to go. You are on the glide path. Continue present rate of descent. Half a mile to go." (Was even the Controller's calm, bedside manner beginning to sound a trifle strained?) "A quarter of a mile to go. The runway is a little to your left; I say again, the runway is a little to your left—go ahead and land."

And now, unmistakably, there was a lifting of the darkness ahead. An ill-defined glow, like the first hint of dawn, had appeared where until a moment before had been nothing but the blackest night. It warmed Alan's heart to see it; they were nearly home. He glanced once again at his companion, wondering how he was reacting. Dennis was

hunched over the wheel, straining his eyes toward that waxing but still-formless light. There was a trace of anxiety in
his stare—but that, surely, was natural enough during these
last critical moments.

The first line of fire appeared so suddenly that it took
them by surprise, even though they had been expecting it.
Marching into the mist both behind and ahead of them, it
lay at an acute angle to their course—and that was absurd,
for they should have been flying straight along it. Something
had gone badly wrong; the aircraft's heading was wildly in
error, and the runway was certainly not "a little to your
left" as the Controller had said.

Dennis was struggling to get C Charlie back over the
runway, but it was too late. The error had been so unexpected, so completely unreasonable, that he had no time to
correct it. One by one the four lines of fire slid by beneath
them; then they had crabbed across the runway and were
once more out in the darkness.

As Dennis pulled back the wheel to gain altitude, he
reached for his mike and called the truck.

"C Charlie to Longstop. Something wrong with your
line-up. The runway was on our *right,* not left. Please check.
Over."

There was a brief silence. Then an abashed voice replied:

"Longstop calling C Charlie. Message received and understood. Am investigating. Continue on course three two
zero and change to Channel D. Out."

Dennis switched radio channels, then spoke to Alan over
the intercom.

"That was a bloody poor effort. Wonder what went
wrong?"

Alan could think of many explanations—too many for
his peace of mind. But he would never have thought of the
right one.

CHAPTER 26

THERE WAS NO particular reason why Squadron Leader Strickland should have driven out to watch the show, but a Security Officer never had to justify his curiosity. He had gone no more than half a mile before he was very sorry to have left his office.

For he was lost, on his own airfield. It was impossible to see through the streaming windshield, and he was forced to use the edge of the perimeter track as his guide. But something had gone wrong (he had been a bit suspicious about that sharp turn to the left a few yards back), and he was afraid he had veered off onto one of the aircraft-dispersal sites.

He was sure of it when he almost ran into the parked Liberator. It was impossible to drive ahead, and he could not see to reverse. But he knew exactly where he was now—the runway was only a couple of hundred yards ahead—and it would be quite safe to take a short cut over the grass. Even in the heaviest rain, this side of the airfield never got bogged.

He had covered a careful fifty feet when there was a sudden "twang," followed almost at once by a metallic crash as something banged into the car. "What the hell!" exclaimed the Squadron Leader, and reluctantly climbed out into the rain to inspect the damage.

It was very slight. He had hooked a steel guy wire, almost invisible in the rain, and pulled down the object it was supporting. Lying under his front wheel was a crumpled pyramid of yellow-painted tin, attached to a six-foot iron pole.

Squadron Leader Strickland looked at it with considerable annoyance. People shouldn't leave such obstacles standing around the airfield, he told himself. He dismissed that childish thought as soon as it materialized; no one did put up contraptions like this except for very good reasons.

He inspected the thing more closely and then, with some discomfort realized what it was. Though he was not a technical man he was familiar with all the airfield equipment, and he knew that this was something to do with GCD. It was also very near the runway in operation; that meant they might be using it now. . . .

The Security Officer groaned. He couldn't take chances, and he'd have to get a message through to the GCD truck somehow. That meant finding his way back to the perimeter track, and then locating the nearest telephone to Flying Control. With the best of luck, that would take at least ten minutes.

It took more like twenty, for the guy wire was tangled around his front axle, and by the time he had unwound it his temper was as filthy as his uniform. He had barely finished when he heard the roar of approaching engines; when C Charlie overshot the airfield and climbed away into the night, he felt vague premonitions of guilt. They were fully justified.

Before C Charlie had passed over the truck, the postmortem was in progress. Somewhat rudely pushing the azimuth operator aside, Corporal Hart examined the glowing images on the display tube with the utmost care. He had done the lining up himself, only ten minutes ago, and had checked it again immediately before the approach.

Runway 320 was somewhat tricky, but did not present any real problems. The touchdown point was just over the brow of a hill, and this meant that it was impossible to place a radar reflector on the center line of the runway itself; it would have been hidden from view. The lining up depended, therefore, on a corner reflector placed at a carefully measured distance to the right of the runway, but in sight of the truck.

Well, there it was, where it should be. No—just a minute —*something* was wrong! Corporal Hart stared at the pattern of glowing blobs and lines, which he had scrutinized so many times; and suddenly he realized that the most important part was missing.

That big, juicy echo on which he had carefully aligned the entire GCD system was *not* their reflector; it was at least a hundred feet off to the right. He guessed that it was a parked aircraft; nothing else in that area could give such a large radar echo. By lining up on *that,* instead of on the proper reflector, he had slewed the whole approach path across the sky.

He felt cold with fright. What would Mr. Bishop say when he heard about it? He might get court-martialed—it was pure luck that C Charlie hadn't crashed on that last approach . . .

But it wasn't *his* fault, he told himself. If the reflector had been there, everything would have been OK. Who would have dreamed that it was missing? Some of their earlier reflectors had been blown down, but nowadays they were all set in concrete and properly guyed. It must be sabotage. . . .

"Well, Hart," called the Approach Controller impatiently, "what's the trouble?"

Corporal Hart broke the news as gently as he could.

"Our marker's missing, sir. Someone's knocked it down or taken it away. That means we can't check our line-up."

"But I thought we were supposed to *be* lined up!"

Hart gulped.

"I'm afraid we used the wrong echo, because we didn't know our own marker was missing. That's why the glide path was so badly off."

"Then do something about it, quickly. They're in the circuit—they'll be making another approach in five minutes."

Do what? thought Hart helplessly. In this filthy weather it would take at least half an hour to get another reflector, locate the right position, and fix it in place.

In an emergency, even the dullest minds are capable of surprising feats, and Corporal Hart was certainly not dull; indeed, he was almost as smart as he thought he was. His hesitation lasted only for a few seconds; then he switched on the intercom to the transmitter truck.

"Mac," he called urgently, "we've lost our offset marker and can't line up the system. Is LAC Jackson there?"

"Yes, but what can he do about it?"

Jackson was an athletic young Canadian who had a passion for physical fitness and was much better than average at almost any sport one cared to mention. The WAAFs thought the world of him, and he had done a good deal to fill the vacuum left by Pat Connor.

"Ask him to grab a bike and head for the runway. When he gets there, tell him to cycle to touchdown just as fast as he can, *keeping exactly in the middle of the runway.* He must get clear as soon as he reaches the perimeter track, unless he wants C Charlie to land on top of him. Make sure he understands."

"He'll understand," Mac replied, rather shortly. He liked Jackson, and somewhat resented Hart's assumption that everything had to be explained to him twice. He had to admit, however, that Hart's suggestion was an excellent one, and the best thing that could be done in the circumstances.

"What's happening?" asked the Approach Controller plaintively.

"Give me a couple of minutes, sir," begged Hart. "Then everything will be OK."

He could only hope so; but an awful lot depended on Leading Aircraftsman Jackson and his bicycle.

Perhaps Alan would have been a little happier had he known what was going on, but he could hardly bombard the ground staff with questions; if he did, it would seem that he was pressing the panic button. He was still, at this stage, more puzzled than worried. The approach system was clearly cockeyed, and this was very surprising, for he had complete confidence in Corporal Hart. Maybe he should have checked the line-up himself before he took off, but he'd been too busy with those generals. Well, they were certainly getting their money's worth.

C Charlie was being vectored around again for another approach, and the Traffic Director seemed to be taking his time. That was understandable; he might be holding them off while the boys in the back room found what was wrong. It was probably something that could be fixed in a couple of minutes—or else it would take hours and they'd better start looking for a diversion airfield. Alan had no idea how much gas C Charlie was carrying in its tanks; still less—and this thought was almost equally disturbing—did he know how much longer FIDO could keep up its hundred thousand gallons an hour. Suppose those walls of fire collapsed, and the fog came rolling back . . .

At the moment they were still going full blast, and no one knew that better than LAC Jackson. He had grabbed one of the bikes parked against the control van, and had hurried it over to the runway as quickly as he could, pushing it ahead of him across the sodden grass. There was no hope of riding here; the tires would sink up to the rims if he attempted it.

He knew exactly what he had to do, and why it was so important. In any event, the raw heat from the burners did not encourage him to linger near the edge of the runway. As soon as he felt its hard surface beneath him, he swung himself on to the bike and raced out into the exact center of the huge, lonely strip of concrete.

It seemed a pity that there was not a single eyewitness of Jackson's Ride, for it was to become one of the legends of

GCD. Since Jackson himself was not a very articulate type, no one ever knew exactly what he felt as he flew like the wind along the axis of Runway 320, with the roar of the flames in his ears and the stars miraculously shining overhead. Probably he felt nothing at all; he could have had little energy for sightseeing or introspection. For it was later calculated that he covered a distance of four thousand feet, on a wet surface, up a slight gradient, in little more than two minutes. And, be it noted, on an RAF bike, which is built for durability rather than speed.

There was no doubt that he was feeling quite pleased with himself, though a little short of breath, when he saw the huge, elongated numbers "320" on the concrete ahead of him, and knew that he had almost reached the end of the runway. He cycled across them, and veered off onto the perimeter track—straight into the arms of the Station CO, who was still waiting anxiously amid the ambulances and Flying Control trucks.

"What the hell do you think you're doing, cycling on the runway in use!" shouted the Group Captain. "Sergeant, put that man on a charge!"

It was fortunate for Jackson that he was not struck as dumb as Billy Budd in a similar moment of monumental injustice. He was still trying to explain matters when the distant roar of C Charlie checked all further conversation.

For there had been a witness of Jackson's Ride, though not a human one. That witness, as Corporal Hart had planned, was the GCD system itself. The fact that it could track individual human beings had been proved conclusively during the defense exercise (though it had not, the Corporal remembered a little sourly, saved *him* from being scragged in his foxhole by the RAF Regiment). A large lump of manhood like LAC Jackson would give him a fine echo; his bike would give an even better one.

The precision system picked him up first at five hundred feet—a small, distinct amoeba of light moving up the runway, approximately where Hart had expected to see him.

"Strewth," he said under his breath, "he's moving!"

Indeed, the echo had shifted appreciably between successive sweeps of the scan. Hart watched it with the utmost satisfaction. There would be no further argument about the line-up, now that LAC Jackson was tracing the runway; 320 had never been pinned down so accurately before.

. Already he was halfway to touchdown point, and now the original error was obvious. The marker that *should* have given them their line-up was undoubtedly missing. Presently they'd find out what had happened to the damned thing, but they had no need of it now that they had a much better way of pinpointing the runway. Maybe they should always send someone cycling along to touchdown before they made an approach. It would take a bit of time, and would annoy Flying Control, but there would never be any doubts.

Hart had already made the necessary corrections and reset the Controller's meters by the time that LAC Jackson was expostulating with the Station Commander. It was a close thing; he had barely finished his adjustments before C Charlie came on the screens once more, nine miles out and lined up for the approach.

Corporal Hart relinquished his seat to the azimuth tracker, who promptly speared the oncoming blip with her electronic pin.

"OK now, sir," he called to the much-relieved Controller. "The calibration's perfect." "I'd stake my life on it," he added beneath his breath. If anything else went wrong, it would not be in *his* department. . . .

Nor was it.

CHAPTER 27

THE SECOND APPROACH was just beginning when the telephone from Flying Control started to ring. Now what? thought Corporal Hart as he picked up the receiver. He wondered ironically if someone was going to raise hell because GCD had not asked permission to overshoot on 320.

"GCD truck here—Corporal Hart speaking," he answered smartly. As he listened, his face relaxed into a somewhat satisfied smirk. "Thank you," he said at last. "Tell him we already know about it."

"What was that?" asked the Controller, who was just getting ready to take over C Charlie.

"Flying Control reported our marker down, sir. The Station Security Officer ran into it."

"Pity they couldn't tell us ten minutes earlier. Still, I'm glad we know what went wrong." He pushed the transmit key. "Longstop calling C Charlie. Are you receiving me? Over."

"Receiving you loud and clear. Over."

"Remain on receive, continue on course three two zero. . . ."

Listening to that familiar and reassuring patter, Alan felt at ease once more. There was nothing to worry about now; he had the best Controller and the best (he had to admit it) pilot, and whatever had gone wrong on the ground had now been fixed. He still wondered what it was, but he'd find out soon enough.

Three miles to go; there had been very few corrections. It was a simple, almost standard approach—if one forgot the bonfire at the end. Suddenly, Alan remembered a little notice that one of the trainee controllers, presumably blessed with a classical education, had pasted above the meter panel. It had read *Facilis descensus Averno,* and one needed no Latin to realize that it might be all too appropriate.

"Three degrees left; I say again, three degrees left. You are slightly above the glide path. Increase rate of descent. Two miles to go."

The memory of that Latin tag brought back another even more ominous phrase which some cynic had once suggested as a motto for GCD—"Nearer, My God, to Thee." Alan's mind dwelt upon it a little uncomfortably. Like most of his generation, he had no formal religion and had put himself down as "Church of England" when enlisting. No one had ever made any determined attempts to save his soul—not even Miss Hadley, who might have been expected to do so. Though she was High Church, she had never attempted to influence Alan in this direction. Having spent much of her life among non-Christian communities, she was unusually tolerant in matters of faith.

"One and a half miles to go. Resume normal rate of descent."

Alan smiled, even now, as he remembered the times he had been exposed to religion in the RAF. When the Flights were drawn up for Church Parade, the Warrant Officer in charge would shout: "Fall out the Jews and Roman Catholics!" All those who considered themselves in these categories would step smartly back two paces, and the C. of E. prayers would be read. Alan often wondered if the Jews and

Roman Catholics felt that six feet of parade ground gave their consciences sufficient insulation.

He wished he could get his mind away from this subject, but he could not help thinking of the plastic tags around his neck—the two tags with his name, number, and C. of E. stamped upon them. For if the worst came to the worst, those letters would decide what happened to his body, in the absence of any other instructions for burial. But enough of that—

"You are on the glide path, runway directly ahead, half a mile to go—go ahead and land."

They were almost there; everything was fine. Alan felt himself reaching for his safety belt; it was a little too tight and he'd slacken it off just as soon as they touched down.

There was the yellow glow of the burners, blasting through the fog. It was all right—the line-up was perfect. In thirty seconds, they'd be down.

Without any warning, the aircraft shuddered violently, as if a giant hand had slapped it. At the same instant the light from below flared up with a sudden dazzling brilliance as the concealing fog whipped away. They might have been flying above the throat of a volcano, looking straight down into the incandescent lava. It could only be imagination, but it seemed to Alan that he could feel the heat of the flames licking against his face.

The buffeting grew more violent. Dennis seemed to be fighting with the controls, like a rider trying to curb a startled horse. He was no longer attempting to land, but, on the contrary, was gaining height—climbing to escape from the turbulence that had suddenly engulfed the aircraft. There was no doubt of what had happened; they had been caught in a manmade gale generated by the heat of the burners. Ten million horsepower, the general had calculated. How many little C Charlies would be needed to match that?

It was over so swiftly that Alan had no time to feel any fear. His only sensation was one of surprise, coupled with an almost dispassionate annoyance that an excellent approach had been aborted at the last moment. Not until the glare of the flames had dwindled to a faint twilight luminosity, soon lost once more in utter darkness, did he consciously start taking stock of the position.

They would have to go around again, of course. The crucial point was—could they do any better next time?

He was about to call Dennis on the intercom when the voice of the Controller, now definitely showing signs of worry, broke through over the radio.

"What's the matter, C Charlie? We hard you overshoot. Couldn't you see the runway?"

Dennis picked up the mike dangling on his chest and threw the transmit switch.

"C Charlie to Longstop," he answered, as calmly as if he had done a normal overshoot on a bright summer day. "The line-up was perfect, but there's such a hell of an updraft from the flames that I got blown off the runway. You'll have to take me round again. I'll be able to cope better, now I know what to expect. Over."

There was a long pause—much longer, it seemed to Alan, than was necessary for the Controller to digest and act upon this information. After all, he had only to tell them to continue on course three two zero and climb to three thousand feet. . . .

But the instruction, when it came, was quite different, and by its very unexpectedness brought back all Alan's apprehensions with redoubled intensity.

"Longstop to C Charlie," said the radio. "I am *not*, repeat not, taking you round the circuit again, but will turn you back on a reciprocal. Change course to one four zero; I say again, one four zero. Use maximum rate of turn."

One four zero! They were being given a hairpin bend—or as close to that as C Charlie could manage. It would take them straight back over the airfield, retracing the line of their unsuccessful approach, but in the opposite direction. Though it was the quickest possible way of getting them into position for another approach, Alan did not like the sound of it at all. It seemed unwise to attempt so unusual a maneuver in such circumstances as these, when it was important to make everything as easy as possible for the pilot.

Was FIDO running short of gas, as he had feared? Well, they could probably get in without it, especially since it seemed to be doing its best to blow them back into the sky. Or had something else happened to the Mark I? This was definitely not their lucky day.

How unlucky it was only Sergeant McGregor realized. He alone knew, as he stood beside the roaring diesel in the transmitter truck, that the Mark I was finished. All the electronic circuits were working perfectly—the signals were coming in clearly, the needles of the meters were steady at their appointed places, the wave forms on the oscilloscopes showed their familiar shapes. Yet none of this compensated for the small piece of broken metal, no bigger than the last joint of a little finger, that McGregor was now holding in the palm of his hand and cursing with a quiet and desperate intensity.

The aircraft banked violently as Collins threw them into their hairpin bend. If the horizon had been visible, it would now have become an endless slope, steep as the roof of a house, bisecting the sky ahead of them. But in this tiny enclosed world the only indication of the turn was the centrifugal pressure forcing them into their seats, and the swiftly changing numbers on the compass card as the aircraft pointed first west, then southwest, then south, and at last almost southeast, as it straightened out on 140, the exact reverse of the course they had flown on the approach.

"And now," said Dennis, barely anticipating Alan, "I'd like to know what the hell's happening." He switched from intercom to RT.

"C Charlie calling Longstop. Steady on course one four zero. Please advise. Over."

Again that long pause, all too suggestive of hasty conferences on the ground. Then the carrier wave of the GCD truck's transmitter broke through, quenching the faint mush of distant interference.

"Longstop calling C Charlie," said the Controller. "Continue on present course. Sergeant McGregor wishes to speak to Mr. Bishop. Over."

The words, though half expected, made Alan cold with apprehension. But his voice—he hoped—was steady enough as he flicked the transmit key and said, "Bishop here. Go ahead. Over." Despite all his fears about the coming message, he found himself hoping that Mac would remember that this was hardly a private circuit, and that scores of people—including the Station Commander—would be listening to every word. The usual Australian adjectives, however merited, might not go over too well in these circumstances.

Mac sounded breathless and—though this was hard to credit—almost on the point of tears.

"McGregor here, sir." (He *had* remembered his audience.) "The search system's packed up, and there's nothing we can do to fix it. The turning gear's bugg—ah—broken, and the whole antenna's jammed solid. We can't move it an inch. One of the teeth snapped off in the main geardrive and chewed up the works before we could switch the motor off. The Controller's sending you downwind and we should be able to pick you up on the precision system in a minute, so there's no need to worry. But I thought you'd better know what's happened."

"No need to worry!" That was a slight exaggeration, if ever there was one. In a single moment of tearing metal, the Mark I had become blind over three hundred and forty of the three hundred and sixty degrees of the sky. The beam of the search system could no longer sweep around the heavens giving a complete picture of everything that lay in each direction of the compass. The Traffic Director's hundred-mile-wide circle of vision had shrunk to a single useless line of light, pointing along the bearing on which the antenna had now frozen.

But what was left might be enough; the precision system's independent antennas were still scanning back and forth across the runway. Though the sector they could ex-

plore was only twenty degrees wide, it was the most important slice of the sky. If C Charlie could be headed into it,
and kept there without wandering off into the blind 95 per
cent of the heavens, it could be landed.

Alan acknowledged McGregor's report without comment; there was nothing he could add, no helpful suggestion
he could possibly make. What had happened could be recti-
fied only by a major overhaul of the antenna-driving mechanism, and the construction of a fresh set of gears—a job that
would take weeks, rather than days.

But there was no point in looking *that* far ahead. The
next five minutes were all that mattered now. . . .

Dennis had heard the whole conversation, and knew exactly what had happened. Yet his voice was perfectly normal
and unperturbed as he reported: "Steady on course one four
zero. Still at three thousand feet."

"Roger," said the Controller. "We're looking out for
you."

How long had it been, thought Alan, since they had
turned back on their course after overshooting the runway?
Surely by now, covering two miles in every minute, they had
passed back over the airfield and must now be entering the
thin wedge of space being searched by the precision antennas! In his mind's eye, he had a vivid, almost photographic
image of the situation. He could picture a giant clock face
centered on the airfield, with twelve at due north. The whole
face of the clock was dark—except for a tiny slice pointing
toward five, and not even covering the space between two
successive fifures.

C Charlie was like a fly crawling over this darkened clock
face. It had been aimed at the narrow illuminated section,
but might already have missed it, to remain lost in the
blackness that covered almost all the dial.

So this, Alan told himself without really believing it, was
probably the most dangerous moment of his life. Introspection was not normally one of his vices; he could worry with
the best, but did not waste time watching himself worrying.
Yet now, as he roared across the night sky toward an un-

known destiny, he found himself facing that bleak and ultimate question which so few men can answer to their
satisfaction. What have I done with my life, he asked himself, that the world will be the poorer if I leave it now?

He had no sooner framed the thought than he rejected it
as unfair. At twenty-three, no one could be expected to have
made a mark on the world, or even to have decided what
sort of mark he wished to make. Very well; the question
could be reframed in more specific terms. *How many people
will be really sorry if I'm killed now*?

There was no evading this. It struck too close to home,
brought back too vivid a memory of the tearless gathering
around his father's grave.

He started the census reluctantly, knowing that it would
not take long. Miss Hadley, of course, would be bitterly
distressed, but Alan realized that her grief would not be
wholly unselfish. She needed him as a focus for the complex
yearnings of her spinstered soul; there were bonds here that
must soon be gently disentangled, lest his own development
be warped, his independence jeopardized. (Was it too late
already?)

His thoughts continued to sweep around the circle of his
acquaintances, as the now-stilled search system had once
probed the sky. Lucille: what of her?

Yes, she might squeeze a tiny tear; he saw that with pitiless logic. And here was the ultimate irony—even this he
would have to share with Dennis.

These unprofitable thoughts had occupied him for no
more than a few seconds, yet it was hard to believe that
minutes had not passed since their last word from the
ground. Surely Dennis should call the Controller to find out
what was happening! He turned to look at the man who now
shared his fate, but he was merely a faint shadow in the
darkness, for the only light in the little cabin was that spill-
ing from the instrument panel. There was no way in which
he could guess what Dennis was thinking, until he spoke
again over the intercom. And even then, his voice would be

subtly distorted, so that his real emotions would be disguised.

It is strange how the mind can leapfrog across the years, selecting from a million, million memories the one that is even faintly relevant, while rejecting all the others. With startling clarity Alan remembered a story from his undisciplined childhood reading; he had long ago forgotten the context, but the disquieting image remained.

The Fates, so the ancients had believed, were three old women with scissors, who determined the moment at which each man's life thread should be snipped. Three women, sharing a single eye among them, which they passed from one to the other. . . .

At this very moment, Alan's fate was being decided by three girls—the trackers in the control van, straining for the first glimpse of C Charlie's echo on their screens. It was as well that they had not one eye, but two —the elevation and azimuth screens, each showing its cross section of the lightless sky.

The three trackers in that darkened room half a mile below would have been surprised at the analogy; it would have scared them to think that they were arbiters of anyone's fate. At this moment, however, they were utterly unconscious of their own personalities or feelings. For each one of them, nothing existed but the luminous rectangle of light upon which all her attention was concentrated.

Ten minutes ago, the elevation tracker had been plagued by an anxiety as old as humanity: was she going to have a baby? But now, all her world was contained in that faint pencil of electrons, scanning up and down the screen from sky to ground, ground to empty sky.

The azimuth screen was equally empty, its operator equally intent, having wholly forgotten sick mother, errant boy friend, and laddered stockings as she stared at the screen in front of her. She was looking at a completely blank map, ten miles long and only twenty degrees wide—that pathetically blinkered twenty degrees of vision now left to a radar system that had once swept the full circle of heaven.

A spark of light flickered for a moment at the edge of the picture. The questing radar beam moved away from that area of the sky; then, two seconds later, it returned. Now there was no doubt; an echo was moving onto the screen from the extreme right-hand edge. With each sweep of the scan it edged in toward the center of the display, and moved a little farther out in range.

"I've got him!" shrieked the azimuth tracker. "Five miles out, over on the right!"

The tension in the van relaxed in a great, silent wave of relief. C Charlie was back in the narrow funnel of vision, no longer lost in the open dome of the sky, beyond help or advice. Now something could be done.

With swift and automatic skill, the three trackers began a furious cranking of their handwheels. Range, azimuth, elevation—within seconds each operator had pinned her electronic pointer upon that luminous oval crawling over the face of the tubes. On the Controller's panel, the lights flashed on. His meters, dark and lifeless until now, were feeding him information again, allowing him to trace every movement of C Charlie through the distant night.

He pressed his transmit key, and sent the message Alan had almost lost hope of receiving.

"Longstop calling C Charlie. We have you at six miles. Continue on present course."

"Continue on present course!" thought Alan. "But we're flying directly away from the airfield!"

Then he realized what the Controller was doing. Six miles was too close to home; if they were turned back on their course now, there might not be time to straighten them out and get them lined up on the runway before they were over the airfield once more. The Controller was giving himself room to maneuver; they still had four miles to go before they would disappear off his field of view, and there were a couple of minutes yet before he need swing them around.

"Now at seven miles," said Ground Control, in a calm and almost lazy voice—though not one so lazy that it ceased

to inspire confidence. "I shall be turning you round shortly.
Are you receiving me? Over."

"C Charlie calling Longstop. Receiving you loud and
clear. Over," acknowledged Dennis.

"Longstop calling C Charlie. Message acknowledged and
understood. Remain on receive and apply maximum rate of
turn to left; I say again, maximum rate left onto course three
two zero; repeat, course three two zero."

Alan felt the floor press up against him. Before his eyes
the compass card began to spin, and the rate-of-turn needle
shot over to its maximum. They were making their second
hairpin bend in the sky.

The pressure slackened; the compass slowed its spin.
Now they were flying straight again, headed back toward
the airfield. C Charlie was coming home.

"I have you at six and a half miles," said the Controller.
"Change course fifteen degrees left; I say again, fifteen degrees left. . . ."

The familiar, almost hypnotic patter had started again.
How many times had Alan heard it before, either on the
ground or in the air? He could not guess; it must be hundreds. But never before, he knew well enough, in circumstances such as these.

"Fife miles to go. Check wheels down. . . ."

Five miles from safety and solidity, crawling down the
lightless sky. Thank heavens there were no hills or mountains in this part of the world. *My God, what about the radar
towers at Filey?*

They were not far from this line of approach, reaching
up into the fog like the masts of some sunken ship. Alan had
a hideously vivid memory of those thin steel girders, with
the curtains of the antenna arrays spread out in a vast net
between them. Against that net C Charlie could smash like
a butterfly into a spider's web.

Don't be a fool, he told himself. We know all about Filey
—the glide path doesn't go within three miles of it. There's
no need to get into a flap—everything's under control. . . .

"Start descent at fife hundred feet a minute. You are

slightly to the left of the runway. Change course fife degrees right; I say again, fife degrees right. Three and a half miles to go. . . ."

In another two minutes it would all be over, one way or the other. Yet all that Alan felt was a great sense of calm. There was nothing he could do to affect the issue, and if the Fates snipped the thread now, he would probably never know; it would happen so quickly.

All the while a part of his brain had been acting as an impersonal monitor, analyzing the approach and noting how the aircraft responded to the Controller's corrections. It was a perfectly straightforward descent, with no complications from cross winds. Indeed, for the last mile they had scarcely veered from the line of the runway, and the Controller had given only the most trifling changes of course. Dennis had nothing to do but to point the nose down and forge ahead.

That was just as well, for it gave him time to work out his plan of action. The approach was no problem: the fun would begin when they were over the runway, flying into the artificial gale of the FIDO burners. But now that he knew what to expect, Dennis believed he could handle the situation.

He had spared only the briefest of thoughts for his passenger. His opinion of Alan had gone up quite a few points, and he was rather sorry that he had got him into this mess. But it would do him good to see, once in a while, what pilots had to do to earn their pay.

"Two miles to go. Change course three degrees left; I say again, three degrees left. You are slightly below the glide path. Reduce rate of descent."

To Alan's surprise, Dennis ignored this last instruction. The rate-of-descent pointer remained stubbornly fixed at five hundred feet a minute. What was Dennis trying to do? Fly them into the ground?

Less than a minute to go. And now, for the first time on this approach, the Controller began to sound a little worried.

"You are nicely on course, C Charlie. But you are still

too low—fifty feet below the glide path. Reduce rate of descent; I say again, reduce rate of descent. Half a mile to go."

Almost grudgingly, Dennis pulled the stick back a fraction of a degree. It was too late now to climb back to the proper glide path, but the Controller could sweat that one out. I'm coming in low and fast, Dennis told himself—it's my best chance of getting the old kite down on the deck before that ruddy gale takes her up into the sky again.

"One thousand feet to go," said the Controller. "The runway is dead ahead of you. *But you are still much too low.*"

C Charlie had received that first warning, for the elevation needle had started to climb upward from its dangerous low point. But had the pilot reacted in time? In a few seconds they would know. The Controller had done his best; until the last mile, it had been a flawless approach.

The lights on the meter panel went dead; the girls in the back room could no longer track the aircraft—its echo had been lost in the maze of reflections from the ground. The Controller leaned back in his chair, suddenly drained of strength. All around him, the crowded van was not only silent, but utterly still. The three WAAF operators were frozen at their screens, their fingers motionless on the tracking handwheels. The NCO radar mechs and the forgotten U.S. Air Force generals, who had scarcely moved a muscle for the last ten minutes, still stood crowded against the walls as silent spectators.

No one knew what had happened to C Charlie; and no one knew that they had all just witnessed the very last approach that would ever be made on the Mark I.

CHAPTER 28

SQUADRON LEADER STRICKLAND was a stubborn man; he was also a rather embarrassed one, for he feared that some apologies would be in order in due course. After he had telephoned his confession to Flying Control, he immediately set off once more toward the end of the runway. Having already got soaked to the skin and well daubed with mud, he was determined to see matters through to the end.

This time he did not get lost, and found his way to the end of Runway 320 without difficulty. The nearest of the FIDO burners was a hundred feet away, yet its heat caressed his face like the tropical sun. From time to time he could hear, above the roar of the flames, the voice of the GCD Controller echoing from the radio truck around which the Station Commander and his cohorts were standing. Beyond that, he knew, were the ambulance and fire wagon; but they were quite invisible in the blinding mist.

At any second, C Charlie would be over the edge of the airfield; it was now only a thousand feet away—too low, the Controller had just said. By God, he was right—there came the roar of the twin Cheetahs, from a point that seemed scarcely higher than the perimeter fence. It moved swiftly closer—now it was past them—louder and deeper than one would expect from an aircraft making a landing. Almost certainly, Strickland decided, the pilot had changed his mind and was attempting to overshoot.

The Squadron Leader was wrong; Dennis Collins had a different plan, and he almost brought it off.

They hit the updraft from the burners and caught their first glimpse of the runway at the same instant. The fog parted before their eyes, so that suddenly they were looking along a glowing canyon walled with flame. There, directly beneath them, was the painted "320" of the compass course they had been following. Those huge, elongated figures, scuffed and worn by a thousand touchdowns, were so beautiful, so heart-warming that Alan almost wanted to kiss them.

But he was still separated from the runway by an infinite thirty feet and an appalling hundred and twenty miles an hour. The concrete slabs flickering backward beneath their wheels might have been a universe away.

In that eternal second, Alan made a surprising discovery. It was not true that men remembered their past lives when they thought they were going to die. At least, it was not true for him, perhaps because he had already scanned his past and found in it little cause for pride. He could think only of the future that now might never be.

There was so much he could have done. The skills he had acquired would have had many uses in the world to come. He had spent much time over those books that Schuster had sent him—as much as he could spare from his duties—and had mapped out the paths of knowledge that he would be able to follow. It was true that he could never be a real scientist, as he had sometimes hoped in moments of envious admiration.

Yet his was the kind of skill the scientists would need, to nurse the strange and complex machines that their brains would create—and which, quite often, their clumsy fingers might break. (Where was Schuster now? He would like to have met him again.) A great, impersonal sadness swept over him, a grief not for himself, but for all those he might have helped, or whose lives he might have made happier.

Now that rising gale was upon them, tearing at wings and fuselage, trying to spin them back into the sky like a child's kite. But this time Dennis was expecting it; he opened the throttle, pouring on the power in an attempt to drag C Charlie through that wall of wind by brute force.

The runway accelerated beneath them, gaining speed instead of losing it. Then, as Dennis had hoped, the turbulent buffeting died away as they left the transition zone and passed into smoother air. But he was using up runway at a terrifying rate—the end of the luminous canyon was only a thousand feet away. Better smack the deck now, before it was too late.

He cut the engines a second before impact. All things considered, it was not too bad a landing. Aircraft tires, however, can stand only so much. C Charlie was still doing a good ninety miles an hour when there was a loud report on the starboard side, followed instantly by a violent lurch and a horrible squeal of metal on concrete. A stream of sparks trailed from the naked wheel hub as it ground itself against the runway, and like a lopsided drunkard, C Charlie veered ever more and more steeply toward the right.

It was losing speed fast, but not fast enough. As Alan stared through the Perspex with fascination, but not the slightest fear (for this all seemed to be happening to someone else), he saw the edge of the runway coming closer and closer, until he could make out every detail of the concrete slabs and the dark, sodden grass bordering them.

C Charlie was moving almost sideways when, with great reluctance, it left the firm safety of the concrete and slithered on to the soggy, yielding earth. The starboard prop turned itself into a plow. There was a fantastic symphony of groaning metal and twanging control cables, and a final lurch as the aircraft tried to stand on its nose, failed, and flopped heavily back on a level keel.

For a moment there was silence in the cabin, save for

tiny, unidentifiable cracklings and tinklings. It was utterly dark; someone must have switched off the FIDO burners, probably as a safety precaution, within seconds of C Charlie's hitting the ground.

"Not one of my better efforts," said Dennis. "Still, it's a good landing if you can walk away from it. Let's see if we can find our way out of here."

They unfastened their seat belts and groped their way through the darkness. The cabin door had stuck and gave them some trouble, but presently they forced it open and lowered themselves gingerly to the invisible ground.

"I suppose we'd better wait here," said Alan, "until someone comes to look for us."

It was not a very intelligent remark, for they had no practical alternative, in a darkness that seemed almost palpable now that the glare of the FIDO burners was gone. Overhead a few misty stars were glimmering faintly, but they were already fading as the fog rolled down like a silent avalanche, to fill the valley that had been briefly blasted through it.

At a moment like this, there was nothing that could or need be said. Even the dripping darkness seemed friendly, now that the firm and wonderful earth was once more beneath their feet. They had shared an experience that they could never talk about, except jokingly, in the days to come. Yet each knew that from now on their relationship was wholly altered.

They would never really like each other, but they would never again be enemies. They were linked now in a comradeship as strong and deep as love itself, though springing from different roots. The proof of that was clear enough in each man's mind, for both Alan and Dennis now knew that they would not grudge each other any share in Lucille's favors.

The Station Medical Officer found them first, only two minutes after they had landed.

"Glad to see you've saved me some trouble," he said, jumping out of the ambulance. "But that's a nasty gash you've got over your eye, Bishop."

"Have I?" said Alan, in great surprise. He put his hand to his forehead, and looked stupidly at the blood smeared over his fingers. "Blast," he remarked. "I hope it doesn't get on my uniform."

"Well, hop in the back, both of you. I'll take you over to the hospital for a check."

"Lay off it, Doc!" protested Dennis. "I haven't got a scratch. And look at my hands—steady as Gibraltar."

"Even rudimentary nervous systems like yours, Collins, can suffer from delayed shocks. So in you get."

They won a short reprieve when the rest of the convoy arrived. The Station Commander glanced at C Charlie and said: "Hmm, not too badly bent; she'll be flying again in a week. Very good show, Collins—glad you're OK. You, too, Bishop—though you'd better hurry up and get that cut fixed."

As they climbed into the back of the ambulance, Dennis exclaimed: "I say, Bish—we forgot to tell the Controller we're down!"

Now that it was all over, Alan felt suddenly very weary, and quite unable to bother about such trivial matters.

"Don't worry, Dennis," he said with a tired smile. "That's one thing he *does* know. He'll find out the rest soon enough."

As the ambulance drove away through the thickening fog, using the edge of the runway as a guide, Squadron Leader Strickland watched it go. His business would have to wait until tomorrow.

CHAPTER 29

WHEN STRICKLAND ARRIVED at the hospital, soon after breakfast, he found Alan deeply engrossed in a textbook on applied mathematics. Being a somewhat cynical person, he wondered if this was meant to impress visitors; as it happened, it was not.

"Sorry to bother you now," said the Squadron Leader breezily, "but the sister said it was OK to see you. How are you feeling, by the way?"

"Fine, thank you, sir," answered Alan, not altogether truthfully. A slight reaction was beginning to set in, and he was no longer so indignant at being confined to bed for a few hours.

"Cigarette?" asked Strickland, in the traditional opening gambit. He sometimes wondered how interrogations were conducted before the discovery of tobacco.

"Thanks—I could do with one; I haven't been able to scrounge any from the nurses."

"I suppose you know," began the Squadron Leader a little awkwardly, "that I was the clot who knocked down that gadget of yours. I gather it could have been serious."

"That's quite all right," said Alan, full of generosity. "As a matter of fact, it was a good thing it happened. The only way we can improve the system is to find out what can go wrong. This has made us rethink the whole line-up problem, and already we've arrived at some better answers."

"I hope the FIDO boys have, too. They seemed to be giving you a rough time last night."

"Oh, they're very happy—we taught them a lot. They say they can fix the burners so you don't get the sudden updraft. But next time, I think I'll let someone else have a go."

"Don't say I blame you."

They puffed for a minute in contented silence. Then the Squadron Leader remarked: "Anyway, that wasn't what I wanted to talk about."

"Oh?" said Alan, showing slight signs of alarm as he remembered his visitor's job. His own conscience was perfectly clear; in any case, after last night almost anything would be too much of an anticlimax to take very seriously.

"I won't keep you in suspense," said Strickland. "So tell me—how much do you know about Mrs.—ah—Buckingham?"

It was several seconds before Alan could remember who Mrs. Buckingham was; he had practically forgotten Olga's married name. (If it *was* her married name.)

As the implications of the question went home, Alan felt an unpleasant sinking sensation. He also felt considerably embarrassed, and a slow flush spread across his face.

Then he saw that the Security Officer was grinning and appeared completely relaxed; *that* was a good sign, anyway. . . .

"I hardly know anything about her," said Alan cautiously. "What do you want to find out?"

"Frankly, old man"—that "old man" was most reassuring—"there's damn all you can tell me. But there's quite a flap on about our friend Olga, and you can help me out."

"Go on," said Alan, still somewhat worried. The only problem he could imagine involving Olga was so serious that the Station Security Officer would certainly not be grinning like this.

"Well, Olga's got a maid called Joan Curnow—"

"She *had*," interjected Alan. "Joan's left. I don't know why."

"I do. Joan's boy friend took a poor view of the setup, and you can hardly blame him."

"Oh," said Alan, a slow light beginning to dawn.

"Now that wouldn't have mattered much, in the ordinary course of events. But Joan's boy friend is a smart young fellow—and he happens to be the local police constable.

"So he decides," continued the Squadron Leader, obviously warming to his theme, "to do something about Olga's ménage, if only to protect his innocent ladylove. I suppose she *is* innocent?"

"Don't ask me," said Alan. "I shouldn't be surprised."

"Anyway, young Sherlock starts thinking. Not only does he disapprove of these goings on, but he begins to wonder if there is more to Olga's than meets the eye. Mata Hari and all that, you know."

Alan understood that very well. He had wondered, too.

"Presumably it never occurs to him that an establishment like Olga's, which you must admit is a little out of place in wild and woolly Cornwall, will have been investigated by about six sets of intelligence teams. The French, the Americans, and the British have all been through Olga's at one time or another; if there had been the slightest suspicion, she'd have been politely asked to move."

Alan felt very much relieved. He had always assumed that *someone* had taken care of this matter, yet at the same time there had been the nagging feeling that he shouldn't take it for granted. As was often the case in the past, he had taken the line of least resistance, and done nothing.

"So P. C. Sherlock starts investigating, with a little reluctant help from Joan. He keeps track of the visitors and compiles quite a dossier. Because he wants to get all the credit, he doesn't even tell his Sergeant. And then one night, with-

out benefit of search warrant—for all's fair in love and war
—he has a look round the inside of the house."

"And what does he find?" Alan asked anxiously.

"Not exactly what he was looking for, but enough to get
Olga into serious trouble. I have the list here."

The Squadron Leader started to read, and for a moment
Alan wondered which of them had gone crazy.

"Butter, 125 pounds; margarine, 46 pounds; lard, 44
pounds; sugar, 112 pounds; five-pound tins Spam, 20; one-
pound tins corned beef, 58 . . . It goes on for quite a
while. And most of it, I might add, from U.S.A.F. or Air
Force stores."

Oh dear, thought Alan. Now the fat's in the fire—several
hundred pounds of it. But what the devil has this got to do
with *me*?

"This means, of course, that Olga can be sent to jail for
black-market offenses, or at least heavily fined. We could
probably get her for receiving stolen goods, as well."

"I suppose you could," said Alan gloomily. He could see
his happy evenings coming to a sudden end. Somehow, it
was hard to imagine Olga in prison, though it was not so
difficult to picture her as a successful food hoarder.

He recalled, with some discomfort, various small black-
market items he had given to the girls. And he had occasionally delivered packages from Mac and others, without
inquiring as to the contents. At this memory, he began to
get apprehensive again.

"Olga's been a naughty girl," continued the Squadron
Leader, "but we'll be able to straighten things out. The main
reason why I wanted to see you was this. You're acting CO
of the GCD Flight, and it's up to you to have a word with
your chaps. I don't care how you put it; tell 'em they can
give the girls their cigarettes and sweet rations, but if they're
caught pinching any more stuff from the cookhouses or
messes, they're in for it. Understand?"

"Yessir," said Alan. "I'll tell them." He wasn't sure how,
but it would be done—probably at a top-secret briefing.

"But there's one thing I don't understand—" he added.

"Why I'm obstructing the course of justice, to put it bluntly?"

"Er—yes."

"Because Olga asked me to, if you want to know."

There was nothing much that Alan could say to this; so he waited patiently.

"Olga doesn't talk much—I mean about herself. One day, I hope someone can persuade her to tell her story. Her place in Paris was part of the Underground for months after the Germans came in. I don't know how many of our chaps she smuggled out—but a lot of them were bloody sorry to leave. Then Jerry got wise to her, and for a while she was in a concentration camp—which helps to explain the food hoarding. Don't ask me how she got to England, but here she is and we're going to look after her—not that she needs much help, usually.

"So now you know; but keep it under your hat. Olga wouldn't like to know that I've been shooting a line for her."

Alan lay back among the pillows, thinking this over. He was astonished, and also humbled. Life still had much to teach him, it seemed. Struck by a sudden wild surmise, he glanced at the medal ribbons below the Squadron Leader's wings. There, beside the DFC, was a tiny Croix de Lorraine, as well as other foreign ribbons that Alan did not recognize. Had Strickland passed through Olga's after the fall of France? "A lot of them were bloody sorry to leave" had a ring of personal experience about it. But this was a question to which he could hardly expect an answer; security officers were good at keeping secrets—especially their own.

CHAPTER 30

WHEN ALAN'S PROMOTION came through the next week, it was not exactly a surprise; indeed, since he had been in charge of the unit for a month, he considered it somewhat overdue. Nevertheless, it was with a great feeling of satisfaction that he took his uniforms along to the camp tailor, and had the second band stitched on the sleeves. Aircraftsman Class II Alan Bishop had certainly not imagined, as he marched back and forth on the parade grounds of Southbridge and Gatesbury, that he would ever become Flight Lieutenant Bishop. He was also quite proud of the little oak leaf on his breast; though he would never acquire any of the more glamorous ribbons, at least he had been "mentioned in dispatches." True, some cynics maintained that MDs were dished out by a man at the Air Ministry sticking pins in the Air Force List—but Alan knew that he had earned his.

He was still earning it, for with the collapse of the Mark I's turning gear the entire training program had had to be revised. With no operational unit, there could be no more circuits and approaches. "D" Flight was out of a job.

This was no longer the disaster that it would have been a

few months ago. They had already trained a substantial
number of operators and controllers, who could keep in
practice on the synthetic devices that were springing up in
ever-increasing numbers. F/O Lebrun now had quite an empire under his command; some of his gadgets were almost as
good as the real thing. Two large huts were stuffed with
replicas of GCD displays and control panels, on which the
novices could be safely broken in. The unit even possessed a
couple of Link trainers, ingeniously coupled to the cathode-
ray tubes and meter panels. A pilot could fly these minute,
captive aircraft without getting more than a foot from the
ground, while the directors and controllers could steer him
around an imaginary sky and head him in for an approach.
All his movements would be reproduced on a chart by a
slowly crawling metal crab, and at the end of a run all concerned could look at the inked record and see how successful they had been.

And there was one very effective device that involved no
technical resources at all. It was simply a matchbox,
crunched at the psychological moment behind the ear of a
controller who had made a particularly disastrous
talkdown. . . .

But though the synthetic trainers could do a great deal,
they were only a beginning; they could not take the operators and controllers beyond the early stages of their instruction. To do that, one had to have real aircraft, buffeted by
the unpredictable winds of the real sky—and a real radar
system to follow them down to earth.

Flight Sergeant (as he now was) McGregor still thought
he could rebuild the Mark I turning gear, and Alan had let
him go ahead. But he did not think it was really worth it—
for the first Mark II would soon be on its way.

They could thank Ted Hatton for that. He had wafted the
Mark I across the Atlantic when no one in the United States
except its inventors was particularly interested in it, and
now he had performed a much more difficult conjuring
trick. No doubt his many influential friends in the Allied
scientific army had pulled strings for him, but even so it was

a remarkable feat. He had managed to divert the very first production model from the U.S. Air Force to the RAF, on the grounds that the RAF already had a training school going full blast and was, therefore, in the best position to utilize it. The U.S. generals who had plaintively asked "When can *we* use it?" were told that they could send their first teams to be trained at Norton Wold.

This station, somewhere in the Midlands, was to be the new home of GCD. Now they were to have an airfield all their own; no longer would they be a parasite—sometimes an annoying one—on a busy operational station. At Norton Wold they would not have to ask the control tower for permission to approach and overshoot on a runway. The control tower would belong to them.

The move would be a major undertaking, and Alan did not look forward to organizing it. Quite apart from the administrative problems, it would mean breaking so many links with the past.

There was Lucille, for example. Yet somehow, this thought did not upset him as much as he had expected. His possessive jealousy had been dissolved away, with much else, during those flame-girt moments above Runway 320. That secret inferiority no longer nagged at his self-pride; he could look at the pilots and navigators and gunners around him with respect, but without envy.

And in return, he had earned their respect. That, perhaps, was more important.

The station band, augmented with talent from Davistowe, had excelled itself tonight. So had the Mess Secretary, in arranging decorations and refreshments. By general agreement, it was the best dance of the season, and the fact that it was also a farewell party to the GCD unit cast only the faintest of gloom over the proceedings. The Commanding Officer had made a very nice valedictory speech, saying what a privilege it had been to have had such excellent fellows at St. Erryn, and the excellent fellows, all of them well-oiled by this time, had shouted "Hear, Hear." Then the dance had begun, and both joy and drinks were unconfined.

Alan's dancing was more enthusiastic than skillful, but that hardly mattered in this crowd. He was quite conscious of the admiring, and occasionally quizzical, glances his guests were receiving. Probably by this time everyone knew who they were, and he couldn't care less.

He was fighting his way through the melee around the bar, in the interval between "The Lambeth Walk" and "The Beer Barrel Polka," when he collided with Flight Lieutenant Collins. Dennis looked very handsome in his dress uniform, with all medals up. He was also more than a little drunk.

"I say, Bish, old boy," he murmured confidentially in Alan's ear, "did *you* invite them?"

"I certainly did."

"Wish I'd thought of it, but I'm not sure I'd have had the nerve. The Queen Bee doesn't like it at all—look at her glaring at Strickey."

Alan glanced across the room. Yes, the WAAF Admin Officer was looking daggers at Squadron Leader Strickland and Olga, who were chatting animatedly together against the far wall. Olga looked stunning, overdressed by exactly the right amount and displaying those impressive rings, earrings, and chokers whose authenticity or otherwise was another of her little secrets. She was also a good deal thinner and none the worse for it now that "Wit's End" had had to jettison its surplus calories.

Thank goodness *that* had been settled, Alan told himself. But where was Lucille, so that he could give her the drink she'd asked for? The music had started up again, and there was no hope of reaching her. She was right there in the middle, more or less surrounded by Dennis, whose idea of dancing seemed to have much in common with all-in wrestling.

Alan looked at them both with a benevolent smile; he was happy that they were enjoying themselves. He couldn't see Elise, but he was quite sure that someone was taking care of her.

And then, without any warning, and for no reason that he could understand, all this music and gaiety seemed suddenly unreal and utterly detached from him. He wanted no part of it, not even as a spectator. The fact that this was his last night at St. Erryn abruptly hit him like a blow in the solar plexus.

He pushed his way out of the crowded anteroom. "Are you all right, sir?" asked the Mess Steward anxiously, as he headed for the exit.

"I'm OK," he said. "I just want some fresh air. If anyone starts looking for me, I'll be back in ten minutes."

Without bothering to check if it was the right one, he grabbed a bike from the rack outside the Mess. It was very dark, but he knew the way with his eyes closed. The sound of music and revelry died behind him; he was alone in the night, as he wished to be.

That ten minutes was optimistic, for he had to cycle halfway around the airfield—no trifling journey even when one took unauthorized short cuts along the runways. By the time he reached his destination, he was sweating despite the cold.

He was in a cemetery of trucks and cars—a kind of knacker's yard of derelict vehicles. If he had been wholly sober, he might have had difficulty in finding his way through this mechanical morgue, but now some instinct guided him unerringly.

For the very last time, Flight Lieutenant Bishop swung open the door of the control van and stepped inside, lighting the way with his bicycle lamp. Dim and lifeless now, the elevation and azimuth displays stared blankly at him. Never again would luminous glowworms crawl across the indicator tubes as aircraft were tracked down the sky; never again would the WAAF operators crank their handwheels as they followed the echoes toward the runway. Half the electronic circuits had already been stripped and the panels removed;

loose wires and coaxial cables hung everywhere, like the tendrils of dying vines.

A quarter of a million dollars' worth of gear was disintegrating, and no one cared; its work was done. There had never been any proper stock-taking on the Mark I, and now its components were vanishing at a quite amazing speed. The more valuable and useful parts, and all the secret tubes, had gone back to Stores; for the rest—well, most of the mechs seemed to be building their private radios, and Mac was assembling a personal cathode-ray oscilloscope. The Mark I was a derelict ship that had been overrun by wreckers.

This dim and dusty truck was full of ghosts. Alan slid into the controller's seat, and swiveled around to look at the meter panel. Upon these needles, now all resting on the zeros from which they would never stir again, his life had once depended. The monologues of a thousand talk-downs mingled and reverberated along the corridors of memory. Ranger calling C Charlie . . . Fife miles to go . . . Reduce rate of descent . . . Three degrees left . . . Check undercarriage down . . . Go ahead and overshoot . . . Change to Channel B . . . Are you receiving me? . . . Over and out . . . *Over and out.* . . .

He stared at the lifeless meters, no longer seeing them. The first time he had stepped into this van, he had been a callow Flying Officer not long out of radar school. Now, so much had happened to him, for good or bad, that he could scarcely remember how he had felt in those distant days, not yet a year ago.

Lovingly, he stroked the worn plastic of the bench. He was saying good-by to an old friend, whose triumphs and disasters he had shared through the most critical, and most formative, period of his life. Whatever the future brought, he knew that he could never feel the same about the factory-built Mark II.

He had not cried at his father's grave, but now the tears were trickling down his cheeks. How strange—indeed, how perverse—to weep for a machine! Even one with as complex and temperamental a personality as the Mark I did not merit the tribute of tears; why, then, was he weeping now?

There was no simple answer; his sadness came from a multitude of causes, and alcohol was the least of them. The sorrow he felt was that which every man must know when a chapter of his life closes and he leaves forever a spot where he has experienced much, of either good or evil.

Some of those tears were for his father—or what his father might have been, had fate ruled otherwise. And some were for Lucille; she had given him happiness, and only fools spurned that—but she had not given him love. Alan suspected, a little uncomfortably, that her memory would warp and color his emotions for years to come. That was a problem he must meet when it arose. No one could foresee the future, or guard himself against all its contingencies.

Alan rose from the swiveling seat, took a last look around the control van, and quietly left. As he closed the door behind him, it seemed to snap the threads of many friendships. Good-by, he thought, to Howard and Pat and Benny; good-by to Doc Wendt and Professor Schuster, wherever they might be. He wondered if he would meet them again, in the unimaginable world beyond the war.

It was quite possible, for he had become entangled in powers and instrumentalities that would surely shape the future. But first the war itself had to be won. In the momentous months ahead, the men he was training would be setting up their equipment on bomb-scarred airfields in liberated Europe, and beside runways of crushed coral on far Pacific islands. And perhaps he might be with them, facing unknown perils and hazards.

There was no GCD to guide him past these, no FIDO to clear away the mists that veiled the future. Nor did he need such aids; and in recognizing that fact, he had come at last to the beginnings of wisdom and maturity.

ABOUT THE AUTHOR

ARTHUR C. CLARKE is one of the most famous science fiction writers of all time. In addition to *Rendezvous with Rama,* he has written such million-copy bestsellers as *Childhood's End, 2001: A Space Odyssey, 2010: Odyssey Two,* and *2061: Odyssey Three.* He cobroadcast the *Apollo 11, 12,* and *15* missions with Walter Cronkite and Captain Wally Schirra, and shared an Oscar nomination with Stanley Kubrick for the film version of *2001: A Space Odyssey.* His most recent novel is *Rama II,* which he wrote with Gentry Lee.

The World of
ARTHUR C. CLARKE

ARTHUR C. CLARKE is legendary. He's a science fiction writer whose imaginings reverberate outside the realm of fiction. A true visionary, he conceived of communications satellites in geostationary orbits—a speculation soon realized. He also cobroadcast the *Apollo 11, 12,* and *15* missions with Walter Cronkite and Captain Wally Schirra.

No less remarkable are his literary works. His 1973 novel, *Rendezvous with Rama,* swept the Hugo, Nebula and Campbell awards. Author of more than fifty books, Clarke has 50 million copies in print. *2001: A Space Odyssey,* is the Oscar-nominated product of his collaboration with film director Stanley Kubrick.

At the heart of every Arthur C. Clarke novel lies a small puzzle with large ramifications. This is an author who takes an idea, and drops it into a quiet pool of thought. There's a splash—that's the intriguing nature of Clarke's scientific genius. Then the ripples spread out, washing up on character, society, soaking the whole book in wonder. It laps around your toes as you read. . . .

A FALL OF MOONDUST

As Clarke points out in his 1986 introduction to A Fall of Moondust, *the book was completed in November of 1960, nearly a decade before the first moon landing. The book theorizes a moon thats surface is covered with an ultra-fine dust, and imagines the fate of a group of visitors that are buried alive in the treacherous stuff.*

"Over billions of years," says Clarke in his introduction, "[astronomers] argued persuasively, the ferocious change of temperature between day and night would break up and eventually pulverize the local rocks. [Dr. Thomas] Gold et al. then theorized ingenious transport mechanisms, involving electric charges, which would allow the resulting dust to flow across the face of the moon, and eventually accumulate to form traps more treacherous than any quicksands on Earth."

In 1969, "Armstrong and Aldrin stepped onto the moon," says Clarke, "As is well known, they did not instantly vanish into a sea of dust. . . ." Clarke's ideas are intriguing, however; and though no longer open to speculation, still make for great storytelling, as the following passage will demonstrate:

In almost total darkness, *Selene* was racing up a narrow canyon—and not even on a straight course, for from time to time she zigged and zagged to avoid invisible obstacles. Some of them, indeed, were not merely invisible, but nonexistent; Pat had programmed this course, at slow speed and in the safety of daylight, for maximum impact on the nerves. The "Ah's" and "Oh's" from the darkened cabin behind him proved that he had done a good job.

Far above, a narrow ribbon of stars was all that could be seen of the outside world; it swung in crazy arcs from right to left and back again with each abrupt change of *Selene*'s course. The Night Ride, as Pat privately called it, lasted for about five minutes, but seemed very much longer. When he once again switched on the floods, so that the cruiser was moving in the center of a great pool of light, there was a sigh of mingled relief and disappointment from the passengers. This was an experience none of them would forget in a hurry.

Now that vision had been restored, they could see that they were traveling up a steep-walled valley or gorge, the sides of which were slowly drawing apart. Presently the canyon had widened into a roughly oval amphitheater about three kilometers across—the heart of an extinct volcano, breached aeons ago, in the days when even the Moon was young.

The crater was extremely small, by lunar standards, but it was unique. The ubiquitous dust had flooded into it, working its way up the valley age after age, so that now the tourists from Earth could ride in cushioned comfort into what had once been a cauldron filled with the fires of Hell. Those fires had died long before the dawn of terrestrial life, and would never wake again. But there were other forces that had not died, and were merely biding their time.

When *Selene* began a slow circuit of the steeply walled amphitheater, more than one of her passengers remembered a cruise in some mountain lake at home. Here was the same sheltered stillness, the same sense of unknown depths beneath the boat. Earth had many crater lakes, but the Moon only one—though it had far more craters.

Taking his time, Pat made two complete circuits of the lake, while the floodlights played upon its enclosing walls. This was the best way to see it; during the daytime, when the sun blasted it with heat and light, it lost much of its magic. But now it belonged to the kingdom of fantasy, as if it had come from the haunted brain of Edgar Allan Poe. Ever and again one seemed to glimpse strange shapes moving at the edge of vision, beyond the narrow range of the lights. It was pure imagination, of course; nothing moved in all this land except the shadows of the Sun and Earth. There could be no ghosts upon a world that had never known life.

It was time to turn back, to sail down the canyon into the open sea. Pat aimed the blunt prow of *Selene* toward the narrow rift in the mountains, and the high walls enfolded them again. On the outward journey he left the lights on, so that the passengers could see where they were going; besides, that trick of the Night Ride would not work so well a second time.

Far ahead, beyond the reach of *Selene*'s own illumination, a light was growing, spreading softly across the rocks and crags. Even in her last quarter, Earth still had the power of a dozen full moons, and now that they were emerging from the shadow of the mountains, she was once more the mistress of the skies. Every one of the twenty-two men and women aboard *Selene* looked up at that blue-green crescent, admiring its beauty, wondering at its brilliance. How strange that the familiar fields and lakes and forests of Earth shone with such celestial glory when one looked at them from afar! Perhaps there was a lesson here; perhaps no man could appreciate his own world until he had seen it from space.

And upon Earth, there must be many eyes turned toward the waxing Moon—more than ever before, now that the Moon meant so much to mankind. It was possible, but unlikely, that even now some of those eyes were peering through powerful telescopes at the faint spark of *Selene*'s floodlights as it crept through the lunar night. But it would mean nothing to them when that spark flickered and died.

For a million years the bubble had been growing, like a vast abscess, below the root of the mountains. Throughout the entire history of Man, gas from the Moon's not yet wholly dead interior had been forcing itself along lines of weakness, accumulating in cavities hundreds of meters below the surface. On nearby Earth, the ice ages had marched past, one by one, while the buried caverns grew and merged and at last coalesced. Now the abscess was about to burst.

Captain Harris had left the controls on autopilot and was talking to the front row of passengers when the first tremor shook the boat. For a fraction of a second he wondered if a fan blade had hit some submerged obstacle; then quite literally, the bottom fell out of his world.

It fell slowly, as all things must upon the Moon. Ahead of *Selene,* in a circle many acres in extent, the smooth plain puckered like a navel. The Sea was alive and moving, stirred by the forces that had waked it from its agelong sleep. The center of the disturbance deepened into a funnel, as if a giant whirlpool were forming in the dust. Every stage of that nightmare transformation was pitilessly illuminated by the earth-light, until the crater was so deep that its far wall was completely lost in shadow, and it seemed as if *Selene* were racing into a curving crescent of utter blackness—an arc of annihilation.

The truth was almost as bad. By the time that Pat had reached the controls, the boat was sliding and skittering far down that impossible slope. Its own momentum and the accelerating flow of the dust beneath it were carrying it headlong into the depths. There was nothing he could do but attempt to keep on an even keel, and to hope that their speed would carry them up the far side of the crater before it collapsed upon them.

If the passengers screamed or cried out, Pat never heard them. He was conscious only of that dreadful, sickening slide, and of his own attempts to keep the cruiser from capsizing. Yet even as he fought with the controls, feeding power first to one fan, then to the other, in an effort to straighten *Selene*'s course, a strange, nagging memory was teasing his mind. Somewhere, somehow, he had seen this happen before.

That was ridiculous, of course, but the memory would not leave him. Not until he reached the bottom of the funnel and saw the endless slope of dust rolling down from the crater's star-fringed lip did the veil of time lift for a moment.

He was a boy again, playing in the hot sand of a forgotten summer. He had found a tiny pit, perfectly smooth and symmetrical, and there was something lurking in its depths—something completely buried except for its waiting jaws. The boy had watched, wondering, already conscious of the fact that this was the stage for some microscopic drama. He had seen an ant, mindlessly intent upon its mission, stumble at the edge of the crater and topple down the slope.

It would have escaped easily enough—but when the first grain of sand had rolled to the bottom of the pit, the waiting ogre had reared out of its lair. With its forelegs, it had hurled a fusillade of sand at the struggling insect, until the avalanche had overwhelmed it and brought it sliding down into the throat of the crater.

As *Selene* was sliding now. No ant lion had dug this pit on the surface of the Moon, but Pat felt as helpless now as that doomed insect he had watched so many years ago. Like it, he was struggling to reach the safety of the rim, while the moving ground swept him back into the depths where death was waiting. A swift death for the ant, a protracted one for him and his companions.

The straining motors were making some headway, but not enough. The falling dust was gaining speed—and, what was worse, it was rising outside the walls of the cruiser. Now it had reached the lower edge of the windows; now it was creeping up the panes; and at last it had covered them completely. Pat cut the motors before they tore themselves to pieces, and as he did so, the rising tide blotted out the last glimpse of the crescent Earth. In darkness and in silence, they were sinking into the Moon.

THE SANDS OF MARS

The Sands of Mars was Arthur C. Clarke's first full-length novel. And not surprisingly, the young Clarke chose to create a hero for his novel that was a famous science fiction writer.

Clarke's premise is fascinating. When Martin Gibson's literary and scientific imagination are confronted with the cold hard realities of space, the clash of opposites results in both disillusionment and a renewed sense of wonder. In the process, Gibson also stumbles upon a secret abiding on Mars—a secret that could threaten the future of that world.

"So this is the first time you've been upstairs?" said the pilot, leaning back idly in his seat so that it rocked to and fro in the gimbals. He clasped his hands behind his neck in a nonchalant manner that did nothing to reassure his passenger.

"Yes," said Martin Gibson, never taking his eyes from the chronometer as it ticked away the seconds.

"I thought so. You never got it quite right in your stories—all that nonsense about fainting under the acceleration. Why must people write such stuff? It's bad for business."

"I'm sorry," Gibson replied. "But I think you must be referring to my earlier stories. Space-travel hadn't got started then, and I had to use my imagination."

"Maybe," said the pilot grudgingly. (He wasn't paying the slightest attention to the instruments, and take-off was only two minutes away.) "It must be funny, I suppose, for this to be happening to you, after writing about it so often."

The adjective, thought Gibson, was hardly the one he would have used himself, but he saw the other's point of view. Dozens of his heroes—and villians—had gazed hypnotized by remorseless second-hands, waiting for the rockets to hurl them into infinity. And now—as it always did if one waited long enough—the reality had caught up with the fiction. The same moment lay only ninety seconds in his own future. Yes, it *was* funny, a beautiful case of poetic justice.

The pilot glanced at him, read his feelings, and grinned cheerfully.

"Don't let your own stories scare you. Why, I once took off standing up, just for a bet, though it was a damn silly thing to do."

"I'm not scared," Gibson replied with unnecessary emphasis.

"Hmmm," said the pilot, condescending to glance at the clock. The second-hand had one more circuit to go. "Then I shouldn't hold on to the seat like that. It's ony berylmanganese; you might bend it."

Sheepishly, Gibson relaxed. He knew that he was building up synthetic responses to the situation, but they seemed nonetheless real for all that.

"Of course," said the pilot, still at ease but now, Gibson noticed, keeping his eyes fixed on the instrument panel, "it wouldn't be very comfortable if it lasted more than a few minutes—ah, there go the fuel pumps. Don't worry when the vertical starts doing funny things, but let the seat swing where it likes. Shut your eyes if that helps at all. (Hear the igniter jets start then?) We take about ten seconds to build up to full thrust—there's really nothing to it, apart from the noise. You just have to put up with that. I SAID, YOU JUST HAVE TO PUT UP WITH THAT!"

But Martin Gibson was doing nothing of the sort. He had already slipped gracefully into unconsciousness at an acceleration that had not yet exceeded that of a high-speed elevator.

He revived a few minutes and a thousand kilometres* later, feeling quite ashamed of himself. A beam of sunlight was shining full on his face, and he realised that the protective shutter on the outer hull must have slid aside. Although brilliant, the light was not as intolerably fierce as he would have expected; then he saw that only a frac-

---

* The metric system is used throughout this account of space-travel. This decimal system is based upon the meter equalling 39.37 inches. Thus a kilometre would be slightly over one-half mile (0:62 mi.).

tion of the full intensity was filtering through the deeply tinted glass.

He looked at the pilot, hunched over his instrument board and busily writing up the log. Everything was very quiet, but from time to time there would come curiously muffled reports—almost miniature explosions—that Gibson found disconcerting. He coughed gently to announce his return to consciousness, and asked the pilot what they were.

"Thermal contraction in the motors," he replied briefly. "They've been running round five thousand degrees and cool mighty fast. You feeling all right now?"

"I'm fine," Gibson answered, and meant it. "Shall I get up?"

Psychologically, he had hit the bottom and bounced back. It was a very unstable position, though he did not realise it.

"If you like," said the pilot doubtfully. "But be careful —hang on to something solid."

Gibson felt a wonderful sense of exhilaration. The moment he had waited for all his life had come. He was in space! It was too bad that he'd missed the take-off, but he'd gloss that part over when he wrote it up.

From a thousand kilometres away, Earth was still very large—and something of a disappointment. The reason was quickly obvious. He had seen so many hundreds of rocket photographs and films that the surprise had been spoilt; he knew exactly what to expect. There were the inevitable moving bands of cloud on their slow march round the world. At the centre of the disc, the divisions between land and sea were sharply defined, and an infinite amount of minute detail was visible, but towards the horizon everything was lost in the thickening haze. Even in the cone of clear vision vertically beneath him, most of the features were unrecognisable and therefore meaningless. No doubt a meteorologist would have gone into transports of delight at the animated weather-map displayed below—but most of the meteorologists were up in the space stations, anyway, where they had an even better view. Gibson soon grew tired of searching for cities and other works of man. It was chastening to think that all the thousands of years of human civilization had produced no appreciable change in the panorama below.

Then Gibson began to look for the stars, and met his second disappointment. They were there, hundreds of them, but pale and wan, mere ghosts of the blinding myriads he had expected to find. The dark glass of the port was to blame; in subduing the sun, it had robbed the stars of all their glory.

Gibson felt a vague annoyance. Only one thing had turned out quite as expected. The sensation of floating in mid-air, of being able to propel oneself from wall to wall at the touch of a finger, was just as delightful as he had hoped—though the quarters were too cramped for any ambitious experiments. Weightlessness was an enchanting, a fairy-like state, now that there were drugs to immobilise the balance organs and space-sickness was a thing of the past. He was glad of that. How his heroes had suffered! (His heroines too, presumably, but one never mentioned that.) He remembered Robin Blake's first flight, in the original version of "Martian Dust." When he'd written that, he had been heavily under the influence of D. H. Lawrence. (It would be interesting, one day, to make a list of the authors who *hadn't* influenced him at one time or another.)

There was no doubt that Lawrence was magnificent at describing physical sensations, and quite deliberately Gibson had set out to defeat him on his own ground. He had devoted a whole chapter to space-sickness, describing every symptom from the queasy premonitions that could sometimes be willed aside, the subterranean upheavals that even the most optimistic could no longer ignore, the volcanic cataclysms of the final stages and the ultimate, merciful exhaustion.

The chapter had been a masterpiece of stark realism. It was too bad that his publishers, with an eye on a squeamish Book-of-the-Month Club, had insisted on removing it. He had put a lot of work into that chapter; while he was writing it, he had really *lived* those sensations. Even now—

The Sands of Mars *is notable as one of the first science fiction novels about Mars "to abandon the romantic fantasies of . . . C. S. Lewis and Ray Bradbury," says Clarke. "By the 1940's it was already certain that the planet's atmosphere was far too thin to support higher animals of the terrestrial type."*

* * *

A Fall of Moondust *and* The Sands of Mars: *two of Arthur C. Clarke's most richly imaginative novels. Even a small sampling from this incredibly prolific author is ample evidence of Clarke's invaluable contribution to imaginative fiction—for any science fiction author*

"The Nine Billion Names of God" *is a short story excerpted from* More Than One Universe: The Collected Stories of Arthur C. Clarke, *available in August from Bantam Spectra.*

THE NINE BILLION
NAMES OF GOD

The title story was written, for want of anything better to do, during a rainy weekend at the Roosevelt Hotel. Its basic arithmetic was later challenged by J. B. S. Haldane, but I managed to save the situation by alphanumeric evasions whose precise nature now escapes me.

"J. B. S." also remarked of this story, and "The Star" (q.v.): "You are one of the very few living persons who has written anything original about God. You have in fact written several mutually incompatible things. If you had stuck to one theological hypothesis you might have been a serious public danger." I am glad of my self-contradiction, preferring to remain a prophet with a small p.

Nevertheless, I appear to have created a durable myth: not long ago, a radio talk on the BBC referred to the opening situation of this story as actual fact. And now that IBM computers have entered the field of biblical scholarship, perhaps this theme is coming a little closer to reality.

"This is a slightly unusual request," said Dr. Wagner, with what he hoped was commendable restraint. "As far as I know, it's the first time anyone's been asked to supply a Tibetan monastery with an Automatic Sequence Computer. I don't wish to be inquisitive, but I should hardly have thought that your—ah—establishment had much use for such a machine. Could you explain just what you intend to do with it?"

"Gladly," replied the lama, readjusting his silk robes

and carefully putting away the slide rule he had been using for currency conversions. "Your Mark V Computer can carry out any routine mathematical operation involving up to ten digits. However, for our work we are interested in *letters,* not numbers. As we wish you to modify the output circuits, the machine will be printing words, not columns of figures."

"I don't quite understand. . . ."

"This is a project on which we have been working for the last three centuries—since the lamasery was founded, in fact. It is somewhat alien to your way of thought, so I hope you will listen with an open mind while I explain it."

"Naturally."

"It is really quite simple. We have been compiling a list which shall contain all the possible names of God."

"I beg your pardon?"

"We have reason to believe," continued the lama imperturbably, "that all such names can be written with not more than nine letters in an alphabet we have devised."

"And you have been doing this for three centuries?"

"Yes: we expected it would take us about fifteen thousand years to complete the task."

"Oh," Dr. Wagner looked a little dazed. "Now I see why you wanted to hire one of our machines. But exactly what is the *purpose* of this project?"

The lama hesitated for a fraction of a second, and Wagner wondered if he had offended him. If so, there was no trace of annoyance in the reply.

"Call it ritual, if you like, but it's a fundamental part of our belief. All the many names of the Supreme Being— God, Jehovah, Allah, and so on—they are only man-made labels. There is a philosophical problem of some difficulty here, which I do not propose to discuss, but somewhere among all the possible combinations of letters that can occur are what one may call the *real* names of God. By systematic permutation of letters, we have been trying to list them all."

"I see. You've been starting at AAAAAAA . . . and working up to ZZZZZZZZ. . . ."

"Exactly—though we use a special alphabet of our own. Modifying the electromatic typewriters to deal with this is, of course, trivial. A rather more interesting problem is that of devising suitable circuits to eliminate ridiculous combinations. For example, no letter must occur more than three times in succession."

"Three? Surely you mean two."

"Three is correct: I am afraid it would take too long to explain why, even if you understood our language."

"I'm sure it would," said Wagner hastily. "Go on."

"Luckily, it will be a simple matter to adapt your Automatic Sequence Computer for this work, since once it has been programed properly it will permute each letter in turn and print the result. What would have taken us fifteen thousand years it will be able to do in a hundred days."

Dr. Wagner was scarcely conscious of the faint sounds from the Manhattan streets far below. He was in a different world, a world of natural, not man-made, mountains. High up in their remote aeries these monks had been patiently at work, generation after generation, compiling their lists of meaningless words. Was there any limit to the follies of mankind? Still, he must give no hint of his inner thoughts. The customer was always right. . . .

"There's no doubt," replied the doctor, "that we can modify the Mark V to print lists of this nature. I'm much more worried about the problem of installation and maintenance. Getting out to Tibet, in these days, is not going to be easy."

"We can arrange that. The components are small enough to travel by air—that is one reason why we chose your machine. If you can get them to India, we will provide transport from there."

"And you want to hire two of our engineers?"

"Yes, for the three months that the project should occupy."

"I've no doubt that Personnel can manage that." Dr. Wagner scribbled a note on his desk pad. "There are just two other points—"

Before he could finish the sentence the lama had produced a small slip of paper.

"This is my certified credit balance at the Asiatic Bank."

"Thank you. It appears to be—ah—adequate. The second matter is so trivial that I hesitate to mention it—but it's surprising how often the obvious gets overlooked. What source of electrical energy have you?"

"A diesel generator providing fifty kilowatts at a hundred and ten volts. It was installed about five years ago and is quite reliable. It's made life at the lamasery much more comfortable, but of course it was really installed to provide power for the motors driving the prayer wheels."

"Of course," echoed Dr. Wagner. "I should have thought of that."

The view from the parapet was vertiginous, but in time one gets used to anything. After three months, George Hanley was not impressed by the two-thousand-foot swoop into the abyss or the remote checkerboard of fields in the valley below. He was leaning against the wind-smoothed stones and staring morosely at the distant mountains whose names he had never bothered to discover.

This, thought George, was the craziest thing that had ever happened to him. "Project Shangri-la," some wit back at the labs had christened it. For weeks now the Mark V had been churning out acres of sheets covered with gibberish. Patiently, inexorably, the computer had been rearranging letters in all their possible combinations, exhausting each class before going on to the next. As the sheets had emerged from the electromatic typewriters, the monks had carefully cut them up and pasted them into enormous books. In another week, heaven be praised, they would be finished. Just what obscure calculations had convinced the monks that they needn't bother to go on to words of ten, twenty, or a hundred letters, George didn't know. One of his recurring nightmares was that there would be some change of plan, and that the high lama (whom they'd naturally called Sam Jaffe, though he didn't look a bit like him) would suddenly announce that the project would be extended to approximately A.D. 2060. They were quite capable of it.

George heard the heavy wooden door slam in the wind as Chuck came out onto the parapet beside him. As usual, Chuck was smoking one of the cigars that made him so popular with the monks—who, it seemed, were quite willing to embrace all the minor and most of the major pleasures of life. That was one thing in their favor: they might be crazy, but they weren't bluenoses. Those frequent trips they took down to the village, for instance . . .

"Listen, George," said Chuck urgently. "I've learned something that means trouble."

"What's wrong? Isn't the machine behaving?" That was the worst contingency George could imagine. It might delay his return, and nothing could be more horrible. The way he felt now, even the sight of a TV commercial would seem like manna from heaven. At least it would be some link with home.

"No—it's nothing like that." Chuck settled himself on the parapet, which was unusual because normally he was scared of the drop. "I've just found what all this is about."

"What d'ya mean? I thought we knew."

"Sure—we know what the monks are trying to do. But we didn't know *why*. It's the craziest thing—"

"Tell me something new," growled George.

"—but old Sam's just come clean with me. You know the way he drops in every afternoon to watch the sheets roll out. Well, this time he seemed rather excited, or at least as near as he'll ever get to it. When I told him that we were on the last cycle he asked me, in that cute English accent of his, if I'd ever wondered what they were trying to do. I said, 'Sure'—and he told me."

"Go on: I'll buy it."

"Well, they believe that when they have listed all His names—and they reckon that there are about nine billion of them—God's purpose will be achieved. The human race will have finished what it was created to do, and there won't be any point in carrying on. Indeed, the very idea is something like blasphemy."

"Then what do they expect us to do? Commit suicide?"

"There's no need for that. When the list's completed, God steps in and simply winds things up . . . bingo!"

"Oh, I get it. When we finish our job, it will be the end of the world."

Chuck gave a nervous little laugh.

"That's just what I said to Sam. And do you know

what happened? He looked at me in a very queer way, like I'd been stupid in class, and said, 'It's nothing as trivial as *that*.'"

George thought this over for a moment.

"That's what I call taking the Wide View," he said presently. "But what d'you suppose we should do about it? I don't see that it makes the slightest difference to us. After all, we already knew that they were crazy."

"Yes—but don't you see what may happen? When the list's complete and the Last Trump doesn't blow—or whatever it is they expect—*we* may get the blame. It's our machine they've been using. I don't like the situation one little bit."

"I see," said George slowly. "You've got a point there. But this sort of thing's happened before, you know. When I was a kid down in Louisiana we had a crackpot preacher who once said the world was going to end next Sunday. Hundreds of people believed him—even sold their homes. Yet when nothing happened, they didn't turn nasty, as you'd expect. They just decided that he'd made a mistake in his calculations and went right on believing. I guess some of them still do."

"Well, this isn't Louisiana, in case you hadn't noticed. There are just two of us and hundreds of these monks. I like them, and I'll be sorry for old Sam when his lifework backfires on him. But all the same, I wish I was somewhere else."

"I've been wishing that for weeks. But there's nothing we can do until the contract's finished and the transport arrives to fly us out."

"Of course," said Chuck thoughtfully, "we could always try a bit of sabotage."

"Like hell we could! That would make things worse."

"Not the way I meant. Look at it like this. The machine will finish its run four days from now, on the present twenty-hours-a-day basis. The transport calls in a week. OK—then all we need to do is to find something that needs replacing during one of the overhaul periods—something that will hold up the works for a couple of days. We'll fix it, of course, but not too quickly. If we time matters properly, we can be down at the airfield when the last name pops out of the register. They won't be able to catch us then."

"I don't like it," said George. "It will be the first time I ever walked out on a job. Besides, it would make them suspicious. No, I'll sit tight and take what comes."

"I *still* don't like it," he said, seven days later, as the tough little mountain ponies carried them down the winding road. "And don't you think I'm running away because I'm afraid. I'm just sorry for those poor old guys up there, and I don't want to be around when they find what suckers they've been. Wonder how Sam will take it?"

"It's funny," replied Chuck, "but when I said good-by I got the idea he knew we were walking out on him—and that he didn't care because he knew the machine was running smoothly and that the job would soon be finished. After that—well, of course, for him there just isn't any After That. . . ."

George turned in his saddle and stared back up the mountain road. This was the last place from which one could get a clear view of the lamasery. The squat, angular buildings were silhouetted against the afterglow of the sunset: here and there, lights gleamed like portholes in the side of an ocean liner. Electric lights, of course, sharing the same circuit as the Mark V. How much longer would they share it? wondered George. Would the monks smash up the computer in their rage and disappointment? Or would they just sit down quietly and begin their calculations all over again?

He knew exactly what was happening up on the mountain at this very moment. The high lama and his assistants would be sitting in their silk robes, inspecting the sheets as the junior monks carried them away from the typewriters and pasted them into the great volumes. No one would be saying anything. The only sound would be the incessant patter, the never-ending rainstorm of the keys hitting the paper, of the Mark V itself was utterly silent as it flashed through its thousands of calculations a second. Three months of this, thought George, was enough to start anyone climbing up the wall.

"There she is!" called Chuck, pointing down into the valley. "Ain't she beautiful!"

She certainly was, thought George. The battered old DC3 lay at the end of the runway like a tiny silver cross. In two hours she would be bearing them away to freedom and sanity. It was a thought worth savoring like a fine liqueur. George let it roll round his mind as the pony trudged patiently down the slope.

The swift night of the high Himalayas was now almost upon them. Fortunately, the road was very good, as roads went in that region, and they were both carrying torches. There was not the slightest danger, only a certain discomfort from the bitter cold. The sky overhead was perfectly clear, and ablaze with the familiar, friendly stars. At least there would be no risk, thought George, of the pilot being unable to take off because of weather conditions. That had been his only remaining worry.

He began to sing, but gave it up after a while. This vast arena of mountains, gleaming like whitely hooded ghosts on every side, did not encourage such ebullience. Presently George glanced at his watch.

"Should be there in an hour," he called back over his shoulder to Chuck. Then he added, in an afterthought: "Wonder if the computer's finished its run. It was due about now."

Chuck didn't reply, so George swung round in his saddle. He could just see Chuck's face, a white oval turned toward the sky.

"Look," whispered Chuck, and George lifted his eyes to heaven. (There is always a last time for everything.)

Overhead, without any fuss, the stars were going out.

New York
May 1952

THE GARDEN OF RAMA

In Rama II, *the stunning sequel to Arthur C. Clarke's 1973 masterpiece* Rendezvous with Rama, *a military and scientific mission is mounted to board the second mysterious Raman spaceship that has entered our solar system. And just like the first Raman ship, the second leaves our neighborhood of space silently and enigmatically—with one minor difference. On board are three humans who have cast their fates with that of the massive spaceship.* Rama II *is leaving our solar system—carrying them to an unknown destination, light-years away.*

In The Garden of Rama, *Richard Wakefield, Nicole des Jardins, and Michael O'Toole are on board* Rama II *for years before even a hint of their destina-*

tion is revealed. Nicole has borne children, and they all have aged considerably on their strange voyage taking them farther and farther from home. What follows is an excerpt from Nicole's journal, in which she recounts the final moments of their long journey and the wonders that are their destination.

8 JULY 2213

The maneuver began four days ago, right on schedule, as soon as the third and final light show was finished. We didn't see or hear any avians or octospiders, as we haven't for four years now. Katie was very disappointed. She wanted to see the octospiders all return to New York.

Yesterday a pair of the mantis biots came into our lair and went straight to the deceleration tank. They were carrying a large container in which were the five new webbed beds (Simone, of course, needs a different size now) and all of the helmets. We watched them from a distance while they installed the beds and checked out the tank system. The children were fascinated. The short visit from the mantises confirmed that we will soon be undergoing a major change in velocity.

Richard was apparently correct with his hypothesis about the connection between the main propulsion system and the overall thermal control of Rama. The temperature has already started to drop topside. In anticipation of a long maneuver, we have been busy using the keyboard to order cold-weather clothing for all of the children.

The constant shaking is again disrupting our lives. At first it was amusing for the kids, but they are already complaining about it. Poor Benjy is in a state of continual distress. He moans often and not even Simone can comfort him. Katie wants to go up and wander around New York. She is irritated that we won't let her.

I am praying that our destination is near. Michael prays that "God's will be done"—sometimes I'm afraid my prayers are more selfish than that.

1 SEPTEMBER 2213

Something new is definitely happening. Again I am so excited that I can hardly sit still.

For the last ten days, ever since we finished in the tank and the maneuver ended, we have been approaching a solitary light source situated about thirty astronomical units away from the star Sirius. Richard had ingeniously manipulated the sensor list and the black screen so that this source is dead center on our monitor at all times, regardless of which particular Raman telescope is observing it.

Two nights ago we began to see some definition in the object—we could tell that there were actually many separate sources of the light. We speculated that perhaps it was an inhabited planet and Richard rushed around computing the heat input from Sirius on a planet whose distance was roughly equal to Neptune's distance from our sun. Even though Sirius is much larger, brighter, and hotter than the sun, Richard concluded that our paradise, if this was indeed our destination, was still going to be very cold.

Last night our target began to resolve itself more clearly. It is an elongated construction (Richard says it therefore cannot be a planet—anything "that size" that is decidedly nonspherical "must be artificial"), shaped like a cigar, with two rows of lights along the top and the bottom and a few more at each end. Because we don't know exactly how far away it is, we don't know for certain its size. However, Richard has been making some guesstimates, based on our closing velocity, and he thinks the cigar is roughly a hundred and fifty kilometers long and fifty kilometers tall.

The entire family sits in our main room and stares at the monitor. This morning we had another surprise. Katie identified the other two vehicles before anyone else. Richard had shown her earlier how to change the Raman sensors feeding into the black screen, and while the rest of us were talking, she accessed the distant radar sensor that we had first used thirteen years ago to identify the nuclear missiles coming from Earth. The cigar-shaped object was at the edge of the radar field of view. Standing right in front of the cigar, almost indistinguishable from it in the wide field, were two other blips. If the giant cigar is indeed our target, then perhaps we are about to have company.

8 SEPTEMBER 2213

There is no way I can adequately describe the astounding events of the last five days. The language does not have adjectives superlative enough to capture what we have seen and experienced. Michael has even commented that heaven may pale by comparison beside the wonders that we have witnessed.

At this moment our family is on board a driverless small shuttle craft, no larger than a city bus on Earth, that is whizzing us from the way station to an unknown destination. The cigar-shaped way station is still visible, but just barely, out the domed window at the rear of the craft. To our left, our home for thirteen years, the cylindrical spaceship we call Rama, appears to be headed in a slightly different direction than we are. It departed from the way station a few hours after we did, lit like a Christmas tree on the outside, and we are presently separated from it by about two hundred kilometers.

We came to a stop, relative to the way station at least, four days and eleven hours ago. We were the third spacecraft in the queue, behind a spinning starfish only one-tenth the size of Rama and a giant wheel, with a hub and spokes, that entered the way station within hours after our final, vernier correction maneuver.

The way station itself was hollow inside. The ends, top, and bottom of the cigar, the portions that we could see from a distance because of the lights, were structures of some kind. When the giant wheel moved into the hollow center (and it just barely fit, so its diameter, according to Richard, must be at least forty kilometers), deployable elements of the way station rolled out to meet the wheel and fix it in place.

While the wheel was entering the way station, we moved up to the second spot in the queue, about three hundred kilometers from the way station. Because of the lights and the superb quality of the Raman telescopes, we were able to watch what was going on in the way station with a resolution of several hundred meters.

A suite of special vehicles in three unusual shapes (one looked like a balloon, another like a blimp, and the third resembled a bathysphere on Earth) entered the wheel during the next twelve hours. We couldn't see what was going on inside the wheel, but the vehicles were there for quite a while. They came out singly at odd intervals over the next two days. When each vehicle emerged, it was met by a shuttle like ours except much larger in all cases. The shuttles were all parked in the dark in the right-hand side of the cigar. Each of them moved into place thirty minutes or so before the appointed time for its rendezvous with one of the special vehicles that had been inside the wheel.

As soon as they were loaded, the shuttles always took off in a direction directly opposite the queue. About an hour after the final vehicle had emerged from the wheel and the last shuttle had departed, the many pieces of mechanical equipment attached to the wheel were retracted and the great circular spacecraft itself eased out of the way station.

Although we nominally took turns sleeping during all the activity, I hardly slept at all. My mind was bombarded by dreams and my high level of excitement made it impossible for me to stay asleep longer than two hours at a time. Each time I woke up I would ask someone if anything significant had changed before trying to force myself to doze off again.

The starfish had already entered the way station and was being handled by another set of gantries and attachments when a loud whistle summoned us topside in Rama. The whistle was followed, as before, by a light show in the Southern bowl, but this one was completely different from the ones that had preceded the maneuvers. The Big Horn was the star this time. Circular rings of color would form slowly near its tip and then glide north, centered along the spin axis of Rama. The rings were huge. Richard estimated they were at least a kilometer in diameter, with a ring thickness of forty meters.

The dark Raman night was illuminated by as many as eight of these rings at a time. The order remained the same—red, orange, yellow, green, blue, brown, pink, and purple—for three repetitions. As a ring would break up and disappear near the Alpha relay station at the Northern bowl of Rama, a new ring of the same color would form back near the tip of the Big Horn.

We stood transfixed, our mouths agape, as this spectacle took place. As soon as the last ring disappeared from the third set, another astonishing event occurred. All the lights came on inside Rama! The Raman night had only begun three hours earlier—for thirteen years the sequence of night and day had been completely regular. Now, all of a sudden, it was changed. And it wasn't just the lights. There was music as well; at least I guess you could call it music. It sounded like millions of tiny bells and it seemed to be coming from everywhere.

None of us could move for several minutes. Benjy began to cry. High in the sky, toward the north, Richard (who had the best pair of binoculars), then spied something flying slowly toward us. "It's the avians," he shouted, jumping up and down. "I just remembered something. I visited them in their new home in the north while I was on my odyssey."

One at a time we each looked through his binoculars. At first it wasn't certain that Richard was correct in his identification, but as they came closer the fifty of sixty specks resolved themselves into the great birdlike creatures we know as the avians. They headed straight for New York. Half the avian hovered in the sky, maybe three hundred meters above their lair, as the other half dove down to the surface.

"Come on, Daddy," Katie yelled. "Let's go see." Before I could raise my objection, father and daughter were off at a sprint. I watched Katie run. She is already very fast. In my mind's eye I could see my mother's graceful stride across the grass in the park at Chilly-Mazarin—Katie has definitely inherited some characteristics from her mother's side of the family even though she is first and foremost her father's daughter.

Simone and Benjy had already started toward our lair. Patrick was concerned about the avians. "Will they hurt Daddy and Katie?" he asked.

I smiled at my handsome five-year-old son. "No, darling," I answered, "not if they're careful." Michael, Patrick, Ellie, and I returned to the lair to watch the starfish being processed in the way station.

We couldn't see much because all of the ports of entry to the starfish were on the opposite side, away from the Raman cameras. But we assumed a similar unloading activity was occurring, because eventually the three shuttles left for some new destination. The smaller starfish was finished with its processing very quickly. It had already left the way station before Richard and Katie returned.

"Start packing," Richard said breathlessly as soon as they came back to the lair. "We're leaving. We're all leaving."

"You should have seen them," Katie said to Simone almost simultaneously. "They were huge. And ugly. They went down in their lair—"

"The avians returned to get some special things from their lair." Richard interrupted her. "Maybe they were mementos of some kind. Anyway, everything fits. We're getting out of here."

As I raced around trying to put our essentials into a few of the sturdy boxes, I criticized myself for not having figured everything out sooner. We had watched both the wheel and the starfish "unload" at the way station. But it had not occurred to us that *we* might be the cargo to be unloaded by Rama.

It was impossible to decide what to pack. We had been living in those six rooms (including the two we had fixed up for storage) for thirteen years. We had probably requested an average of five items a day using the keyboard. Granted, most of the objects had long since been thrown away, but still . . . We didn't know where we were going. How could we know what to take?

"Do you have any idea what's going to happen to us?" I asked Richard.

My husband was beside himself trying to figure out how to take his large computer. "Our history, our science —all that remains of our knowledge is there," he said, pointing at the computer in agitation. "What if it's irretrievably lost?"

It weighed only eighty kilograms altogether. I told him we could all help him carry the computer after we had packed clothing, personal items, and some food and water.

"Do you have any idea where we're going?" I repeated.

Richard shrugged his shoulders. "Not the slightest," he replied. "But wherever it is, I bet it will be amazing."

Katie came into our room. She was holding a small pouch and her eyes were alive with energy. "I'm packed and ready," she said. "Can I go topside and wait?"

Her father's affirmative nod was barely in motion when Katie bolted out the door. I shook my head, giving Richard a disapproving look, and went down the hall to help Simone with the other children. The process of packing for the boys was an ordeal. Benjy was cranky and weepy. Even Patrick was irritable. Simone and I had just finished (the job was impossible until we forced the boys to take a nap) when Richard and Katie returned from topside.

"Our vehicle is here," Richard said calmly, suppressing his excitement.

"It's parked on the ice," Katie added, taking off her heavy jacket and gloves.

"How do you know it's ours?" Michael asked. He had entered the room only moments after Richard and Katie.

"It has seven seats and room for our bags," my ten-year-old daughter replied. "Who else could it be for?"

"Whom," I said mechanically, trying to integrate this latest new information. I felt as if I had been drinking from a fire hose for four consecutive days.

"Did you see any octospiders?" Patrick asked.

"Oc-to-spi-der," Benjy repeated carefully.

"No," answered Katie, "but we did see four mammoth planes, real flat, with wide wings. They flew over our heads, coming from the south. We think the flat planes were carrying the octos, don't we, Dad?"

Richard nodded.

I took a deep breath. "All right then," I said. "Bundle up, everybody. Let's go. Carry the bags first. Richard, Michael, and I will make a second trip for the computer."

An hour later we were all in the vehicle. We had climbed the stairs of our lair for the last time. Richard pressed a flashing red button and our Raman helicopter (I call it that because it went straight up, not because it had any rotary blades) lifted off the ground.

Our flight path was slow and vertical for the first five minutes. Once we were close to the spin axis of Rama, where there was no gravity and very little atmosphere, the vehicle hovered in place for two or three minutes while it changed its external configuration.

It was an awesome final view of Rama. Many kilometers below us our island home was but a small patch of grayish-brown in the middle of the frozen sea that circled the giant cylinder. I could see the horns in the south clearer than ever before. Those amazing long structures, supported by massive flying buttresses larger than small towns on Earth, all pointed directly north.

I felt strangely emotional as our craft began to move again. After all, Rama had been my home for thirteen years. I had given birth to five children there. I also have matured, I remember telling myself, and may finally be growing into the person I have always wanted to be.

There was very little time to dwell on what had been. Once the configuration change was complete, our vehicle zipped along the spin axis to the Northern hub in a matter of a few minutes. Less than an hour later we were all safely in this shuttle. We had left Rama. I knew we would never return. I wiped the tears from my eyes as the shuttle pulled out of the way station.

The Garden of Rama, *a Bantam Spectra hardcover, will be available in August 1991.*

The Classic Works Of
ARTHUR C. CLARKE

Bantam Spectra is proud to present brand new editions of Arthur C. Clarke's landmark novels and story collections. These new editions feature stunning new covers which no collector will want to miss.

"A master for a new generation of SF. His skills hold the hope of wonders to come." -- *Analog*

The Extraordinary Fiction of Ian McDonald

☐ *Desolation Road* (27057-5 * $4.99/$5.99 in Canada) Set on a terraformed Mars of the distant future, here is the history of one isolated town, its colorful inhabitants, its rise and premature fall. Reminiscent of the best of Ray Bradbury, *Desolation Road* will constantly surprise and delight.

"*Desolation Road* is wild, original, exuberant, profound, moving, magical." -- *The Denver Post*

☐ *King of Morning, Queen of Day* (29049-5 * $4.99/$5.99 in Canada) In the myth-ridden hills of Ireland, three generations of young women struggle to tame the ancient magical powers that course through their blood. Each must face the darker side of the human mythconsciousness. One will embrace it, one will destroy it. And one will be swallowed whole.

"The man is a poet masquerading as a novelist."
-- Katherine Kurtz